AN UNSETTLING SUMMER

The Story of a Poor Boy

By Alan Bell

DEDICATION

Dedicated to my father, Marvin Bell, and to my family: My mom, Cleta; my sisters, Brenda and Linda; my wife, Debbie; and my sons, Andrew and Troy.

I couldn't have finished this book without the constant love and support of my wife and my two incredible boys … all right, my two incredible adult sons.

This is a work of fiction. All characters are nothing more than fantastic imaginings about how certain plausible Missourians may have lived in the 1930s.

Excerpt from "Hills (Summer in the Ozarks)"
(Used with the author's permission)

It's summer in the Ozarks, it's hot between the hills
You can't go back tomorrow, strolling through the hills
You can't turn back the sorrow, neglecting how it feels
It's just a distant vision, barefoot in the hills

TABLE OF CONTENTS

Chapter 1

THE STILL

Deep in the woods, on top of a small hill, stood a tiny clearing just big enough for Hiram Brodie's carefully hidden still.

It was past midmorning on a sunny Saturday in early May of 1938. The sun was filtering through the canopy, just shy of breaking into the small opening overhead. The day was heating up rapidly. It soon would be time to take a break. Hiram planned to retreat to the shade and have a sip or two from the jug that held a sample from one of his previous batches of white lightning. He'd rest under a sturdy tree for a few hours. Hiram believed that working through the hottest part of the day wasn't good for a body.

Once more, he stirred and checked the 55-gallon barrel holding the mash. Despite the repeal of Prohibition more than four years earlier, Hiram – like many of his neighbors – continued to produce illicit moonshine. He sold most of it, making a better living than he could farming, raising livestock or cutting timber.

While citizens were once again free to purchase liquor in the open, Hiram and lots of likeminded country and backwoods bootleggers continued to evade the law and sell their black-market booze.

Hiram had started up the still again just a few days ago. He had been tending the mash for three or four days, letting the cracked corn, malt, sugar and yeast work their magic. This afternoon, toward evening, he'd syphon off the mash. Tomorrow, he'd fire up his pride and joy, a state-of-the-illegal-industry copper still. Then he'd start producing some of the finest moonshine in the county.

While he was guiding the wooden paddle around the barrel, he heard the sound of brush moving somewhere lower on the hill. Hiram was always listening for unusual or foreign noises when he was tending the still. This sound had been faint, but he was certain it was produced by some intruder. The question was whether it was a deer or a bird or a more dangerous creature: a law officer. The noise had come from the southern slope of the hill.

Hiram froze. His still was well concealed: He'd chosen this spot carefully. But that didn't mean an enterprising revenuer couldn't stumble upon him. Or maybe one of the few neighbors who knew the location of his outdoor workshop had betrayed him. He had told several of those neighbors on certain occasions that if he ever found out someone had turned him in, it would be one of their last acts on Earth. That wasn't a boast, that was a vow.

Hiram moved silently around to the base of a big pine tree, which provided shade from the afternoon sun. He pickup up his .20-gauge shotgun. If the intruder turned out to be a revenuer, he'd fire. There were plenty of places in these hills to hide a body. If it was the sheriff or his deputy, Hiram might be able to talk his way out of the situation. In some ways, though, he'd rather shoot the government man than argue with local officials.

Listening carefully, he heard more movement, slightly to the right of the primitive trail he'd made to haul his equipment up to this secluded spot. He listened hard. Again, he heard faint sounds. They were slowly but persistently coming nearer, approaching through the undergrowth from the direction of a wide dogwood tree.

As the creature drew closer, Hiram saw the brush moving, beginning to part. The trespasser was visible between the branches of the dogwood. Hiram raised his gun to his shoulder and took aim. The interloper was only 20 yards away and showed no sign of realizing Hiram was waiting. It would be an easy kill shot.

Hiram sited the shotgun and waited for the intruder to break into the open. Finger on the trigger, Hiram was ready to fire when something made him stop. As the small figure emerged, a flash of recognition hit him.

It was Dusty, his 12-year-old son. A wave of relief swept over Hiram, followed by a stronger wave of anger.

"What the hell are you doing here?" Hiram bellowed at the boy.

"I almost shot you. You know better than to sneak up here like that."

Dusty's eyes widened in surprise. He thought he'd been completely silent coming up the hill. How had his dad heard him? Why was he pointing the shotgun at him? Why was he so mad?

The truth was it didn't take much to make Dusty's father mad. Hiram was strong-willed with a temper that flashed easily when provoked. Everyone in the area knew that you didn't rile Hiram Brodie unless you wanted a fight. Now that he was riled, he looked ready to lay into Dusty.

"Don't NEVER come up here unless I tell you," Hiram continued yelling at Dusty. "I orta whip the hell out of you."

He stomped toward Dusty, reaching for the wooden paddle still sticking up from the barrel of mash. He grabbed the paddle as he strode toward the boy, still hollering.

"Do I need to knock some sense into that empty head of yours?"

Hiram raised the paddle. Dusty had two choices: take a licking or take off. He chose the latter, knowing it might only delay the former. But who wants to stand still while an enraged moonshiner raises a club to hit you?

Dusty sped back into the trees, dodging and leaping over obstacles, breaking a new trail down the hill. He didn't slow down until he got to the clear-running spring that flowed down from an adjacent hill. The boy scampered along the stream bank until the watercourse turned eastward toward his family's house.

Finally, Dusty sat down and got a long cool drink from the flowing stream. He kept an eye out for his dad, ready to rise and sprint away again if necessary.

Hiram didn't follow. He hoped his tirade had taught the boy a lesson. He also hoped no one had followed Dusty … or heard him yelling at the boy. His anger slowly, gradually subsided. He put the paddle down by the mash barrel, went back to the pine tree and took a long tug on the jug. Whether drinking made him calmer or meaner was a fair question. Either way, the alcohol – for now – kept him on the hill near his still. And that's all that mattered at the moment to Dusty.

Chapter 2

THE BOY AND HIS GRANDMOTHER

Dusty rested by the spring, wondering if his dad would stay mad or get drunk and forget about his appearance on the hill. The unintentional interruption was a rarity: Dusty usually stayed away from his dad's still. There were better places to be. Hiram was unpredictable at the best of times. A drunk Hiram could be a mean Hiram, and he was apt to take that meanness out on Dusty.

The only reason he'd gone on up the hill this particular Saturday was to ask if he could borrow his dad's .22 rifle to go hunting. Not exactly receiving permission, Dusty thought it best to forget hunting for now and find something else to do.

Dusty decided to go to one of his favorite places: his half-Cherokee grandmother's house. Louellen Brodie lived in the original Brodie cabin at the initial Brodie homestead. It had been her home for almost 40 years, ever since she'd married James Brodie back in 1899. They had produced three sons: Hiram was the oldest, Martin was the middle boy and Cleve (short for Cleveland) was the youngest.

James had died back in 1911 at age 37. A horse had thrown him during an impromptu and ill-advised race with a neighbor. Louellen's husband survived his injuries a few days, just long enough to impress on his three sons the obligation they had to take care of their mother after he was gone. While his body was buried in the family's section of Wheaton Cemetery, not two miles from his home, James' strong spirit continued to reside over the home, a constant reminder that his sons should watch over their mother.

Because of that duty, the middle brother, Martin, lived with Louellen at the old cabin. His mother was now 59 years old and still fairly independent. But she needed occasional help, which Martin provided. The problem was that Martin was obliged to be away from home most days. He worked at the post office in Avery, the nearest town, which was a couple of miles away.

With Martin absent so much, other relatives routinely called on Louellen throughout the week. Although she was thankful for the attention, she sometimes wished they would allow her a little more solitude. She enjoyed the peace and quiet of her home as she toiled through her daily household chores.

Always stoic and reserved, Louellen could appear cold and detached. She often greeted visitors with a stern nod of the head. She didn't speak much unless she had something to say. She wasn't quick to smile and rarely laughed. But Louellen did enjoy seeing her grandchildren: Dusty and his sisters, Nancy and Jenny.

Seldom did the trio go more than two or three days between visits. Louellen would leave her chores to get them something to eat or a cup of milk. Often, she would sit and listen patiently to tales about their youthful adventures. When she needed to get back to work, she would lead them around the property, performing her tasks with her eager grandchildren at her heels.

Louellen was proud of her sons, proud of her grandchildren and fiercely proud of her Cherokee heritage. She had been born Louellen Farrell in 1875, the daughter of Jefferson Farrell and his full-blooded Cherokee wife, Miriam Lat-ho-ke. Louellen had had three brothers and two sisters, with two brothers and one sister surviving into adulthood. Beyond her parents and siblings, she had little information concerning other relatives. Her aunts, uncles and cousins were scattered throughout Arkansas and Oklahoma. Quite likely most of them had died since the day her mother had married Jeff Farrell and left her Cherokee family.

Though usually quiet and solemn, Louellen Brodie would sometimes sing old Cherokee songs that her mother had learned from her mother and so on for untold generations. She liked to sing when she was alone, feeling kinship with her ancestors as she repeated words of their deeds and beliefs.

When Louellen wasn't alone, she worked to make certain all her relatives were also proud of their Cherokee heritage. On occasion, she could turn uncharacteristically talkative, telling her grandchildren stories about her ancestors.

She particularly liked to talk about her grandparents and great-grandparents. She recalled how they had owned land and were prosperous farmers in Tennessee. She told how the white men tried to take their land. The Cherokee had gone to the Supreme Court to challenge this thievery. And the Cherokee had won: The court agreed the natives owned the land.

Then she told of how the evil president, Andrew Jackson, had ignored the high court. His treachery allowed white governments to take Cherokee lands. Then, a century ago in 1838, the white men had forced her ancestors to undertake a terrible journey of hunger, thirst, cold and exhaustion. Had driven them west like animals to the wide Mississippi River. Had forced them to cross in brutal conditions. Had pushed them 1,000 miles to be settled unceremoniously in the wastelands of Oklahoma.

She told them how so many had died along the way, their bleak graves scattered along a trail of tears. Families were forced to leave the bodies of loved ones behind in unhallowed ground. Forced to continue worn and spent toward an uncertain, dispiriting future.

Along the way, here and there, an individual or a family might abandon the exodus. Her grandparents had done so, settling in Arkansas in the late 1830s. To survive, they had to assimilate into white society to some degree. But not completely.

Louellen reminded her grandchildren how her grandparents had remained unbowed, had retained much of their heritage and had passed their culture, as best they could, to their children. Many of the Cherokee ways were gone, but the Cherokee spirit survived in her. It survived in her brothers and sisters. And she would make sure it survived in her sons and grandchildren.

Louellen expected Dusty to carry on the Cherokee heritage, and he was a willing learner. Dusty loved his grandma, and he loved her stories. Although his sisters visited their grandmother regularly, Dusty walked over to see her nearly every day. Excepting Martin, the old woman spent more time with her grandson than with anyone else.

XXX

At 12 years old, Dusty still had a lot of little boy in him. He liked to fish and set traps and was learning to hunt – when he could get permission to borrow his dad's rifle. He still enjoyed catching frogs, skinny dipping in the river and getting dirty.

The latter habit had earned him his nickname. Especially when he was younger, he seldom arrived at school as clean as when he left home. He almost never arrived home cleaner than when he left the schoolhouse. The youngster had a real fascination with mud puddles. Once, during second grade, he talked his mom into letting him wear a new pair of shoes to school. The shoes were supposed to get him through winter, after which every kid and most adults kicked off their footwear, spending the bulk of summer barefoot.

It was a cool October day. In the morning, the weather had been cloudy but dry. Dusty proudly wore his new shoes all through the school day. Early in the afternoon, however, the clouds thickened and the skies opened up. It rained hard. By the time school let out, the rain had stopped, but the path home was full of fresh, new, inviting puddles.

Dusty, overflowing with natural boyish energy, ran and jumped and sloshed his way home, testing almost every little muddy pool along the way. He nearly ruined the shoes. His mom was fit to be tied, and she had switched him good. It seemed like a small price to pay for the fun of playing in the puddles.

Though generally well-behaved, Dusty could create mischief on occasion. There was the time he caused a ruckus with one of the few store-bought toys he ever owned. The boy had helped Martin with some chores one weekend. For an eight-year-old, he'd done a pretty fair job, in Martin's opinion. His uncle rewarded him with a toy firetruck. When you ran the wheels across the floor, a siren screeched and a red light lit up on top of the truck's cab.

Dusty played for hours with this wonderful novelty. Eventually, like all boys, he decided to experiment. He wanted to see if he could get one of the family's cats to pull the vehicle through the living room. Dusty went out to the barn, found some leather straps and fashioned a nifty little harness that he could attach to the firetruck.

He corralled a young, black and white cat, hauling it into the house. He locked the screen door so the cat couldn't get away. He then set up his assembly in the front room, a large room that doubled as his sisters' bedroom at night.

First, he attached the leather harness to the front bumper of the truck, making sure it was secure. Then he placed the cat in front of the truck and threaded the uncooperative feline's head through the harness. The cat clawed, scratched and wiggled, but Dusty finally maneuvered the homemade tack into position. He held the cat in his left arm while he turned the truck's switch on. He let go of the cat.

Even Dusty was unprepared for what ensued. The cat tried to walk away, shaking its head to free itself from the harness. Slowly at first, the cat moved a couple of steps forward and the firetruck followed, the friction of its wheels starting the siren up. The animal looked behind to identify the source of the sound. The concerned cat took a couple more startled steps away from the sound.

The quicker the cat scampered, the louder the siren wailed. Suddenly, the terrified tomcat took off, bolting toward the screen door – flashing light and whining siren right on its tail. The poor creature didn't wait for anyone to open the door. It bounded through the screen, taking most of the harness with it and leaving the truck wedged in the tangled wire mesh.

Dusty roared with laughter, falling back on the floor. He'd never seen anything so funny. Tears poured from his eyes. He had trouble catching his breath. The cat's apprehension, its confounded expression, its sheer panic – the whole of it took less than three seconds. Then the traumatic exit through the screen. It was all too much.

Dusty was still laughing, inside at least, when his mom came home. Eliza Brodie was not one to accept excuses in the best of times. Seeing the damage to the screen door, Eliza figured her son was the likely culprit. She knew he had a mischievous streak. He was a Brodie boy: Trouble seemed to follow them like little ducklings follow their mother.

When Dusty heard his mom's footsteps on the porch, he was still clearing screen door mesh from the bumper and grill of the toy. He slid the damaged vehicle – sideways so the siren wouldn't sound – under the bed in the corner of the room just as his mom came through the damaged door.

"Dusty, what did you do to the door?" she yelled, not giving him any benefit of the doubt.

Dusty's eyes widened. He tried to think of an answer that wouldn't involve an out-and-out lie.

"I never touched the door," he said. "The cat did that."

"Which cat?" his mom demanded.

"The black and white one," Dusty replied. "He's kind of jumpy."

"And what was the black and white cat doing in the house?" his mom persisted. That was a harder question to answer.

"Well … I suppose he was curious about my firetruck," Dusty said, wondering if he'd revealed too much.

"And what made him tear through the screen that way?" Would his mom's questions never cease?

"Well, the sound might've scared him," Dusty said as innocently as he could manage. Eliza thought her young son was acting just a bit too innocent.

"Where's the truck now?" she inquired.

"Uh, somewhere around here," Dusty said. His eyes unwillingly darted toward its hiding spot under the bed.

Eliza followed his eyes, walked over to the bed, bent down and pulled the toy out.

"This looks strange," she said with a grim frown. "It looks like you tried to attach something to it. Maybe a harness? For a cat?"

She glared at Dusty. He couldn't stand any more grilling. He told her, in what he hoped was a pure and angelic manner, more or less what had happened.

"I didn't know the cat would take off through the door," he explained to her with wide eyes. "I thought it would just pull the firetruck around the room."

Dusty got a severe thrashing with a thick birch. When his dad got home, he got another whipping, this time with a leather strap. He had marks on his back end for several days. But Dusty was convinced it had been worth it. He still laughed to the point of tears every time he thought of that cat, its eyes wide with fright, skedaddling through the screen door trying to escape the firetruck and its wailing siren.

XXX

Gradually, such juvenile antics became less common. Youthful romps through the mud were a thing of the past. Dusty was coming upon his teen years. He was starting to recognize and learn more of the habits and customs of the adults in his life. He grew a bit more judicious about when to engage in shenanigans.

By age 12, Dusty understood that while most people were poor, some were poorer than others. And a few were significantly better off. He realized his family wasn't one of those. Money was perpetually scarce. He knew clothing, shoes and many other items were always in need. He realized luxuries weren't in the cards for his family.

He also knew sufficient food was never guaranteed. A bad growing season could mean fields and gardens might produce a meager harvest. Sickness among the livestock or poor hunting luck could curtail meat supplies. And financial volatility could result in the inability to buy the barest necessities at local stores.

Though aware of all this, Dusty often unwittingly took advantage of his grandma's limited larder. When he visited, she rarely failed to offer him something to eat and drink. If not for Grandma Louellen, Dusty and his sisters would have fared much worse than they did. She supplied them with fresh or canned fruit, milk and biscuits – staples of their diet. And in the hardest of times, she could offer only a scant supply of these.

Hill folks understood want. Bad times often meant limited offerings on the tables of the Brodies and their neighbors. Like beggars, hungry people can't be choosers. So boring, repetitive fare didn't bother most of them, as long as they could fill their bellies.

But slim pickings bothered Dusty more than most people. He was finicky about food. It wasn't that he turned his nose up at what was offered. It was just that he tended to eat only what he liked. Some foods he hated so much that he avoided them unless he was almost literally starving.

Grandma Louellen knew this, of course, and tried to make sure she had a few things on hand that Dusty liked. One of his favorites was chocolate gravy and biscuits. Many people claimed Louellen made the best biscuits in the county. Whether that was true or not, she'd definitely had a lot of experience baking them, using her simple, frugal recipe.

Chocolate gravy was a different matter. No one could match her skill at stirring up a batch of chocolate gravy. She didn't share the exact recipe, but family members and a few nosy, old crones eventually learned the dish consisted of flour, cocoa, sugar, butter, milk and – if available – a bit of vanilla.

It was less gravy than thin pudding, served piping hot from a pot with a ladle. Smother a biscuit or two in the rich, dark brown sauce then dig in with a fork … or better yet a spoon to clean up every drop. It was breakfast, dinner and dessert all in one. And Dusty could never get too much. Louellen loved to see people enjoy her cooking, but none of her table guests showed more appreciation for her kitchen skills than her grandson.

XXX

While Louellen kept Dusty relatively well-fed, her grandson kept her up to date on all his adventures. She liked to hear about his friends and the fun he had with them before, during and after school. Though not naturally boastful, Dusty did tell his grandma how he often won the games they played, beating the other boys – and the few tomboys who hung out with them – in races and games like tag, hide and seek or crack the whip.

He also regularly bested his schoolmates when skipping rocks downstream or throwing them at trees, birds or squirrels. The latter sometimes provided the entrée for supper. At times, squirrel meat was a godsend. Dusty was slim and wiry, but he had an unusually strong arm. Just as important, it was an accurate arm. He liked to play baseball and show off that arm.

And he loved to run. Though on the smallish side, no one at the one-room Avery schoolhouse was faster. Whether it was in a straight line, across the hills and dales or around makeshift bases on a ball field, Dusty was the fastest runner in his school.

It's true a couple of the older boys who went to the high school in Kenneth, about five miles north, could outrun him in longer races. But up to 100 yards or so, no one could keep up. His secret was a quick start: His short legs would propel him like twin pistons, seemingly churning at twice the speed of other runners. He would sprint quickly to an early lead and generally hold on for the duration of the race as others contestants attempted to make up ground.

While he was indeed fast, he was also more agile than most other kids around Avery. He could dart, shift, cut or reverse directions with ease. This made him nearly impossible to catch in games of tag and difficult to defend in the version of sandlot football they all played.

Louellen, of course, attributed these physical skills to his Indian blood. He was a Cherokee, and Cherokee boys – like Cherokee men – were fierce and talented athletes. She particularly liked to watch her grandson play baseball. This game showed off his skills best. On the football field, larger and stronger players had some advantage. If they could latch on to Dusty, they could lay some painful bruises on the skinny boy.

When Louellen got the chance, she liked to go to the local ball field and watch Dusty play in pickup games. She sat stoically behind the backstop, never cheering or booing or applauding. She just watched her grandson.

On the baseball diamond, Dusty possessed an ideal skillset. He was no slugger, but his speed could disrupt a game in ways that Louellen could appreciate. She saw in Dusty the ideal of a young Cherokee buck, and it warmed her heart. He liked having her behind home plate, watching him. When he did well, she patted his head. When he had a subpar game, she patted his head the same way. But Dusty knew she was with him and for him. And he imagined he played better when she attended his games.

Dusty's physical feats cheered his grandma, but she was also interested in her grandchildren's schoolwork. She enjoyed hearing about all the things they were learning in the classroom. Despite – or perhaps because of – her lack of formal education, everything about school interested Louellen Brodie.

Her mother, Miriam, valued the traditional Cherokee ways to the point that she didn't think her daughter needed to attend school. Her father, with his European heritage, thought a couple of years of education would do his daughter good. Being the head of their household, Jefferson Farrell had gotten his way. Louellen had attended school and learned the very basics of reading, writing and arithmetic.

However, Jefferson was not truly progressive concerning education for females. He pulled his daughter from school in the winter of her fourth-grade year. Miriam had fallen ill and would remain so until spring brought her revival.

All through that winter, nine-year-old Louellen handled the lion's share of the housework, including cooking, cleaning and laundry. This period defined her future: She would never return to school. She was able to read and write, poorly perhaps, but with some pride. Still, from that winter on, Louellen worked at being a good daughter and, later, at being a good wife.

XXX

After his cold welcome at the still, Dusty had walked over to his grandmother's home, arriving a bit before noon. He realized he was just about in time for lunch. Louellen was busy working in her large garden. It was warm work, and she wore a wide-brimmed straw hat to shade her dark, wrinkled face.

Dusty came trotting up the path that ran up from along Dermot's Branch. He stopped about 30 yards from the house to watch his grandma. She worked the hoe through the soil, chopping and raking and smoothing the rows. A few plants were up and growing. Others, planted more recently, were just battling to emerge. Louellen expertly handled her hoe to cut down competing weeds, eliminating their ability to use up precious water and nutrients her vegetables required.

Dusty had never realized how small she looked, bent over and laboring under the hot sun. He knew his grandma worked hard, but he never heard her complain about the work itself, only about the aches and pains this lifestyle brought her.

He had a sudden wish that he could help her, take over working the garden, let his grandma sit on the porch and rest. He thought about running up to her, taking the hoe and sending her into the shade. But young boys with good intentions don't always follow through. It was getting awfully warm to work in a garden. He could think of lots of things more fun than chopping weeds. As his good intentions faded, he ambled to the corner of the house and called out to her.

"Hi, grandma!"

Louellen turned and looked up. She nodded at Dusty, turned back to her garden and kept working. Dusty strode up to her and gave her a hug. That pleased Louellen, though she only responded by patting the boy's head. She resumed her work.

"It's kinda hot today, isn't it?" Dusty inquired.

"It's hot enough," she said without stopping.

"You gonna take a break soon?" the boy asked.

At this, the grandma stopped work, leaned against the hoe and eyed the far end of the garden.

"I'll finish this row. Almost time for lunch. You hungry, boy?"

"I sure am," Dusty admitted. "You want me to get the other hoe and help you with this row?" He was careful not to volunteer for a longer shift in the garden.

"No. Run and get the milk from the springhouse," his grandma replied. "I'll be in directly."

A slightly relieved Dusty scampered down to the springhouse, where Louellen kept milk, butter, cream and other foodstuffs that tended to spoil in the heat. She and Martin had electricity in the cabin, but no refrigerator or ice box. The springhouse was the only cold storage technology on the farmstead.

By the time his grandma came in from the garden, Dusty had a jug of milk on the kitchen table, along with two tin cups and two plates. Louellen took a towel off a bowl, revealing three biscuits left over from breakfast. She retrieved a butter knife and cut a biscuit in half. She opened a mason jar of blackberry jam and smeared the sweet, dark paste on both halves, handing the first – with the most jam, of course – to Dusty. Then she poured them each a little more than half a cupful of milk. They proceeded to eat.

After a few bites, Dusty got a curious look on his face. Louellen noticed but said nothing. Soon enough, the boy gathered his thoughts into a question.

"Grandma, why does Dad make moonshine all the time?" he asked her.

Louellen took another bite of her half biscuit and chewed for a few seconds.

"He is under a spell," she said. "Hiram thinks he needs liquor. He does not."

"Then … why does he drink it?" Dusty asked.

A few more seconds of chewing brought only a brief answer.

"He is unsatisfied," the grandmother shrugged.

"But why is he unsatisfied? He's better off than some folks," the grandson said. Dusty knew lots of people with fewer worldly good than his father. Lots of them got by without moonshine.

"Hiram had great dreams," his grandma explained. "He wanted something more than a home, a fire, food, a family. When his dreams did not come true, he was disappointed. Now he is not satisfied with the things he has."

"But why does that make him drink?" Dusty asked.

Louellen stopped eating and stared out the kitchen window for a long time before answering. Then, still looking out the window, she seemed to see something far, far away.

"He drinks to forget his life and remember his dreams," she said. "Too many Cherokee have done so."

Dusty pondered this response a bit before saying, "Well, that'll never happen to me. I'll always be happy with what I have. I won't wish for things I don't have."

His grandmother turned to look at the boy, perhaps appraising his resolve. "It is good to be thankful. But even the little we have can be taken away. This I know."

"No one will take you away from me, will they grandma?" Dusty asked.

"No one knows, my boy," she said, taking his young hand in her grip. "But, for your father, I see troubles. I see troubles for all my sons. I hope my visions are false."

Louellen slowly patted her grandson's hand. Then they sat silently together for a few minutes. Dusty eventually broke the stillness.

"Dad may want to whip me tonight," he said. "I sneaked up the hill to his still. He ran me off."

"Don't go there," his grandmother said sternly. "There is nothing but trouble there."

Louellen didn't know how right she would turn out to be. Her visions were not false.

Chapter 3

THE STILLNESS

Louellen always paid attention to her premonitions. It was part of her heritage and part of the belief system entrenched in the people of the region. Like other Ozark families, the Brodies lived in relative isolation. Generations had occupied the same hills or dells, growing closer to the land and learning a few of its secrets. They always listened, trying to learn what the land was telling them. Attempting to foresee troubles. Trying to forestall those troubles if they could.

Summer always seemed to deepen the sense of isolation. As the weather warms up in the spring, the trees of the Ozark hill country begin producing dense, leafy canopies. The greenery extends from the ground to high into the sky. The lush landscape rolls and curves up and down the hills, which undulate from modest to moderate to mountainous elevations. The land is blanketed with awakening plants and the ground is obscured from sight.

From late March, when dogwood trees begin to bud in the undergrowth, the internal workings of the timberland become increasingly concealed. Grasses green first. Then dogwoods, with their large, white, intoxicating blossoms, overshadow a backdrop of reviving trees. Bare winter branches begin to bud, gently accelerating their activity until the trees display a multitude of shades of green. Soon, the aroused forest bursts forth as its foliage blends the myriad hues into a beautiful natural camouflage. As the timber closes in, this verdant vista veils the terrain, denying observers more than a vague impression of what lies deep in these woods. At this point, it seems you can't see the trees for the forest.

But it's not just the camouflaging canopy that isolates these hills in summer. The advancing calendar also brings heat and humidity.

Almost daily, the intense sun bakes the sky and toasts the treetops. Degree by degree, the warmth seeps down onto the hills and collects in the hollows between them. When it's summer in the Ozarks, it's nearly always hot between those hills. And seldom will a cooling breeze infiltrate the layers of woodland to relieve the oppressive heat.

Above the vast woodland, the scorched sky turns a deep, almost tangible shade of blue. From a distance, a spectator almost believes he might ascend the tallest of the trees, reach out and touch the cerulean sky. More than one poet has considered snatching a little piece of this low-hanging heaven for a perpetual muse. But such efforts rarely bear lasting fruit. Some things can't be explained with words alone.

And then there's the sound. On the surface, you may hear the gentle swish of lilting leaves or quivering brush if, on occasion, a feeble breeze filters through the woods. Or you may hear the sharp notes of birds perched unseen in the upper limbs or soaring haughtily overhead. Or you might discern the buzz of insects welling up all around, fading as you walk by then swelling up again in your wake. Occasionally an old tree may creak or groan, complaining of some old and ancient malady.

But the overarching sound of these hills is silence. On still days, with the sun beating down and with no breeze reaching the ground, most people hear – or at least sense – a quietude, a remoteness, even a bittersweet sense of loneliness. This real sound of the Ozarks is a tentative silence. It's the soundtrack to life in these parts. Most every southern Missouri hillbilly feels it strongly.

To the stranger passing by, the sounds and scenery are no more than a fleeting fancy. A thing to wonder at then move on. The allure of the magnificent landscape is only a snapshot in time, a brief moment. It will fade to mere memory or perhaps be forgotten altogether as the twists and turns of daily living wear it into a small hazy image of a bygone summer day.

The wooded hills and the forests also serve another purpose. To most of the inhabitants, the close vegetation and hot, humid weather amount to the price of privacy. The nature of the woods ensures the solitude required to maintain their sense of independence and self-determination. This goes double for a particular segment of the population: These thick, heavily veiled hills and valleys provide a haven for local moonshiners.

The Ozark mountains have been home to countless liquor stills over uncounted decades. The distillation of spirits evolved into a solemn ritual bred into the fabric of the land. Generation after generation took to the hills or hollows to establish and stoke homemade contraptions to turn corn or other grain into powerful drink. Young lads and, yes, young lasses accompanied parents or grandparents to the family still to help feed the fire, ferment the grain and collect moonshine into jugs and jars.

These spirits were mostly produced for use of the local clan, but in times of need, they were a convenient currency that bootleggers could use to improve their family's financial condition. You could sell more corn more easily for more money as moonshine than as cattle or hog feed. Moonshine was easier than shelled corn to transfer to a ready "market."

In times of economic distress, an enterprising hillbilly could make a significant profit selling a few jugs of "stump liquor" or "white lightning" or "mountain dew" or whatever label the sellers chose to use for their production.

XXX

The ancestors of Hiram Brodie and his two brothers – including Louellen's husband, James – had handed down a long, even proud, legacy of alcohol production. Hiram, in particular, took to moonshining as a way of life. He used the seclusion of the family's cabin and the nearness of three isolated hills to keep his liquor enterprise concealed.

Hiram was the firstborn son of the firstborn son and so on for seven generations of Brodies, back to the point where knowledge of the family hierarchy was lost. Hiram was a thick-bodied and powerful man. Though he was half Scottish, he had inherited thick black hair and a dark complexion from his Native American relatives.

Hiram had his mother's dark blackish-brown eyes. He often wore a stony, expressionless countenance borrowed from her. Despite the deadpan expression, people looking into his face often sensed a smoldering resentment. Something fierce hid deep in those eyes. No one who looked closely doubted that Hiram had a hot temper that could flare suddenly.

In 1938, Hiram boasted a stout 36-year-old physique. His build was due partly to genetics and partly to rigorous manual labor. Hiram had worked for several years as a logger – or lumberjack, if you prefer. He retained the muscles he'd developed at that occupation, though he didn't maintain the intense work ethic that cutting timber required. When he needed money, he'd work. If he didn't particularly need anything, he would hunt, fish and drink. And make moonshine.

Hiram had found an ideal spot on the crest of a small but steep hillock, densely populated by trees and underbrush. The hill's sides were undisturbed by any natural pathways or manmade trails. Just north of this nameless, obscure hilltop was a taller and larger prominence, called Todd Hill after a local family that long ago homesteaded the northern (or far side) of the hill. This hill was a fairly formidable obstacle for those trying to locate Hiram's manufacturing center.

In addition, several branches of the Todd family had homes scattered up, down and around the sides of Todd Hill. Most were close friends of Hiram's, who would sound the alarm if any strangers – particularly lawmen – appeared on their side of the hill. This allowed Hiram and a few other moonshiners scattered about the area to escape into the thicker sections of the woods.

To the southwest of Hiram's hillock was an even bigger elevation, Dermot's Bluff. This eminence was not only larger and steeper than other two hills, it was choked on the near side with gullies and small ravines. These were old watercourses and were wet only during spring runoff or intense flooding. One significant stream, Dermot's Branch, flowed all year. It ran down the bluff and alongside the hillock that hid Hiram's still. Then the stream cut eastward and swept along very near Hiram's cabin. It was at this stream that Dusty had stopped to rest as he had retreated from his dad and the still.

The two larger hills and the stream flanked Hiram's little hill on three sides: north, west and south. That left only the eastern approach as a likely avenue for strangers or snoopers. Hiram's own cabin lay about a mile and a half east of the hill.

When he had discovered this favorable position, he had begun moving his still from a dense hollow a half mile closer to his home. With help from obliging relatives (and a conscripted Dusty), he had hauled his equipment up to the new location. He left some odds and ends and remnants at the old site in case agents of the federal government, the so-called revenuers, stumbled onto his land. He hoped they'd take the vacated site for an active still and, if they had to bust up something, they could destroy bits of useless materials.

Hiram had been careful to avoid wearing an obvious path to the hill where he had placed his new still. If he were feeling a bit wary, he would take indirect routes to his hideaway. If he were feeling slightly more paranoid, he might even cancel a planned trip up the slope. But the lure of liquor always brought him back sooner or later.

In the spring of 1938, Hiram had taken his last stash of corn, sugar, malt and added the requisite yeast to start a new batch of mash. It was this mash that he was tending when Dusty had surprised him on the hill.

In addition to officers of the law, many moonshiners had one more adversary to guard against. Competing moonshiners didn't always get along. Some minor squabbles turned into moderate rivalries. Occasionally, all-out feuds might ensue. The Brodies were not immune to this type of animosity. Their antagonists were another hill family with conflicting views on the distillation and trade of illegal alcohol.

Chapter 4

THE HOG AND THE TRESPASSER

An incident that rekindled the animosity that spring had already occurred. Just a few weeks earlier, it had been Cleve who had almost shot someone. To no one's surprise, it was a member of the Jennings family.

The Brodie and Jennings clans had been sporadic adversaries for decades. Their conflict was never as violent and bloody as the classic Hatfields and McCoys feud, but the members of the two families didn't like, trust or tolerate each other easily.

One storied confrontation involved a disagreement involving Tom Brodie, the father of James and grandfather of Hiram. He had come to loggerheads with Earl Jennings, the great uncle of Kyle and Jake, who were about the same age as the Brodie brothers. Tom had accused Earl of stealing watermelons, apples and peaches from Brodie land. Earl had denied it. Furthermore, he told neighbors that if Tom Brodie ever accused him to his face, he'd leave Tom Brodie "laying in the dust looking at the sky."

One day, Tom showed up at the Avery store while Earl was standing outside shooting the breeze with some friends. One member of the congregation saw Tom walking up the road and alerted Earl. Startled, Earl hurried into the store, grabbed an axe and stood barring the front door. The gossipers moved aside at Tom approached. When the latter looked up, he was facing his armed adversary.

"You ain't comin' in here, Tom Brodie," Earl said, hefting the axe for emphasis.

Tom Brodie considered the threat. Would Earl really take a swing at him? If he did, could Tom counter the attack? Valor got the better part of discretion. Tom stepped up on the porch of the little store, reached out quickly and snatched the axe from his slow-reacting foe.

"Earl, if you wanna fight me, next time bring something more dangerous than this," Tom said, shoving his way past the shocked Mr. Jennings. Tom walked into the store and handed the unused axe back to the proprietor.

Nothing came of this incident. Tom didn't get his melons or fruit back. Earl didn't leave Tom in the dust. It was just one more encounter that split the families, increasing their mutual ill will.

Despite such episodes, for the most part, the Brodie and Jennings factions coexisted. Neither side particularly wanted an all-out confrontation. Both bloodlines deserved their reputations as folks you just didn't tangle with. Especially when they were drunk.

A neighbor who knew both clans well, put it this way: "The Brodie boys and Jennings boys can cut more timber, drink more whiskey, get up the next morning and still cut more timber than any other bunch in the county."

But the distrust ran deep. So, when Cleve found a hog was missing in the early spring of 1938, it was preordained that he would suspect a Jennings of thievery. Cleve took his rifle and tramped the perimeter of his property, looking for any signs of the patriarch, Lem Jennings, or his sons, Jake and Kyle.

Kyle happened to be taking a shortcut through a corner of one of Cleve's fields. In truth, he was more likely heading for a romantic rendezvous than sneaking around snatching livestock. But Cleve didn't feel inclined to give the man the benefit of the doubt. He called to Kyle to stop in his tracks and keep his hands in plain sight. Kyle, though unarmed, wasn't the type to yield so quickly. Recognizing Cleve, he waved off the armed enemy and continued ambling across the newly planted field.

Cleve felt a flush of anger at the trespasser's impudence. He took careful aim with his rifle and sent a bullet into the ground not five feet ahead of Kyle. The interloper stopped in his tracks and turned to face the furious Brodie brother. They both knew Cleve could have hit Kyle – or at least come much closer – if he had intended to. They glared at one another, neither willing to back down. Finally, Cleve broke the tense silence.

"Kyle, you get offa my land right now," he yelled. "By God, I'll shoot you if you don't."

"I ain't hurtin' your land," Kyle replied, as bravely as a man could with a rifle pointing at him.

"I'll be hurtin' you if you don't hightail it out of my field," his foe countered. Cleve, in his late 20s, was a small man with a big mouth. He was a few inches shorter and several pounds lighter than his older brothers. He had the disposition of a banty rooster and the vocabulary of a sailor. He had started his share of arguments and fights in his short life, some of which he had finished and some where his brothers had been obliged to support him to even the odds. Still, he was a scrappy opponent and not one to be taken too lightly.

"Listen, Cleve, I'm just walking here," Kyle said with a serious frown. "I ain't doing no harm."

"You're trespassing," Cleve snarled. "If you don't get going, you'll be carryin' lead with you when you leave."

Just then a voice from Cleve's left – the direction Kyle had come from – called out.

"Hold on there, Cleve. Put the gun down." It was the sheriff, John Lawson, coming up the hill toward where the two contestants were squared off.

Lawson was a likable, level-headed man of about 40 with dark brown hair, sharp narrow eyes and a sharp nose that may have been broken two of three times during the many altercations that accompanied his job. He was cool, softspoken and unpretentious. But he was as tough as any man in the county. As he slowly stalked up the hill, carefully walking between rows of newly planted corn, he mapped out in his mind how best to diffuse this touchy situation. He finally stopped when about 15 yards from either of the combatants.

"First off, Cleve, tell me what's going on here," he said.

"I caught Kyle trespassing," Cleve said brusquely.

"That a good reason to point a gun at him?" Lawson asked.

"Well, I believe he stole one of my hogs," Cleve said. "I found one missing yesterday, and this is the only person I've seen on my land since then."

"That's not enough proof, Cleve, and you know it," the sheriff countered.

Kyle started to respond and give his side of the story, but the sheriff held his hand up to silence the unarmed trespasser. He let Cleve have his say about protecting his land and wanting his pig back. Then the sheriff turned to the accused.

"What about it, Kyle? You steal any of Cleve's livestock?" Lawson asked the accused man.

Kyle vehemently denied the charge, punctuating his rebuttal with a string of curses. Kyle's ardent insistence on his innocence seemed overblown to Lawson – so much so that it raised serious doubts to the sheriff concerning Kyle's possible guilt. But, as Lawson had told Cleve, there was no proof. Just suspicion.

"All right, there's no way to tell what happened to the hog," Lawson said. "Cleve, you take your gun and go back home. Kyle, you get off Cleve's property and don't come back without an engraved invitation. I don't want to hear about you two trying to settle this with violence. Try that and you'll both land in jail. And … I have to warn you … the food there ain't too great."

Lawson looked hard at both men, waiting for them to move. Slowly, Kyle started retracing his steps back across the field toward the fence that marked the limit of Cleve's land. Just as slowly, Cleve started backing away toward his home, finally turning to stomp off as the sheriff watched. Lawson stayed until he was fairly sure neither would double back to renew the encounter.

The situation diffused, at least temporarily, Lawson exhaled deeply. He became aware for the first time how tense he had been while standing between the sworn enemies.

"All in a day's work, sheriff," he told himself.

Then he headed back down to the road where he had left his car when he'd heard Cleve's warning shot.

Lawson knew it was likely that the enmity between Brodie and the Jennings families would cause him more heartburn eventually. As he made his way back to his car, that concern continued to grow. One day, sooner or later, these families would spill blood. And Lawson would have to try to clean up the mess.

XXX

Cleve wasted no time telling his brothers of his run-in with Kyle Jennings. Hiram and Martin were more than sympathetic, especially regarding the loss of the hog. They felt their brother had every right to run Kyle off his land. Proof or not, they believed the lost porker was the work of Kyle, his brother or his pa.

However, none of the Brodies took exception to the sheriff's interference. He was only doing his job. Besides, his arrival hadn't altered much. Had he not shown up, Cleve would have accomplished the same thing, driving the villain away with the muzzle of his rifle.

In the long run, the event only served to rekindle their distrust and suspicion of their rivals. That summer, they'd be on the lookout for any other Jennings shenanigans. And they'd make darn sure to protect their land and property from their long-time adversaries.

XXX

For his part, Kyle was only slightly annoyed by his expulsion from Cleve's field. He had bigger fish to fry. He was courting a local woman, and his priority was the eventual conquest of this handsome gal.

Kyle reluctantly strolled home, no worse for his encounter with Cleve and Sheriff Lawson. He had time to figure out ways to even the score with the Brodies. For now, all he cared about was getting home. His mother would have dinner on the table soon. And his palate was anticipating the wonderful taste of fresh pork chops.

Chapter 5

THE YOUNGER SISTERS

On the day his dad had run him away from the still, Dusty had stayed with his grandma until early afternoon. Despite the possibility that his dad may have returned from the hill, he decided he should go home. He hugged Louellen and left her to her gardening and housework. Dusty followed the familiar path through the woods. A short, half-mile walk brought him to a structure that was essentially a cabin, but a solid, substantial cabin.

It was constructed of split logs with boards covering the inner walls. The home was essentially a three-room affair. It featured a large, broad sitting room that took up the front half of the building. This room doubled as a bedroom, with a big, comfortable bed in the corner on the left side of the room.

Dusty had slept there when he was younger, but now his two sisters shared the bed. The kitchen took up a large section of the back half of the cabin. His mom and dad's bedroom claimed the remaining space in the back right corner of the building.

In the front room, a large pot-bellied stove occupied the right side of the room. A flue rose to the ceiling and over to a stout chimney against the north wall. Other than the wood stove in the kitchen, which vented up to the ceiling, this was the only source of heat.

The front of the house featured a wide porch that ran the length of the residence. The last 10 feet on the left side had been enclosed to provide another little room. This cubicle had served as a closet, storeroom and/or mudroom over the years. But as Hiram Brodie's family had grown, he had converted it into a bedroom for Dusty.

Unlike the original main structure, three of the four walls comprising this room contained no split logs – only the same sort of planks that covered the inner walls of rest of the house. This room was hot in the summer and cold in the winter. Of course, there was no air conditioning in the main cabin, but at least it had doors and windows front and back as well as windows on either side to let in the breeze.

The door of Dusty's room, also made of thin planking, opened onto the porch, near the front door of the cabin. Hiram had rigged a screen door so that Dusty, on hot nights, could take advantage of the cooler outside air. The only interesting feature of the room was a small window, with real glass, facing the front. It was not meant for opening, and early-morning sun often warmed the room quickly. The window's only real value was that it gave Dusty a chance to look out at the road when anyone drove, rode or walked by.

XXX

When Dusty neared the cabin, he noticed smoke coming from the vent on the left side of the roof. That meant his mother had the kitchen stove burning. It was strange for her to be cooking this early in the afternoon, especially on such a warm day.

He headed toward the front door, hoping his dad hadn't returned from the still. He was in luck. With production of his latest batch well under way, Hiram wouldn't leave his still for another two days.

Dusty pulled open the screen door, which squeaked softly.

"Mom? I'm home," he said, walking into to the front room. His eyes hadn't adjusted to the dark interior of the house, so it was hard to make out any details. He smelled something appetizing coming from the kitchen and he walked across the room to look inside.

It wasn't his mother. It was his two sisters. There was flour all over the table along with all kinds of bowls and cooking utensils. He saw a jar on the table. Both sisters looked comical. Their hands and arms, up to their elbows, were dusted with flour … as were their faces.

"What's going on?" Dusty asked.

"Can't you tell?" said Nancy. At 10, she was the older sister.

"Looks like a sack of flour exploded while you two were in range," Dusty replied. His sisters exchanged sour looks, and younger sister Jenny stuck her tongue out at him. "What are you two up to?" Dusty asked suspiciously.

"We're baking a peach pie," Nancy retorted. "If you're not nice, you don't get any."

"Not a single bite," added Jenny, frowning the way only a girl of seven can.

"Lucky me," Dusty said smiling at them. "At least I won't get food poisoning."

"Ha-ha," Nancy said. She liked her brother, but he could be a rascal at times. And he wasn't as funny as he thought he was.

"Does mom know you're messing up the kitchen?" Dusty asked doubtfully.

"She sure does," Nancy said, her nose righteously in the air. "She wants the pie done when she gets home from the store."

"Why'd she go to the store?" the boy said half to his sisters and half to himself. He knew money was tight. His mother was pinching pennies these days. She and his dad had bought what supplies they needed – or at least what they could afford – just a couple of days earlier. They'd gone to town when he and his sisters were at school. What could his mother possibly need today?

"I dunno," Nancy said as if she didn't care. "Jenny, did you hear mom say why she was going?"

"Not me," Jenny said with wide eyes. She thought her answer was important and gave it solemnly.

"Well, how long's she been gone?" Dusty asked.

"I don't know," Nancy said. "Maybe a couple of hours. We wanted to go with her, but she said if we stayed here, we could bake a pie. She even opened a jar of peaches for us before she left."

"Because you're too weak, with those chicken arms," Dusty prodded his sister. He knew she hated it when he called her Chicken Arms. It was a meaningless term, but it made his sister mad, so he liked to say it when he had the chance.

"I don't have chicken arms!" Nancy yelled, just as Dusty had expected. "Besides, you have a mule head."

"Mule head, mule head," Jenny joined in. She liked to take sides when her brother and sister teased each other. This time, she was on Nancy's side. She figured that was smarter since her sister would decide who got the first piece of pie and how big that piece might be.

Dusty didn't like to be called Mule Head any more than his sister liked to be called Chicken Arms. His mom sometimes said he was mule-headed, which he hated. It hurt his feelings. But he didn't want his sisters to know this, so he changed the subject.

"So when does the disaster come out of the oven?" he said, once again taking a dig at his sister's cooking skills.

"Let me look again," Nancy said, taking a towel and opening the stove door. The pie was light brown on top, but the edges were beginning to burn. Was it done in the middle? Would more time burn the crust beyond edibility? She wasn't sure. She decided to take the pie out now and put it back in if it wasn't done enough. She fumbled with the towel and a pot holder to secure the pie tin and pull it out of the oven.

"Need any help?" Dusty asked, not sure his sister could handle the task.

"Not from you," Nancy sneered. Just then the pie tilted to her left. She moved to keep it from falling. In the process, the hot pan touched her left palm near her thumb. She yelped but manage to lift the pie and drop it on the top of the stove. The pie bounced and did quarter turn before gravity pulled it safely to rest atop the stove.

Jenny jumped back in fear as if the pie could burn her too. Dusty, however, moved quickly to help Nancy. A red burn mark was appearing on the meat of her hand. Dusty grabbed her wrist and pulled her to the sink, pumping the pump until the water began to flow. Then he stuck Nancy's hand under the water.

She yelped again and beat her brother's shoulder with her right fist. His sister knew how to throw a punch, and her jabs actually hurt a bit. But Dusty held her hand firmly under the water. When the flow slackened he pumped the handle again to release more cooling water on the wound.

"Jenny, fetch me the butter," he commanded. "Bring it over here right now."

Jenny stood still, petrified by the scene in front of her.

"Jenny, I need you. Bring the butter NOW!" Dusty yelled.

Startled, Jenny finally stirred, grabbing the butter off the table and taking it to her brother. Dusty took a generous dollop with his fingers. He looked at Nancy, still crying but no longer hitting him.

"This may hurt a little bit," he said. "Are you brave?"

Nancy simply looked at him through her tears and pouted, "Braver than you."

Dusty almost smiled. That was his sister: Putting up a defiant front in the face of pain.

The brother softly applied the butter, slathering the soothing balm over his sister's injured hand. The heel of her hand had turned an angry red, but the water followed by the improvised balm was dulling the pain.

"Jenny, I need one more thing," Dusty said to his little sister.

"What?" Jenny asked, now ready to provide any help she could.

"Get a chair and get in the top cabinet, the one to the right," Dusty instructed. Jenny pulled a wooden chair to the spot and climbed up. She opened the cabinet door.

"Now what?" she asked.

"I need the aspirin bottle, it's St. Joseph's Aspirin, I think. Can you read the bottle?" Dusty said, still holding his sister's hurt hand.

"I know what aspirin is," Jenny said. "I've seen mom take it." It's true their mother used aspirin liberally for severe headaches. She often complained, and some days she'd lie in bed for hours. Not many household chores got done those days until Nancy and Jenny got big enough to help.

Jenny climbed back down with the medicine bottle and ran it over to Dusty. He let go of Nancy's arm, poured out two pills and had her swallow them with a cup of water.

"That'll help soon, sis," he said. "How's it feeling now?"

"It still hurts some … but not as bad," she said. Her tears were drying up. "Thanks."

"No problem," Dusty said. Wanting to take her mind off the residual pain, he added, "Let's see about that pie now."

The pie had continued to cook slowly from the heat of the oven below it. Dusty cut into it and found it was good and done. Jenny got the first piece. Nancy got the biggest piece. They left about 60 percent of it for supper. Dusty told his sisters it was a good peach pie. It wouldn't have won any prizes at the county fair, but it wasn't bad. Not bad at all. And it certainly helped relieve the distress caused by his sister's accident.

XXX

In many ways, Nancy Anne Brodie was a typical middle child. Dusty was the eldest and a son to boot. In the 1930s, that made him the unchallenged luminary, the pride of the family, so to speak. Nancy was a girl, thus viewed as a lesser child. She was the second born, meaning she would always be less experienced and therefore less trustworthy than her older brother.

While not a tomboy, Nancy was no fragile female. She didn't sob when she got a splinter or recoil from creepy crawling critters or flinch when baiting her own hook with a live worm. She did her chores with minimal complaint. She didn't grumble excessively about sweltering days or frigid nights. Most of the time, she was a real trooper.

But she was capable of jealousy. She envied Dusty for the amount of freedom she perceived him to enjoy. She resented the praise he earned for making good marks in school when, in truth, she was also at the top of her class.

Nancy thought her lot in life was a little unfair. She was expected to help her mother in the kitchen, with the laundry or with other housework. She washed and dried dishes, swept the floor and learned to iron and fold clothing. She wanted to learn more substantial things. In fact, she envisioned herself as a lawyer or doctor or – almost as thrilling – a librarian.

But perhaps most galling of all was the expectation that she should perpetually look after her younger sister. Nancy in no way felt she should be her sister's keeper. They shared a bed. They shared their few toys. They walked to and from school together.

What was even more aggravating was the fact that Jenny practically worshipped Nancy – until the younger girl reached the age of 11 and a small, predictable sibling rivalry arose. But for now, Jenny followed Nancy everywhere. It seemed Nancy never had a minute alone. Even when she went to the outhouse, Jenny usually followed. At least the facility was a two-holer.

XXX

Jenny Joy Brodie, the youngest daughter, was the impish one, the pugnacious one. She was almost equally comfortable following around behind her big brother as she was shadowing her sister. She stuck to whichever sibling struck her fancy or seemed to offer a better advantage. For instance, if Dusty had a dime, she'd follow him to the store in case he was in the mood to buy a soda pop … or two.

Jenny lived very much for the here and now. Tomorrow was too far away to worry about. She concerned herself with the immediate world and immediate gratification. Consequences be damned.

She would do things that could get her in trouble without considering the ramifications or costs. For some reason, this seemed to endear her to her parents. While they didn't have the means to spoil the baby of the family, Hiram and Eliza did favor Jenny is some ways. Her punishments were less severe and her sins more quickly forgiven.

Dusty and Nancy could never figure out how she got by with it all, especially the backtalking. Jenny could make a sarcastic comment to her mom or dad, and often they'd just laugh it off. Or at worst, give her a quick glower. If either of the elder siblings had done so, the best they could hope for was a loud scolding – and there was always the threat of a severe whipping.

Dusty and Nancy sometimes resented Jenny because of what they believed was her preferential status as the baby of the family. When they were particularly vindictive, they would ramble through the woods, leaving Jenny lagging behind and alone. Or they would play games, intentionally leaving Jenny out of the fun.

Jenny would complain to her mother, or sometimes to her father. In the former case, Eliza almost always ordered the two to play with their younger sister. She even suggested – and occasionally insisted – they let Jenny win. When the young girl whined to her father, his verdict usually favored Jenny. The worst outcome was when Hiram ordered all three kids to stop playing and perform some needless chore. Jenny would have to help and, thus, also would be unable to play, but at least she had the satisfaction of ruining her siblings' fun.

In her early years, Jenny was a bona fide tomboy. If Nancy could abide slimy fauna, her younger sister was positively entranced by them. Any creature – insect, reptile or mammal – filled her with curiosity and wonder. Little Jenny would turn over rocks to find scummy bugs and worms. She started collections of various type of insects, amphibians and reptiles.

Sometimes she brought her menageries of tiny creatures indoors. A couple of times, the captives escaped and scattered throughout the cabin. This caused Eliza a great amount of grief. Jenny often tried to blame Dusty or Nancy for these insect incursions, but her parents knew their youngest was most likely to blame.

One incident, when she was five years old, almost took Jenny away from the family. She was playing on the north side of the house when she saw a movement in the low brush. She stalked the motion through the grass and leaves into thicker vegetation. Suddenly the movement stopped. Jenny peered into the brush and slowly moved the weeds aside. Nothing. She moved a little to her left and parted the greenery again. Still nothing. She took another step left and saw a quick movement near her foot.

She had almost stepped on a copperhead. The snake had tried to hide, but Jenny had tracked it too well. With a quick strike, the snake nailed her on the foot, near her big toe. Being barefoot as usual, she had no protection from the snake's fangs. She ran into the house, screaming for her mother. Eliza recognized the cause immediately: a snake bite. But what kind of snake?

Although there were several species of snakes in the hills, copperheads were the greatest danger. There were some rattlesnakes, but they gave the characteristic warning before attacking. Anyone familiar with rattlers knew to stop, figure out where the snake was and move away from it. Many bites were prevented by a rattler's distinctive alarm.

Then there were water moccasins, also called cottonmouths. Though lacking the loud alert of the rattlesnake, cottonmouths usually adopted a defensive attitude. They either tried to slither away or coiled to raise and wave their tails while opening their mouths wide to show their perilous fangs. They rarely bit unless cornered or handled.

Unfortunately for Jenny, the copperhead had given her no obvious warning. Some people claimed they could smell an angry copperhead, but – like Jenny – most people never knew the danger existed until it was too late.

Eliza started to treat the wound, sending Dusty to the barn, where Hiram was working. When Hiram and Dusty returned, Eliza had slit the bite marks with a knife to bleed away the venom. Hiram began to squeeze more blood from Jenny's foot to expel as much of the toxin as possible. The next treatment didn't appear in any medical volume, but it was a viable option for hill folks.

Eliza retrieved a large potato from the root cellar and cut it into four pieces. Over the next 36 hours, she and Hiram kept a piece of raw potato bandaged tightly to the bitemark. Each slice eventually grew dark grey to black. The Brodies took this as proof the potato was drawing the venom out.

Jenny grew sick and feverish, but she never succumbed. By the time the last slice of potato came off her foot, she was rallying quickly. Whether the potato was effective or whether the bite simply wasn't fatal, no one ever knew. But the Brodies made sure to have a few potatoes in the cellar from then on … just in case.

Once Jenny recovered, she went right back to hunting small animals. In a different world or a different time, she might have had a future as a veterinarian, a zoologist, perhaps a zookeeper. Then again, maybe she'd just turn out to be another hillbilly with a houseful of woodland critters.

Chapter 6

THE DISTANT MOTHER

After they ate the peach pie, the Brodie kids sat on the porch talking and watching the birds come and go. Eventually, they saw their mom walking along the dirt trail that headed northward toward Avery. Jenny ran up the road to meet her mother while Dusty and Nancy stood up and waited for her to get to the porch.

On the way back to the cabin, Jenny had told her mother – in no chronological order – what had happened with the pie, the burnt hand and the use of butter and aspirin on the patient. When Eliza reached the two older children, she was greatly confused.

Nancy took over, telling most of the story, emphasizing how brave she had been and how her hand hardly hurt at all now. Dusty filled in the details he thought were pertinent. Eventually, Eliza was able to piece together nearly the whole story. Then she led her kids on into the house.

If she was surprised by their story of the afternoon's goings-on, she was shocked by the state of her kitchen. She had thought Nancy, and even Jenny, knew better than to leave such a mess. With the burnt hand situation, and the obvious need to sample the pie at once, none of the kids had given much thought to cleaning up.

Eliza was uncharacteristically restrained. Did she feel guilty for leaving her young daughters alone to operate a hot oven? Whatever motivated her, she calmly and simply asked Jenny to help Dusty clean up the mess. Meanwhile, Eliza sat in the front room, holding her injured daughter on her lap, embracing and murmuring to Nancy. No matter how brave she wanted to be, Nancy couldn't help enjoying the doting attentions of her mother.

By the time Hiram came home – after two nights at the still – and found out about the incident, Nancy was fast on the path to healing. His only complaint was that the family had left him just one little piece of peach pie. He grumbled about that for a few days before dropping the subject completely.

XXX

On the third day after the kitchen accident, all three kids went to visit their grandmother. When Louellen saw Nancy's hand, she insisted on soothing it with honey and making a bandage to hold the honey to the wound. She explained to Nancy and Jenny that honey helped heal burns and open wounds.

Nancy told her that Dusty had run cool water over the burn, then applied butter to it. Their grandmother nodded at him approvingly, a silent form of praise.

"I helped get the butter and aspirin," Jenny said, wanting her contributions recognized. Louellen didn't disappoint the child.

"It is good to bring medicine when someone is hurt," she said, touching Jenny's cheek in affection.

But when Louellen heard that Eliza had been gone at the time, in town for two or three hours, she frowned. Like Dusty, she wondered why her daughter-in-law would need to go to the store – and be gone so long – when Hiram had taken her to the store just a day or two before the accident. She pondered a moment then looked at Dusty.

"What did your mother bring home from the store?" Louellen asked him.

In the commotion with his wounded sister, Dusty hadn't noticed. Now that he thought about it, he couldn't recall his mom carrying anything when she came in.

"I don't know," he said. "Whatever it was, I didn't see it."

"Maybe she had it in her bag," Nancy offered.

"Maybe so," Louellen said. "Well, it doesn't matter."

But her mind continued to work over Eliza's reasons for going into town and leaving two young girls at a hot kitchen stove.

XXX

Eliza Jane Cottrell came from an Ozark family that could trace its hill-billy lineage back seven generations. The original settler was Ambrose Cottrell, who had come to the Ozarks before Missouri was a state.

Ambrose had staked his claim in the hills along the Eleven Point River in the late 1810s. He had scratched out a farm and made a go in the rugged wilderness. Ambrose never got rich or even close to it, but he sank deep roots from which six more generations had sprung.

As a whole, the Cottrell clan was fiercely independent and private. That didn't make them much different from other settlers who were populating the hills and bottoms along the Eleven Point. But they were regarded as a little odd – in a land where curious folk were not rare.

The Cottrells seemed to hold some strange beliefs. They tended to bend the Bible to suit their immediate needs. Again, this wasn't uncommon. But many of the Cottrell men – as well as most of the women who married into the family – adopted odd spiritual doctrines. One thing their neighbors learned was never to enter a religious conversation with a Cottrell unless you wanted an impromptu sermon that might present a passel of dubious theological beliefs.

Eliza came from a branch of the family that carried their divine dogma even further. Her father, Grant, read the Bible each and every evening. He would ponder the passages during the night, sometimes rising from his bed to re-read a few verses. Then he would ponder some more.

On many occasions, he would wake the next morning with a new realization. This fresh understanding would dominate his thoughts, his conversations and sometimes his actions all day. Then, back at his table that evening, Grant would read another chapter and deliberate anew, quite likely forgetting the epiphany that had led him throughout that day.

More than one neighbor had come upon Grant Cottrell in his fields or out in the woods preaching to a nonexistent congregation.

His passion and fervor were enough to unnerve most of these accidental witnesses. Some people took to avoiding Grant – and his family – if at all possible.

At home, Eliza's mother backed up her man, no matter how bizarre his notions. She made sure the children listened to their father when he expounded on spiritual matters. The kids, two boys and three girls, were expected to comprehend his ramblings even when they changed from day to day. Thus, the whole lot of them learned early on to parrot their father's beliefs and fake an understanding of his odd philosophies.

Each of the confused children invariably left home at the first opportunity, abandoning the irrational world in which their parents had raised them. One boy joined the military, another set off to ride the rails in search of adventure and the eldest sister married at the age of 15. Another sister simply disappeared. It was assumed she'd run off to get away from her oppressive parents, but no one ever knew for sure what happened to her.

As for the youngest, Eliza, while she remained at home, she toed the line and feigned conviction to her father's bizarre universe. She secretly coped by developing an obsession that pacified her mind and provided a haven from her zealous father's world. She began dreaming of boys.

Young Eliza developed crushes at the drop of a hat. Early on, these were harmless little infatuations. They rarely lasted long, and she kept them mostly to herself … except for a few cryptic comments to other girls at school.

Even the boys noticed Eliza's coquettish behavior. She joined in conversations and games with her schoolmates, but her attention was frequently focused on this or that boy, depending on her mood. She was known for boldly asking a boy – whichever one caught her fancy – to walk her home from school. The next day, however, she might invite another lad to see her home. Or at least partway home if their paths soon diverged.

Then she set her sights on Hiram Brodie. In his early teens, Hiram was somewhat handsome, in a rough-hewn sort of way. He had the coal black hair of a Native American, with wide, muscular shoulders. He had a confident, even brash, air about him. Hiram wasn't a charmer, but he liked to tease the girls. Before long, he began to take greater interest in the opposite sex, much greater interest than he took in his education. For Hiram, school was about the four R's: Reading, Writing, 'Rithmatic and Romance.

Again, it was harmless stuff. Tease a girl about her hair, compliment her dress, make much ado about a correct response to a teacher's question. At recess, Hiram spent lots of time with all the "pretty" girls. When he was captain, choosing sides for baseball or some other contest, he always picked the girls he liked. His teams didn't always win, but Hiram sure enjoyed his recesses.

He had a rival in this amorous pastime. Naturally, it was a member of the Jennings family. If two bloodlines were going to tangle in this neck of the woods, it most likely would be the Brodie and Jennings clans.

Jake Jennings also liked the young ladies. For Hiram, it was mostly a mischievous game. However, Jake took flirting very seriously. He sized up the girls, learned what lines worked on which ones and tried to entice the receptive ones away for a little kissing and cuddling. People weren't surprised. Jake came by his libido honestly.

His older brother, Kyle, was a famous (or infamous, if you had a daughter) little Casanova. His reputation was well-established and well-deserved. By age 18, Kyle was married to a pretty but ignorant young thing. She was already "with child" when the wedding was held. Rumors were rampant in the community that at least two other careless girls were carrying Kyle's seed.

Younger brother Jake was eager to make his own conquests. Even when he was 12 or 13, he was talking about how he was going to have his way with this or that attractive female student. The "good girls" avoided being alone with – or even particularly near – Jake Jennings. The "bad girls" … that was another story.

By the time he was 15, Jake appeared to be trying to equal his brother's record. Some girls, hormones driving strange new thoughts and feelings, didn't so much mind Hiram's teasing or Jake's advances.

A few adventurous ones allowed young Mr. Jennings to lead them to secluded nooks for a little fooling around.

XXX

One of the girls Hiram liked to tease was Eliza Cottrell. Although two years younger than Hiram, Eliza was blossoming early into a fairly pretty girl. She would never achieve what most people would call true beauty. She had dull brown hair and too-thin lips, but her eyes were captivating. They were a soft brown with green specks that seemed to wax or wane in different lighting. Sometimes the green flecks seemed large and bright, sometimes tiny and timid.

When Eliza reached the age of 14, boys – and other girls – started to notice the enchanting quality of those eyes. Her face seemed lovelier as she ripened. One day at recess, Hiram became aware of the magnetic pull of those eyes.

Most of the students were playing an intense game of Red Rover. Hiram's team had called out Eliza. "Red rover, red rover, we dare Eliza over!" Eliza had run almost straight toward Hiram. He and another girl had snagged Eliza as she tried to break through their arms. Eliza had fallen back, and Hiram had instinctively reached out to catch her. He ended up on one knee staring down into those bewitching eyes, the green speckles in full radiance.

"Are you awright?" Hiram asked in a tone more tender than he had intended.

"Yeah, I'm fine," Eliza replied staring deep into Hiram's dark eyes. "Just got the wind knocked out of me a little."

Hiram forgot all about the other students. The only thing he saw was Eliza.

That was the start of a tentative courtship. In time, it developed into a relationship pockmarked with mercurial moments. Their on-again, off-again infatuation brought both of them repeated ribbing from their peers. Some of their friends even made bets on whether Hiram and Eliza would be "sparking" during certain events such as the school picnic, Fourth of July, the first day of school in September.

After about 18 months of this, things came to a head. One day Hiram was teasing another cute girl, which filled Eliza with envy. She began flirting openly with Jake Jennings, especially when she suspected Hiram was watching. Hiram got mad and threatened Jake. When Hiram saw them together again a few days later, he began ignoring Eliza. This time, the ice was slow to thaw. The animosity went on for weeks then months. Everyone assumed it was over between the couple. They were wrong.

XXX

During this time, Hiram was struggling to stay interested in school. He had been a decent but unmotivated student. But by his mid-teens, he was weary of book learning. Playing hooky was normal for Ozark lads, and Hiram made sure to do his fair share. As time went by, he began skipping school more often. By 10th grade, his mom was the only thing keeping him in school.

Louellen valued education, as had her deceased husband, James. He had made her promise to send the boys to school as long as she could make them go. But now, she was losing control of Hiram. He was too big for her to whip. He was too stubborn for her to lecture. He was too selfish to consider the feelings of an "old woman" (his words) when fun and adventure beckoned.

When he turned 17, Hiram decided he'd had enough of school. He joined several other men and older boys on a logging crew. It was hard work but good money. Hiram learned the finer points of logging, of cursing and of drinking. Within a year, he had become very good at all three.

Slowly, he started seeing Eliza again. They couldn't deny their mutual attraction. Eliza was still mildly interested in Jake Jennings, but she made the cold calculation that Hiram would be a better mate. Although she was increasingly desperate to get away from her parents, she wanted to make a wise choice for a husband.

She started being much sweeter to Hiram. She complimented him often and laughed at every corny joke he told. She quickly wrapped him around her finger. The young Brodie man couldn't resist those brownish green, greenish brown eyes. Hiram resolved to have her. He asked Eliza to marry him. She didn't put up much of a fight. Shortly after Hiram turned 18 – and a few days before Eliza turned 16 – they were married.

Hiram moved out of the house that he shared with his mother and brothers, Martin and Cleve. The newlyweds took over a rundown shack and made their initial home together. Over the next couple of years, with money earned from logging, Hiram and his brothers had built a relatively substantial cabin where Dusty and his sisters were eventually born.

Both Eliza and Hiram were stubborn. It was difficult for them to express the love and affection they felt. They continued having disagreements and disputes. Their first years together were hard. Hiram thought a few times about moving out and leaving Eliza for good. But something always stopped him. During this time, Eliza was learning how far she could go and still be able to pull her husband back home.

What saved the marriage in all likelihood was Eliza's first pregnancy. It ended with a stillborn baby boy, but the thought of having a son mellowed Hiram enough that he chose to put up with Eliza. Soon she was pregnant again. This time, she delivered a healthy baby boy. They named him Joshua James Brodie. As a toddler, they began calling him Dusty.

Hiram was a happy if often absent father. Like many fathers in the 1930s, he wasn't overly affectionate toward his kids. But he was proud of them. When he was around. And sober.

Eliza on the other hand, viewed motherhood as a chore. She liked to show off Dusty – as well as her daughters when they were born – but she seemed only to tolerate the responsibilities of parenthood.

Eliza wasn't exactly a bad mother. She clothed and fed her children. She nursed them when they were ill. She taught them what little she knew about life and living. But she kept her emotions mostly closed off. She was sparse with praise and maybe a little too liberal with criticism. She didn't mind using a paddle or switch to get her point across. As the three children grew up, they rarely experienced overt examples of Eliza's love and affection for them.

There are good and bad things about being the oldest child. You may get more attention than your younger siblings. You may be favored when there's an inheritance to bequeath. But you're also a guinea pig of sorts. New parents have to learn everything about being parents from the ground up. They often make their mistakes on the firstborn. If they're good parents, they learn from those mistakes and correct them when dealing with succeeding children.

This was the case for both Eliza and Hiram. They loved Dusty, but they expected a lot out of him. At times, they may have asked too much. He was expected to be quiet when they wanted quiet. He was expected to learn without missteps or errors. He was not expected to misbehave, although all boys inevitably do.

When Hiram was drunk, he expected absolute obedience from Dusty. When the girls came along, his inebriated ire didn't die, but he shifted more toward using abusive language rather than to using abusive language plus a whipping.

Eliza, too, seemed to spare the rod with the girls. She toned down the fussing and hollering with them, though she didn't mind leading them on a guilt trip if she wanted their behavior to improve.

True, some kids had it much worse than the Brodie trio. The hills and hollows held plenty of dysfunction. A few families were really off the rails. But in truth, many families also instilled more self-esteem in their children than Hiram and Eliza. Their offspring eventually developed a protective bravado, but they struggled to develop real self-confidence.

Chapter 7

THE PESTERING PUPIL

All in all, the Brodie siblings liked school. It was a place to see other kids, both in the schoolyard and in the classroom. Situated a quarter mile from town, the Avery schoolhouse was a cozy wooden building barely big enough for a classroom. It served children from first to eighth grade. On most school days, somewhere between 20 and 30 students attended, depending on who was absent due to sickness, weather, farm chores or good, old-fashioned truancy.

The schools in Avery and three other nearby villages taught kids through the eighth grade. The larger town of Kenneth – just four miles north of Avery – had a similar grade school, as well as the area's high school. Unlike the scattered simple grade schools, the high school was housed in a substantial brick building. Kenneth's population was nearly 600, compared to just under 200 in Avery and anywhere from 60 to 230 people in the other towns that fed the high school.

Of all the grade-school students in those towns, only about 50 percent to 60 percent ever attended so much as a day of high school. Of those, maybe 20 percent graduated. Some kids dropped out as early as third grade.

Not Dusty and his sisters. They were destined to graduate from high school. While their parents supported their schooling, it was Grandma Louellen who fervently encouraged their education. Attendance wasn't enough for the old woman. She insisted they achieve good marks. She was constantly asking them what they were learning. Deep down, she knew she was a little envious. She wished she had been able to attend school longer. Louellen didn't want her grandchildren to miss the chance for an education.

For his part, Dusty didn't have to be prodded. He took to books easily. No subject was very difficult. Like most kids, he didn't like remembering dates for history tests. And sometimes he couldn't see any value in advanced mathematics. Still, Dusty applied himself and got top grades in every subject.

Nancy also excelled at schoolwork. She was interested in literature, poetry and music. She was the only Brodie child gifted with a clear singing voice. When she was younger, before Jenny had started tailing her everywhere, Nancy had a secret spot in the woods behind the cabin. She would stand on an old stump and sing to the surrounding trees, bushes and flowers. Birds, butterflies and insects were also part of her audience. Their little noises and the various sounds of the woods were her accompaniment. She imagined herself singing in a big auditorium in front of a microphone, with the music floating on the airwaves to reach the radios of thousands of listeners.

While her passion was for the arts, Nancy also applied herself to other subjects. She was above average in both math and sciences. And, as she was one of only three students her age, her excellent marks easily topped the other two pupils in her class.

Jenny, too, did well in school, but it was more touch and go. Her mind flitted from here to there, often making schoolwork a challenge. In today's world, she might be diagnosed with an attention deficit syndrome. But she could pull her head down from the clouds periodically, especially when the subject was science. Biology was especially wonderful. Jenny loved to learn about animals. Other subjects paled in comparison. Still, Jenny's grades were generally decent.

The same couldn't be said for all students. Yes, there were some very smart kids: Elton Lawson, son of the sheriff, stood out. A couple of years ahead of Dusty, he was destined to attend the University of Missouri and obtain a law degree. Elton would fashion a successful law career. He later dabbled in politics. That ended when he was caught having an affair with a married woman. After his wife divorced him, he stuck strictly to legal work and remained a bachelor lawyer the rest of his life.

Another top student was Shirley Winger, daughter of the mayor. She was in the grade between Dusty and Nancy. Shirley stood out as a student. And she knew it. She felt superior to her rural classmates. Shirley was a city girl whose misfortune was being raised in a country environment. Like Elton, she also attended college. She married a fraternity snob from St. Louis and settled in his hometown. The childless couple lived an affluent life, and Shirley cultivated plenty of friends among the upper classes. Her former Avery classmates thought her life was charmed, and she wouldn't have disagreed.

Others didn't have such comfortable futures in store. Avery produced more struggling students than intellectually gifted individuals. One boy who possessed less mental acumen became a particular nuisance to Dusty. Will Todd was the same age as Dusty, but he was a few inches taller and maybe 20 pounds heavier. Will was a nephew of Billy Todd, a good-old-boy moonshiner and one of Hiram's occasional drinking buddies. Billy was a likable and decent fellow although an unapologetic alcoholic. Billy's brother, Charley, was not so likable. He was simply a miserable man.

Charley Todd routinely beat his wife and kids. And he didn't need to be drunk to do it. He needed no excuse to haul off and cuff one of them to "keep them in line." This attitude extended beyond his family. Charley got into plenty of fights: as a kid, as a teen and as an adult. Some he won. Some he lost. But whatever the outcome, he was always ready to fight again. And there was no one to stop him from taking out his frustrations on his family, no child services or battered wife clinics to protect them.

As the oldest child, Will bore the lion's share of the old man's abuse. This rough treatment soon turned Will into a savage creature and a loner. The beatings may or may not have been partially responsible for his slow thinking. One thing was certain: The constant abuse hardened him to the point that he was tougher than all the other kids. Like his father, Will would start fights for little or no reason. Once he did, he would continue to dish out punishment no matter how much he received in return.

Dusty and Will never got along. Nobody really got along with Will. Everyone tried to avoid him. The good news for his classmates was that Will skipped school a lot. Sometimes, his father would keep him home to work on their small, ramshackle farm. Sometimes, he was likely too battered to attend school. On many mornings, when he did set out for the schoolhouse, he chose to bypass it and go hunting or fishing. He wanted most to get away from his father and the farm.

Though he would challenge almost any boy to a fight, Will for some reason resisted physically abusing any of the girls. Maybe he had seen his mother mistreated too much. Maybe deep inside he had a conscience after all. He certainly didn't mind insulting, belittling and often terrifying the girls. Will was an accomplished bully. A favorite pastime was picking out a poor passive victim, usually one of small physical stature. Will would badger them mercilessly. The target could be a boy, a girl or – on one memorable occasion – a schoolmaster.

XXX

In the fall of 1937, a young professorial type fresh out of college had taken over as headmaster of the Avery school. This man stood barely five-foot-four and weighed no more than 130 pounds. Will Todd was about the new teacher's equal in height, but he was at least 10 or 15 pounds heavier.

One day Will was being particularly disruptive, and the young teacher decided discipline was in order. He demanded Will come to the front of the class to be taught a lesson in manners. Will, who was sitting at the back of the room, got up and approached the teacher slowly at first then more rapidly, gathering speed like a steam locomotive heading down the track. By the time Will reached the front of the room, he was in a headlong bullrush toward the teacher.

The unnerved educator ran around to the other side of his desk, pursued by Will, who was easily catching up to the ungainly little man. As Will roared around the teacher's desk, he stopped long enough to liberate the thick wooden paddle the schoolhouse's teachers had for years used to maintain discipline. That paddle had meted out punishment to countless students in its day. Will apparently felt the score needed settling. He raised the shaft over his head, let out a devilish whoop and resumed his pursuit of the teacher.

Bewildered classmates sat in awe, shocked by the violent outburst. No one moved to defend or protect the young teacher, who continued making tracks toward the door, sniveling and gasping in fear. He only looked back once to gauge the distance between himself and his stalker. Then he was out the door. Will rapidly followed. It took a few seconds for the students to react and scramble from their desks to the door and windows to watch the chase.

The long and the short of it was that Will got in three or four sound licks before abandoning the assault. The young teacher never returned to the schoolhouse again. In fact, he left town the next day, vowing to give up the business of education forever. That, everyone in town generally agreed, was for the best.

Will Todd earned a severe reprimand from the school board, along with a month of suspension. He viewed it as a paid vacation. His old man, predictably, viewed it as another excuse to lay a whipping on the boy. This just deepened the abused-turned-abusive child's animosity and hatred.

XXX

In the meantime, the school board began searching for a replacement. They eventually secured the services of a Mr. Cameron to finish the school year. Knox Cameron was in town tending to an ailing mother, who was staying with her sister. He had decided to take a semester off from college to help his aunt nurse his mother. He needed money and realized he could teach and still help his aunt. So, as of Jan. 1, 1938, Mr. Cameron became the new teacher at Avery School.

Cameron was the physical antithesis of the previous teacher. The new headmaster possessed a solid five-foot-ten frame that easily carried about 170 pounds of flesh, mostly well-toned muscle. Cameron had athletic bona fides. He was the starting catcher on the Drury College baseball team, as well as a lineman on the football team. His face bore the scars of his football collisions. A couple of his fingers were gnarled and pointing the wrong direction due to encounters with foul tips while catching. It would have been foolish for most of the adult males in the county to tangle with Mr. Cameron. The grade schoolers were even more intimidated.

In any case, Mr. Cameron turned out to be a sound educator. He kept discipline more by stern looks than by harsh words or threats of corporal punishment. In fact, he removed the paddle – yes, the one used few weeks earlier by Will Todd. He made it clear he had no need of the instrument. That worried the students more than the paddle's constant silent promise of pain.

Soon after the semester started, Cameron devised a tactic to help ensure good behavior. He planned to reassign desks to isolate the known troublemakers and talkers from each other. They would become islands in a sea of meeker, more obedient students. This new landscape would limit interruptions during lessons.

While he was still considering how to reorder the students, the new teacher made a discovery that every other observer had missed. A young girl, a third-grade student, was performing poorly in every subject. Janey Forsythe sat in the back row, showing little interest and no aptitude for learning. Her classmates found her to be a little slow, unfriendly and very timid. She almost never spoke unless someone spoke to her first. All her answers were short, quiet and benign. If she were a color, it would be beige.

Cameron, soon suspected that the girl's inability to read, do math or answer questions had less to do with a lack of smarts than with impaired eyesight. One day, he made the girl stay after school. He stood by her and had her open her reader. He asked her to begin reading. The results, as usual, were horrible. Cameron stopped Janey before she grew too discouraged. He handed her a magnifying glass.

"Try again, Janey," he said quietly.

The girl took the instrument and hovered it over the page. Her eyes widened and she bent down closer to the words. She could make them out now. They weren't just grayish shadows on the white page. She began to read. Not perfectly, but much better than before. As she continued, she seemed to get more interested in the material and more excited about her own abilities. Cameron saw her confidence grow almost sentence by sentence. After a short while, he stopped her.

"Janey, that was very good," he said. "A really good job." She smiled up at him, proud of her schoolwork for the first time.

"I'm going to move you to the front of the class," the young teacher said. "You'll be able to see better and you'll do better in all your subjects. And, I think one more thing could help. I want to see if your father will get you a pair of glasses."

Janey frowned. It was like the teacher had popped a beautiful bubble she was floating in. Her joy crashed to the floor. Janey knew the cost of a pair of glasses were beyond her means.

Janey lived on a small patch of land with her docile and weak father. Albert Forsythe, known by most people as Bert, was a widower who could no longer run his small farm. He also didn't quite know how to raise a daughter. Bert was a frail man, often too sick to tend his fields. They were plowed carelessly, planted late and haplessly weeded. They produced disappointing yields. In a good year, his income barely paid bank loans and taxes.

Bert did better with his reasonably large garden. If the weather cooperated, the yields would feed him and his daughter through the winter. Then they would scour the countryside in spring for any manner of food that nature might provide.

They would often be undernourished – if not actually starving – by the time the next year's garden began to produce. They would harvest and feed off of it through the early fall. All the while, they would can, pickle or preserve everything they could spare to hold them through the winter and into the next spring. In a bad year, if the garden didn't provide enough, they went hungry.

The folks nearby generally liked the Forsythes. Some of their neighbors would try to look out for them. But if the Forsythes faced a bad year, it was likely their neighbors' yields would be slim as well. It was harder to lend a helping hand in times of need than in times of plenty.

Bert was a simple man with almost no education. He was practically illiterate. He struggled to keep Janey fed and clothed. He taught her the arts of cooking and housework as he knew them. He sent her to school because he really wanted her to have a better life, though he had no idea what that might mean. When Janey continually struggled and brought home poor grades, he scratched his head and had no answers to help her.

Cameron would learn all this gradually. For now, he was wondering about glasses for Janey. After sending her home, the teacher walked back toward his aunt's house in Avery. On the way, he stopped by the general store to ask Ivan Reynolds, the proprietor, what he knew about Janey and her father.

"Well," the storekeeper frowned, "they struggle. More than most around here, I guess. Her pa's sickly. Not much of a farmer. He tries, but he's a broken-down man."

"So they wouldn't have money to buy something like a pair of eyeglasses?" Cameron asked.

"They don't have money to buy food," Ivan replied. "They don't get enough to eat. I can't see Bert spending money, if he had any, on matches for the stove, much less a pair of glasses."

"Well, thanks," Cameron said, turning to leave. Then he had a thought. "How much does a pair of glasses cost?"

XXX

About a week later, Mr. Cameron picked up Janey and Bert in his old Model T Ford, a noisy rattletrap even on good roads. They bounced and jerked along the pitted, uneven track to Kenneth. Cameron pulled up at a secondhand store. It was situated in a dilapidated wood building, squeezed between a service station and a barber shop.

Cameron realized it would be best to take Janey to an eye doctor for an exam and new glasses. But he couldn't afford that any more than Bert Forsythe could. So the trio entered the thrift store, and the teacher asked to see some used eyeglasses. Cameron had come prepared with a couple of books and a couple of pieces of cardboard with words and numbers written on them. The clerk, the teacher and the father had Janey try on every pair of glasses in the store to find which offered the greatest improvement to her near, middle and distant vision.

The pair that helped Janey see best made her look the worst. The spectacles featured tortoiseshell frames with a wide and intrusive keyhole bridge. When sitting on her nose, more than half the lenses sat above her eyes, making it look like the glasses were focusing the world on her eyebrows and forehead. The style – if that word even applied – reminded Cameron a little bit of Groucho Marx without the mustache and cigar.

But Janey was so amazed at how well she could see that she didn't think of how they looked. She was just glad to have something approaching normal vision.

Cameron asked the storekeeper how much he wanted for the glasses. The man twisted his face, thinking for a bit. He took a look at Janey and saw a smile that would not leave her face.

"Well …," the old merchant pondered, "I suppose I could give 'em to you for … 75 cents?"

Cameron, like most people in the 1930s, didn't have much spare cash. But he, too, had been watching Janey looking around with an expression of awe on her face.

"It's a deal," he said, reaching into his pocket to retrieve a good portion of money he had available. Bert Forsythe thanked the teacher profusely and insisted on buying him and Janey soda pops for the return trip. Cameron noted he didn't buy one for himself.

As for Janey, the smile didn't leave her face all the way home.

XXX

The next Monday, the first Monday of February, dawned warm and dry – it was a wonderful weather for the time of year. Janey was so anxious to get to school that she left with only a thin sweater over her threadbare dress.

She had a lightness in her step as she walked the winding path around a hill to get from her home to the schoolyard, which was just under a mile away.

Janey proudly wore her new eyeglasses to school. She was unprepared for the reaction of her schoolmates. They looked quizzically at her spectacles. She saw a lot of frowns.

"Janey got glasses," one girl exclaimed. A group of about five other girls turned their heads to look. They stared at Janey like she was an alien.

"Where did you get those things?" one girl said gawking at the odd-looking eyewear.

"Maybe she stole them from somebody's grandpa," said another.

"I think she dug them up out of the cemetery," suggested a third.

These comments made Janey's high spirits dip. She went into the school and sat at her desk in the back row. She stayed there alone until school started. But she couldn't help being amazed at how well she could see. She could even make out a blurry vision of that day's lesson written on the chalkboard at the front of the room. Her view of that lesson would soon get even better.

This was the morning Mr. Cameron implemented his new seating plan. He assigned the children their new places row by row. He placed Janey in the middle of the front row, where she could see the chalkboard much more clearly. Cameron continued to fill each row, putting Will Todd immediately behind Janey. Dusty ended up immediately behind Will.

Cameron was actually surprised to see Will that morning. Since his suspension, the vicious young man had been skipping school more frequently. No one expected him to show up on an ideal day for playing hooky. Will had come to school in a foul mood. It only got worse when the teacher moved him from the back of the classroom to the second row. He also decided he didn't like having Dusty behind him; he wasn't sure why, but it added to his dissatisfaction.

Cameron knew relocating pupils would cause some agitation. He was prepared for some griping and whining. But he wasn't prepared for the turmoil moving Will would create. Will took a long time to get settled into his new desk. Some of the younger students also were slow to roost. But even after they were mostly settled, Will kept fussing with his desk. He repeatedly lifted and closed the lid, fiddling with his books and moving his pencil from one corner to another. He muttered to himself the whole time, his resentment building with every fidgety movement.

Finally, Cameron had enough. He told Will to sit still. The surly boy resentfully complied. The teacher then started class. Cameron turned his back to the class, lecturing and adding details to the lessons on the chalkboard. This was when Will noticed Janey's glasses for the first time.

She was still looking the room over, awed by the many things now revealed. The petty barbs of her classmates were momentarily forgotten as she took in the scenery from her front-row seat. She could actually see what Mr. Cameron was writing on the board.

Will pecked her on the shoulder. When Janey turned around, he whispered with a sneer, "What are you lookin' at, Four Eyes?"

Janey gave him a quick frown and turned back around. Will gave her shoulder a harder peck. She ignored him, so he delivered a rough shove. Dusty and several other students saw him badgering the younger girl. Finally, Janey turned around, and Will grabbed the glasses from her face.

"Hey!" Janey hissed. "Give 'em back!"

"Shut up, Janey Four Eyes!" Will growled at her.

This exchange caused Cameron to turn around, but Will had quickly hidden the glasses in his lap before the teacher's eyes lit upon his too-innocent face.

"What's going on, Will?" he asked.

"Nothin'," the bully replied, trying to look even more innocent. He only looked guiltier.

"Janey, where are your glasses?" Cameron asked. The girl looked up but didn't say anything.

"Will has them," Dusty said. Everyone stared at him as if he'd challenged Lucifer to a firefight.

Will turned halfway in his seat and glared at Dusty. "Stay out of it, Brodie," the bully snarled.

"Will, turn around and give those glasses back to Janey," Cameron said in a stern and even voice. The kids saw Cameron's eyes narrow. Will took notice, too. He turned a quarter way back in his chair and pushed the glasses back at Janey.

"Here, Four Eyes," he muttered.

"All right. That's it," the teacher said firmly. "If I hear anymore outbursts, someone is staying after school." He was looking straight at Will, but to make sure, he went on to scan the entire classroom with a severe frown.

As soon as the instructor turned back to the chalkboard, Will regained his courage and flicked Janey's ear. She winced and shrunk in her seat but didn't let out a sound. Checking to make sure the teacher wasn't looking his way, Will then turned to his left and gave Dusty a backhand punch to the left side of Dusty's head. Like Janey, Dusty remained silent.

A few minutes later, Will thumped Janey hard on the back. It was the first time he had ever hit a girl at school. It would be the last. Dusty reach forward and whopped Will on the shoulder. The blows were loud enough for Cameron to hear. He turned in time to see Will swivel and draw back his right fist to wallop Dusty.

"Mr. Todd!" No one had ever heard such a cold, icy blast of anger from their teacher. "You will turn around now and keep your hands to yourself!"

Will seemed to consider his options, but under Cameron's stony stare, he slowly lowered his right arm and turned away from Dusty.

All was quiet for the next half hour or so, but few students paid much attention to their teacher. They kept one eye on Will and Dusty to see what might happen next. A couple of boys near the back of the room even made a bet on whether Will would trounce Dusty before or after lunch.

Once the current lesson ended, Cameron announced a surprise math quiz. All the students grumbled and groused as the teacher handed out the tests, a different version for each grade.

"This is a timed exercise," he informed them. "You have 20 minutes to complete these problems. I'll be available if you have questions. No talking, no copying, no cheating. And no one leaves their seat without permission. Anyone breaking the rules will fail … or worse. Got it?"

Most of the students uttered variations of "yes sir" in response. Will and Dusty did not reply.

Dusty positioned his test paper, got his pencil ready and waited for the teacher to say begin. As soon at Cameron did so, Dusty started working on the problems. They were relatively easy and he was moving through them rapidly. He only got hung up once or twice, soon figuring out the correct answer and moving methodically to the next question.

Suddenly: Wham! Will had turned around and hit Dusty across the forehead. Dusty was shaken, slightly dazed, but basically unhurt. He looked up to see Will quickly turn back around as if nothing had happened. Dusty scanned the classroom left to right. He didn't see Mr. Cameron anywhere. Only a couple of problems remained on the quiz. Dusty plowed through both questions, the hardest of the test. Satisfied with his answers, put his pencil down.

He again looked carefully from one side of the classroom to the other. No teacher.

He quietly opened his desktop and took out the thickest, heaviest book. American History. After another quick glance from side to side. Dusty raised the book with both hands and brought down as hard as he could on the top of Will's head.

THUMP! And almost simultaneously, "OW!"

The sudden noise filled the room. The startled students all looked at Will. The bruised bully turned around to confront Dusty then suddenly stopped. His gaze rose to look at something above Dusty. At that point, Dusty felt hands – big, gnarly hands – grasp his ears. It was Mr. Cameron. How long had he been standing behind Dusty?

As the teacher gave Dusty's ears a rough rub, he said, "You think you can be a little quieter after finishing your test, Mr. Brodie?"

Dusty just nodded. He couldn't bring himself to speak.

Then Mr. Cameron let go of Dusty and moved slowly toward Will Todd.

Suddenly, he grasped the boy's shirt and with one hand roughly yanked Will to his feet. The irate teacher pulled Will's face close to his own and with the voice of Armageddon said, "Mr. Todd, you are excused from class. You will NOT return for the rest of the school year. You will NOT terrorize Miss Forsythe. You will NOT lay a hand on any of my students. Is that clear?"

Will had finally met someone who could be as forceful and violent as his own father. He feared the teacher as much as he feared his dad. Wide-eyed and whipped, Will just nodded yes. Like Dusty, he couldn't find words to respond to the fierce teacher. When Mr. Cameron finally released his grip, Will hurried from the schoolhouse. The teacher insisted the students finish their quizzes, allowing them an extra five minutes due to the "interruption."

XXX

Mr. Cameron never spoke to Dusty about his role in that day's adventures. He spoke to Janey only long enough to ensure she was unshaken and would continue to wear her glasses – no matter how students teased or bullied her – to complete her schoolwork.

After letting school out, Cameron went to speak to Will's father. He knew he couldn't make the miserable brute stop abusing his family. He knew Will would only be free of the man's tyranny when he left his home for good. He worried that the abuse may have permanently damaged Will, physically and emotionally. But he had something to say to Charley Todd, and he said it.

Whatever it was, Charley never responded to the boy's suspension. No physical threats or violence: to the teacher, to the school board or to any of the students.

As for Janey? The girls at school gradually realized – with Mr. Cameron as their constant reminder – that they shouldn't taunt the girl over her glasses. The boys likewise left her alone. They all were cowed by their new teacher, dreading another burst of his fury.

Though Janey's classmates weren't much friendlier to her, no one ever called her "Janey Four Eyes" again.

The effect of improved vision was remarkable. Janey continued to raise her grades as she moved through the school system. She and her dad eventually accumulated enough money to buy prescription glasses that were a little more stylish.

Once again, she was amazed: The new glasses offered even better sight than her secondhand specs. Janey's confidence grew and she overcame the worst of her shyness. She even developed a few friendships among her classmates.

As the years went by, Janey's eyes weakened, and she required thicker and thicker lenses. But, despite having "coke bottle spectacles," she could see well enough to read and write. She finished 10th grade before getting married. As an adult, Janey enjoyed all the sights and scenes of God's green earth, including, eventually, the lovely faces of her own children.

Chapter 8

THE BASEBALL TOURNAMENT

As the school year wound down and the weather warmed up, the Avery boys – and several of the girls – turned their thoughts to baseball. The Great American Pastime was everyone's game in the 1930s. Kids measured each other's prowess on the baseball diamond.

Never mind that there were very few real baseball diamonds in the hills. The best most communities could do was a nearly level lot or pasture with an improvised home plate and, if they were lucky, sand-filled sacks for bases. The worst might be a rough pasture with too-tall grass and any number of hidden holes in the outfield. Most of these depressions were courtesy of the livestock who periodically "mowed" the field.

Avery was a step ahead. On a small patch of land just outside of town, the local fanatics had fashioned a level infield with a functional chicken-wire backstop that even curved in on each side. Primitive bleachers sat in back of home plate and along the foul lines, extending about half way to first base on one side and to third base on the other. Squarish sandbags were anchored at all the bases, while a flat wooden home plate had been driven into the dirt 60 feet and six inches from the center of the pitcher's box. The field could be scaled down for smaller kids and softball games. The dirt infield was generally smooth and the outfield grass kept more or less trimmed.

The Avery field even boasted an outfield fence of sorts. A line of hedges curved around from left to right field. The shrubs were three to four feet high and stood 250 feet from home plate down the leftfield line to just over 300 feet from home in center field then back to about

240 feet in right field. Though batted balls, and occasionally an out-fielder, could get lost in the hedges, the configuration made the field look like a real ballpark. It was certainly better than most small-town teams could boast.

However, the real baseball cathedral in the area was in Kenneth, next to the high school. This field had a real, rubber home plate, a regulation mound with a real pitching rubber and genuine, accurate-to-the-inch 90-foot baselines. On special occasions, the Kenneth Field foul lines were chalked all the way to the outfield grass. Sturdy wooden bleachers curled from behind the backstop down the foul lines beyond first and third base. The grounds could seat maybe 500 to 600, with plenty of room for overflow crowds to stand.

Just two weeks before the end of the school year, on an idyllic Friday, the city fathers of Kenneth announced they were holding a tournament featuring four grade-school teams from the area. It had been an early spring, and planting of fields and gardens was nearly complete. This plus good weather should ensure substantial attendance, the town's leaders believed.

They decided the games would be played on a Saturday, just eight days away. The contestants would be Kenneth, Avery, Richfield and a fourth team composed of players from the smaller towns of Everleigh and Mortons Mill. This latter squad dubbed itself EverMort – which the wiseacres in the area quickly translated as "Always Dead."

EverMort indeed was expected to field the weakest lineup. The first game would pit them against the host and favored team, Kenneth. Richfield and Avery, who would likely be competitive with one another, would play the other first-round game. Losers would meet to vie for third place. The winners would play for the title. Everyone expected Kenneth to win handily … everyone in Kenneth anyway. The other towns relished the idea of knocking off their bigger rival.

Folks in Avery bubbled with enthusiasm. With just a week to prepare, they set about selecting a coach for their team. Someone suggested the new school teacher, a college baseball player, would be a good choice. Knox Cameron knew baseball, and he also knew the students who would make up the team. Plus, his selection would avert a potential dispute over which town official should get the job.

When approached, Cameron at first demurred. With a little cajoling, he eventually accepted. The question was how to determine the nine Avery kids who could match up with the best Kenneth and the other teams had to offer. And, how to do so in only one week.

When Dusty heard about the tournament, he could barely contain his excitement. Playing baseball with local kids was great, but playing in a real, organized tournament against other towns? What could be more fun?

There was little doubt Dusty would be on the team. He was one of the best ballplayers the small Avery school could provide. There were a couple of other no-brainers. George Todd, son of moonshiner Billy and cousin of the infamous Will Todd, was a strapping 13-year-old with a cannon for an arm. He would likely be the squad's pitcher.

Ronnie Schwartz was a powerful seventh grader who could anchor the batting order. Lanky lawyer-to-be Elton Lawson could be counted on as well. Just about anyone with any baseball smarts could figure out that much. Selecting the rest of the team would be more challenging.

Cameron scheduled a quick practice/tryout session at the local diamond after school let out on Monday. The new coach had no shortage of "assistants" who wanted to discuss "strategy" and offer opinions on who should make the team and who should play each position.

"My Scotty is small, but he's fast," said one fellow. "He should hit leadoff."

"Amos has good power; make him the cleanup hitter," said another, referring to his grandson.

Cameron listened to their insights, nodded stoically and promptly flushed their advice from his brain. The teacher remained quiet as he shifted players around the field, judging their virtues and inadequacies. Sixteen kids were trying out, three of them girls.

One of those girls had caught the youthful coach's eye. Donna Bakken was a 12-year-old seventh-grader. She was neither sleek nor slender, neither fast nor strong-armed. She was a stout (which meant fat) girl who showed she wasn't afraid of the ball and could catch anything within her reach. She was agile without being graceful. Cameron began to see a role for this hefty girl. If she could handle first base, it would free up another player with more range and a better arm to shore up the rest of the defense.

And Donna could hit. She didn't have home run power, but line drives flew off her bat; sometimes through the infield, sometimes over it and occasionally between outfielders. The trouble was she seldom managed more than a single. She was that slow.

"If she gets on first base, it may take three doubles to score her," Cameron thought to himself. Still, the idea was interesting.

Some things Cameron decided early: George Todd indeed would pitch. Ronnie Schwartz would play left field and bat cleanup. Dusty Brodie would play shortstop or maybe center field, depending on how hard the other team was hitting George's pitches.

After a spirited two-hour practice, Cameron called everyone in to gather around home plate. His "advisors" hovered on the fringes.

"That was a great workout!" the coach enthusiastically told the 16 aspiring ballplayers. "Everyone played hard. You all showed me something today. I think we've got a good chance against the other teams. I'm going to work out who will start and where. I'll also put together a batting order. We'll practice after school Wednesday, and I'll announce the lineup. Now the good news: Everybody made the team!"

The young ballplayers cheered and hurrahed. The many advisors were shocked. There were clearly three or four children, mostly younger and smaller, who didn't belong on a ballfield – not representing the grand town of Avery. Was there a screw loose in this teacher? Did they make a mistake in appointing him as coach? Would his decisions make the whole town look foolish?

XXX

At Wednesday's workout, Cameron started with batting practice for everyone. He called on them to hit in no particular order. All the while, he moved the players who were not hitting around in the field. About 45 minutes later, he called everyone in to home plate.

"Nice job again everyone," Coach Cameron said. "Remember, don't swing at any bad pitches, but when you do swing, use a nice level swing and try to hit the ball solid."

As he spoke, Cameron looked specifically at players who were swinging and missing or barely getting the bat on the ball.

"Now, here's how we're going to line up," he said. "George: pitcher, Hal Wilson: catcher, Elton: third base."

At this, some of the adults shifted uncomfortably, frowned or even muttered. Most had pegged Elton Lawson to play first base, mainly because he was a tall boy with a good reach. Meanwhile, Cameron kept on.

"Dusty: shortstop, Junior Thomas: second base, Donna Bakken: first base."

This last announcement brought an audible gasp from the adults. Even four or five of the players looked at each other puzzled. Cameron, allowing no time for discussion, continued.

"Ronnie: left field, Amos Lane: center field, Ben Winger: right field. The rest of you will be my bench. Stay ready. We likely will need you at some point."

The muttering and gossiping rose in the background. The kids who made the starting lineup were excited. Those that didn't, even though disappointed, congratulated the starting nine.

"All right, I want the starters out on the field," Cameron finally ordered. "The rest of you get ready to run the bases. We're going to see if this bunch can get anybody out."

Cameron turned to the bench players and arranged them from fastest to slowest runner. He then began hitting balls to his fielders. For the next half hour, he drilled his team, always praising good plays, always encouraging those who flubbed a play, always teaching.

Eventually, the baserunners replaced the fielders and practice continued another half hour until the sun hovered above the horizon. Cameron let them go so they could get home before dark.

The team practiced again the next day, but on Friday – the day before the tournament – Cameron chose not to put his team through arduous drills. Instead, he held a short strategy session. He taught them rudimentary signs so he could tell them to take a pitch, bunt or steal a base. The teacher also reiterated that they were ALL part of the team and ALL had a job to do if the team was to emerge victorious.

The players were responding to Mr. Cameron's coaching. Recalling his stern manner in the classroom, many of them had been afraid to make mistakes. However, his upbeat, encouraging attitude lifted their confidence and made them work harder. His pep talk lit a fire in his team. They went home determined to play their best for their teammates, their teacher and their town.

XXX

Fans from all the surrounding towns and the rural areas in between began arriving in Kenneth early Saturday morning. Two local diners had a dozen or so customers lined up outside waiting for a table and some breakfast. A somewhat swankier restaurant, usually open only for lunch and dinner on Saturdays, was also doing brisk business. Any little store or gas station that served sodas or sweets or coffee also took advantage of the crowds to earn a few extra dollars.

Coach Cameron had arranged rides for all his players, and there was no shortage of volunteers who offered their trucks, automobiles or wagons to transport the home team. Dusty's family all attended: his mom and dad, his sisters, uncles Martin and Cleve and, of course, Grandma Louellen. The same kind of turnout was expected for just about every family who had a player on one of the teams. The game also drew a host of fans who had no particular player to root for.

The games were smartly played for the most part. Every squad showed some talent plus a good bit of aptitude for and knowledge of how to play the game. In the opener, EverMort put up a stiffer fight than most fans expected, but Kenneth's overall superiority began to show. A tight contest eventually ended in a 10-3 win for the hosts.

As the second contest started, most of Dusty's family gathered in a section of seats just behind the Avery team's bench. Hiram, who'd had a nip or two during the first game, hollered and rode the umpires as well as the opposing team throughout the second game. Nancy and

Jenny cheered, even more loudly when Dusty was batting or involved in a play.

Eliza and Dusty's uncles were more reserved, cheering now and then, but mostly just watching intently. Martin and Cleve shared comments on good plays, bad plays and any mistake they deemed the umpires to have made. Louellen, as usual, sat stoically, watching like a hawk but internalizing her emotions. Dusty was aware of his family's presence, and it made him proud. He wanted to win whoever was watching, but winning in front of his family would be special.

The Richfield-Avery contest was tight from the start. Richfield got two early runs. Avery came out of the gate more slowly, scratching out a single run in the first when Dusty walked, stole second, went to third on a wild pitch and quickly scored on a long sacrifice fly by Ronnie Schwartz.

Richfield scored two more in the sixth. As Avery came up to bat in the bottom of the inning, they trailed 4 to 1 with just two more turns at bat. Then the tide began to turn. Fortune started to smile on Coach Cameron's team.

Donna led off and took a mighty swing, topping the ball for a slow roller to third base. It should have been an easy out, but the third baseman's throw to first was in the dirt. Before the first baseman could corral it, Donna was standing on the bag.

The Richfield pitcher walked the next two hitters, loading the bases. It was Dusty's turn to bat. He hit the first pitch hard toward left field. The third baseman stuck his glove out and knocked it down before throwing Ben out at second. Dusty beat the relay to first, avoiding a double play. Donna scored to make it 4 to 2.

After a strikeout, Ronnie ripped a ball into the outfield between fielders. One run scored easily. Meanwhile, Dusty got a great jump from first base. Coach Cameron knew it would be a close play at the plate, but he sent Dusty home. The outfielder's throw was true. The crowd cheered as Dusty went into a slide.

Dust rose as Dusty and the ball arrived home at the same time. The umpire hesitated a second before signaling safe. The game was tied. The Avery fans roared. The Richfield fans cursed the umpire.

The next batter, George Todd, lifted a high fly ball into left field. It looked like the third out. Ronnie Schwartz, who had been on second base, rounded third and then slowed to see if the ball would be caught. The left fielder was under it, but a gust of wind took the ball a few feet toward center field. The outfielder staggered to his left and stumbled as the ball bounced off his glove. Ronnie scored, giving Avery the lead heading into the last inning.

George Todd took the mound determined to shut the Richfield hitters down. He got two quick outs. With Richfield's best hitter up, George grooved a fastball. The batter hit the ball deep over Amos Lane's head. The Richfield runner rounded the bases as Amos chased down the ball. Amos fired the ball to Dusty, whose relay throw to home was perfect. Little Hal Wilson was blocking the plate, but the Richfield runner was bearing down on him. The ball hit Hal's mitt about the same time the runner rammed his left shoulder. Somehow Hal held onto the ball. The runner was out. Avery had won.

Their fans celebrated wildly.

Among the spectators was Percy Jennings, son of Hiram's rival Jake. Percy was at the game with his friend, Henry Franks. They had decided to watch a little baseball before moving on to what they hoped would be a riotous, fun Saturday night. They were boisterous teenagers who loved baseball and had keen eyes for talent.

When Dusty had cut loose the throw to nab the Richfield baserunner at the plate, they exchanged wide-eyed looks.

"Did you see the arm on that Brodie kid?" Percy said.

"I never saw a better throw," Henry replied.

"Do you suppose that was a fluke?" Percy asked. "Of course, you can see he's got a good arm, but to be that accurate …"

"I know," Henry nodded. "He had to get that throw off in a hurry, and it was right on target."

"I gotta stay to watch the championship game," Percy said. "I want to see if that arm is real."

"If it is …" Henry didn't even finish his sentence.

Percy and Henry first had to wait for the game to decide third place. Richfield overcame its fielding woes, and its bats came alive. They clobbered the weaker EverMort team 18 to 2. The magic Ever-Mort had conjured for those early innings against Kenneth was long gone.

The crowd – many of whom had gone to find refreshments during the third-place game – was trickling back to the field for the championship game. Dusty's family had stayed put, still in their seats behind the Avery bench. The smart money was on Kenneth to win, but some of the gambling patrons were betting on Avery to stay within three runs. Those bettors thought they had a fair chance of winning.

Coach Cameron called his team together for a short pep rally.

"We played pretty well in the first game, but we just barely won," the coach said. "We'll have to play a lot better to beat Kenneth." He paused to look each young player in the eye before continuing. "And we can do it."

The Avery squad dutifully nodded, some saying, "Yeah," or "That's right," or "You bet." George Todd voiced it a little differently, loudly exclaiming, "Hell, yes!" Cameron did not admonish him but nodded at his confident pitcher.

"I noticed one weakness during their first game," the coach said. "Their catcher can't throw. We're gonna run on him when we can. If the ball ever gets away from him … take off."

The game was a tight, tense affair. Runs were hard to come by. George Todd was matching the big Kenneth hurler pitch for pitch. Avery was the visiting team and went down in order the first two innings. In the third, they broke a scoreless tie.

Donna Bakken had suffered through an inauspicious performance during the first game. Other than reaching on the error, she had struck out and popped up. She had also muffed a throw to first, costing Avery a critical out. She was about to atone for those miscues.

The Kenneth pitcher was a big, raw-boned man-child who threw hard and true. Most of Avery's batters were having trouble making contact with his deliveries. Leading off the top of the third inning, Donna leaned into one of his heaters and drove it hard into right-center between the outfielders. It was clearly a solid hit: The question was how many bases the slow-footed girl could get out of it.

Donna lumbered to first, where Elton Lawson was coaching for Avery. He cheered her on to second. Meanwhile, the rightfielder had tracked the ball down near the fence and heaved it in the general direction of the second baseman. Donna hesitated as she hit second base, but Coach Cameron was yelling, imploring her to try for third. She put her legs back into gear – though she only had one speed – and managed to reach the bag ahead of the throw with a stand-up triple.

The Avery fans went wild. The Kenneth crowd moaned. Then it was the Kenneth's turn to cheer as the next two Avery hitter made outs. Donna was still standing at third base. It was Dusty's turn again. He had popped out to first base in his first chance against the Kenneth pitcher. He, too, had had trouble catching up to the big hurler's fast ball. This time, Dusty was determined to get on top of the pitch. His team needed a run.

The first pitch was inside and nearly nailed Dusty before he spun out of the way. The Kenneth pitcher smiled at him, clearly trying to intimidate Dusty. And it almost worked. Nobody wants to get hit by a fast one.

Dusty took a moment before stepping back up to the plate. A sudden flash hit him. In earlier innings, after throwing inside pitches, this hurler had followed with a fast ball on outside corner. Would he try that again? Dusty leaned over the plate a bit to make sure he could reach the outer half of the plate. If the pitcher threw another one high and tight, it might get Dusty in the head. But the young, wiry hitter ignored the fear and looked for the outside pitch.

He got it. The contact between bat and ball was loud and solid. The ball shot like a cannonball past the second baseman and into right field. Donna plodded home as fast as she could as Dusty reached first easily. Avery led 1 to 0.

Coach Cameron applauded and cheered with the rest of the team and the Avery fans. But he also got Dusty's attention and gave him a signal to steal second. On the first pitch, Dusty took off. The weak-armed catcher flung the ball into centerfield. Dusty didn't even slide, he just kept running, rounding second and heading for third.

When Cameron saw the centerfielder bobble the ball for a second, he waved his arm and told Dusty to keep going. The youngster never slowed down, cutting the corner of the bag perfectly. He easily beat the throw home. The crowd roared. Avery led 2 to 0.

The score stayed that way until the fifth inning. George Todd had been mowing Kenneth hitters down, but he was using a lot of pitches. The young pitcher was walking too many batters, and his stamina was being challenged.

In the bottom of the fifth, he came to the end of his rope. He had thrown 11 innings that day, and he was clearly gassed. He walked the first two hitters and went to full counts on the next two before getting them out. Then he walked the next batter on four straight balls. That brought up Kenneth's best hitter.

Cameron decided to make a change, calling Ronnie Schwartz in from left field to take over. He also called Dusty and Elton over to the mound.

"Ronnie, this guy can hit it a ton," the coach warned. "Keep the ball low and throw strikes. George, you're going to have to play deep in left field. Don't let anything get over your head. Elton. Dusty. I want both of you to play deep and play him to pull. If you can't catch it, knock it down and keep the ball on the infield. All right, let's get this guy out."

The players took their positions, and Ronnie stood on the mound alone. The Kenneth hitter stepped up to the plate, relishing the moment. He raised his lumber over his head and actually snarled at Ronnie.

The great thing about baseball is how one play can turn a game around. If one critical instant goes a team's way, the momentum can carry it on to victory. Such a moment was about to occur.

Ronnie threw a fastball right down the middle. The pitch practically begged, "Hit me." The Kenneth hitter did just that.

It was a scorching liner, barely two feet high, heading rapidly toward left field. But Dusty saw it all the way, having swung over toward third base as Coach Cameron had ordered. The young shortstop only had time to take a quick step toward third, dive and try to gauge where the ball would be. His reflexes and intuition served him well. He got his glove to the spot, now about 18 inches from the dirt, and snared the ball like a hawk snagging a running mouse.

The crowd was silent for a short interval, not quite understanding or believing what they had seen. Then a lusty roar erupted from the Avery fans (and many of the uncommitted spectators as well), only to be echoed softly by the groans of the Kenneth contingent.

In the bleachers, Dusty's family was probably the loudest and certainly the proudest of all the Avery rooters. Even Louellen, the reserved Cherokee matriarch, jumped to her feet, clasped her hands together and bounced up and down yelling and celebrating. It was a thrill she would never forget: Her brave, athletic grandson turning in the highlight of the day. Her heart swelled with pride. She cherished Dusty's display of skill, which she saw as a gift from her ancestors through her to her grandson. It was her heritage on display, and she reveled in the Dusty's sudden glory.

Among the others awed by the play were Percy Jennings and Henry Franks. They gaped at each other, mouths open, no words coming to them. It was as impressive a play as they had ever seen.

Meanwhile, Dusty's teammates were all over him as he made his way to the bench. They were celebrating as if the game were already over. Still, two innings remained.

XXX

After Avery went down quickly in the top of the sixth, Kenneth came up. Ronnie's control began to abandon him. He gave up a walk, got an out, gave up second walk before getting the next batter to swing at three pitches that were out of the strike zone.

The Kenneth coach sent up a pinch hitter, a lanky, gangling, awkward looking kid who batted lefthanded. He swung at the first pitch and looped a popup over second base. Junior Thomas ran out as Amos Lane and Ben Winger sprinted in. It fell amid the three, scoring Kenneth's first run and making the score 2 to 1 with runners on second and third base.

Now it was the Kenneth fans who were whooping and hollering.

Ronnie, clearly disgusted, did the thing that gets so many pitchers in trouble. He started trying to throw harder. His first three pitches to the Kenneth leadoff hitter were high or wide or both. Coach Cameron tried to calm him and reminded him to keep the ball down. Ronnie took the coach at his word and unleashed a pitch that hit the dirt three feet in front of the plate.

The ball skipped by Hal Wilson, who was trying to block it. The young catcher scrambled to track it down as it bounced off the fence behind the plate. The runner from third got a late break toward the plate. Ronnie had sprinted from the mound to cover the plate as Hal gathered the ball and launched it sidearm to his pitcher. The ball jammed into Ronnie's glove just as the sliding runner's foot slammed into Ronnie's ankle. That effectively blocked the runner from the plate, and the Avery pitcher applied the tag for the third out of the inning, preserving the one-run lead.

But Ronnie's ankle would never be quite the same. The umpire later said he heard a snap as the bone broke. Coach Cameron, a few of the Avery players and Ronnie's parents ran onto the field to help the suffering player. It was apparent he couldn't finish the game. In fact, it would be more than a year before he could run without a pronounced limp. Ronnie was carried off the field and was on his way to Doc Tebbetts' office before the game resumed.

In the top of the seventh, Avery again went down meekly. It all came down to the bottom of the seventh inning: Avery needed three outs to win bragging rights over the mighty Kenneth team.

Cameron had to shuffle his lineup. He considered putting George back on the mound, but he decided that he had thrown enough for one day. The best remaining arm belonged to Dusty. Cameron made his decision.

"OK, one more inning," he encouraged. "Amos, you move to third base. Elton, you go to shortstop. Scotty, I need you to take right field. Ben, you're playing center now. And Dusty, you're pitching. Let's wrap this up and go home."

Many of the Avery fans were fine seeing Dusty take the mound. They or their kids had seen him play and knew he had a good arm. Others, who hadn't seen him on the diamond, were worried he might not be able to hold a one-run lead. His family, of course, was thrilled and cheered with gusto as he took his warmup tosses.

Percy nudged Henry when he saw the young Brodie boy striding to the mound.

"Now we'll really get a look at this kid's arm," Percy said. "Let's see if he can throw strikes."

From the first hitter, it was apparent that he could. He struck that batter out on three pitches, the last being a slow changeup that had the batter swinging too early. The second batter fouled a couple of pitches off before fanning on a high fast ball. Strike three again.

Percy and Henry were looking at each other and nodding. Hiram, having taken another nip or two along the way, was yelling on every pitch. So were Nancy, Jenny and even their mother. The more restrained Martin and Cleve were mostly exclaiming after pitches using a syllable or two: Yeah! Awright! That's it! And Grandma Louellen stayed silent, simply raising a skinny wrist with each delivery Dusty made to the plate.

But there was one more test for Dusty. Kenneth's cleanup hitter was up again.

This time the big guy was in the mood to hit one where no one would catch it.

Dusty had been watching this batter for almost two complete games now. He didn't have many weaknesses. He hit the fastest pitches George and Ronnie could throw. He hadn't been fooled by Ever-Mort's pitcher, who had a good curve ball and had changed speeds effectively. This hitter seemed to know a strike from a ball, so he was unlikely to swing at too many bad pitches.

Fans were in a near frenzy as Kenneth's would-be hero strode to the plate. Compared to the small and wiry figure of Dusty out on the mound, the batter seemed like a Goliath come to life. The hulking hitter took his stance and swung his bat menacingly toward Dusty, who responded by staring intently in at Hal for the sign.

Dusty tried to control his breathing as he went into his windup and zipped a fastball low and inside, just off the plate. The anxious hitter whipped his bat around and lined a foul ball that had the Kenneth coach lunging out of the way as the ball whizzed past. That was strike one.

The batter got back into his stance and readied for the next delivery with two more practice swings. Once more, Hal dropped the fastball sign. Dusty shook him off. It would be the changeup. Dusty pursed his lips, glared in at the hitter and wound up like he was going to try to launch the ball as hard as he could. But he held it deeper in his palm than usual.

When his armed whipped around and the ball came out, it looked flat and straight like a high fastball. But the pitch seemed to float through molasses. The batter swung hard and corkscrewed himself into the ground as the ball landed softly in Hal's mitt. That was strike two.

Now Dusty had the big hitter thinking … but he didn't quite know what to think. Dusty had already decided what he wanted to throw before his catcher had fired the ball back to the mound. Dusty didn't even wait for a sign from Hal. He went into a quick, short windup and let fly with his hardest pitch. It seemed to rise as it approached the plate.

The uncertain hitter, saw it coming in chest high, a good pitch to wallop. He tried to react fast and hit the ball hard. But the ball was too high and too fast. The bat came around well under the ball: a swing and a miss. The ball made a loud pop as it hit Hal's glove and stuck. And that was strike three.

The frustrated hitter froze in an awkward stance. The Avery crowd erupted. The team swarmed to the mound to congratulate Dusty. And the residents of Kenneth realized that for at least the next year – and maybe longer – the town of Avery would have bragging rights when it came to baseball.

Percy Jennings and Henry Franks grabbed each other and jumped up and down. They were caught up in the excitement and the celebration. Watching that Brodie kid play ball had been fantastic entertainment, a great way to spend a Saturday. They'd remember this day. And that memory would benefit them in just a few weeks.

Meanwhile, Dusty reveled in the cheering. Teammates, friends, opponents and total strangers pushed forward to shake his hand, slap his back or tousle his hair. It took several minutes for his dad and uncles to make their way to him. Hiram lifted him in a rare hug, while Martin and Cleve added their enthusiastic praise. His mom, his sisters and his grandma had to wait their turn.

Though darkness was gradually approaching, a spontaneous celebration began that kept many Avery folks in town longer than they had planned. The whole Avery team received one accolade after another, but the biggest cheers went to a tired, dirty youth with a wiry build and a rifle arm.

What a glorious night. It would be wonderful to say that it was just the start of a long career in baseball. But that was not to be. Dusty would always be a good ballplayer, usually the fastest on the field. But he would never become a star, never be sought out by birddog scouts, never be offered a professional contract. In many ways, the tournament in Kenneth was the high point of his baseball experience. But that didn't matter tonight. Tonight the world – or at least a small part of it – belonged to Dusty Brodie.

Chapter 9

THE CEMETERY

As the celebration slowly died down, most of the tournament attendees headed home. The sun was dropping quickly toward the horizon, and it would be twilight or darker before many of them would get home.

Martin and Cleve walked their mother back to Martin's Model T, sat her on the bench seat between them and headed home. The brothers continued to talk about the game, specifically about their nephew's heroics.

"Can you believe how that boy played today?" Cleve said.

"Sure done us proud," said Martin, always frugal with his words.

"He's a Brodie, that Dusty is," Cleve added. "My, how he played. Hitting, getting on base, running. I tell you, that boy can run."

"Didn't see anyone faster out there," Martin replied.

"And that catch he made on that line drive," Cleve continued. "I never, NEVER, saw a play like it."

"Yep," Martin agreed. "Timely too."

"But what surprised me was his pitching," Cleve couldn't stop talking about his young nephew. "I mean, I knew he could throw, but Jeez. He mowed them Kenneth boys down."

"He sure done us proud," Martin repeated.

"He done us proud for sure, right mother?" Cleve echoed.

"He has Cherokee blood," Louellen said firmly. "He has the strength and agility of his ancestors."

Martin and Cleve nodded. Louellen didn't say much more, but she had a small, satisfying smile on her face the whole trip home.

Meanwhile, Hiram and Eliza kept their daughters in town a little longer to celebrate with their son. Hiram had a few more drinks. He was in a good mood. He opened the purse strings and took Eliza and his three kids to a little diner that was packed with exuberant Avery fans. He even splurged for ice cream.

Although Nancy and Jenny were genuinely proud of their brother, they were just as excited about the uncommon treats Dusty's performance had occasioned.

With the sun having set and darkness approaching, Hiram gathered his family for the seven-mile trip home. They should get home before darkness fell. Dusty asked his folks if he could stay with some of his teammates, who were still celebrating.

"How you gonna get home?" Eliza asked.

"Elton's dad said he'd drop me at Avery," Dusty replied. "I can walk from there."

"You be home by 9 o'clock, not a minute later," Eliza said.

"Ahh, Eliza, let him have some fun tonight," a well-lubricated Hiram said. The proud father was feeling happy and generous – he was in a rare good mood. Eliza decided not to argue. Dusty could stay in town and enjoy the continuing jubilation.

At around 9:30, long after darkness had fallen, Fred Lawson began rounding up and piling his passengers into his truck. In addition to his family, Dusty and a few area kids were hitching a ride. Elton, Dusty and three others rode in the back of the truck, feeling the breeze as they moved along, talking and excitedly reliving the details of the day over and over.

It was nearly 10 p.m. when the loaded truck reached Avery. Fred slowed down to let Dusty and Ben Winger off near the crude road that led to Dusty's home. The kids yelled goodbyes and final hoots and hollers as Fred and the rest of his passengers drove off.

Normally, Ben would turn east and walk the half mile to his home, while Dusty headed south up the bumpy dirt road. But Ben was somewhat afraid of the dark.

"Say, uh, Dusty, you wouldn't mind walkin' with me to my house, would you?" Ben asked.

"Gee, Ben, it's just up the road," Dusty said, a little annoyed.

"You can go that far alone."

"Well … sure I could. I mean it's not that I'm scared or nothin'. I just thought it'd be fun to talk more about the game."

"I'm tired," Dusty said. "I'm all talked out. I just wanna go home and go to bed."

"I thought we were friends," Ben said plaintively.

"We are, but …" It would add about a mile to his walk home, but Dusty didn't want to hurt Ben's feelings.

"OK, let's go, but hurry up. It's getting late."

The nearer they got to Ben's house, the less frightened the boy was and the more fatigued Dusty was. After saying good night to Ben, Dusty looked back down the road leading to the intersection that would take him home. He hated the idea of retracing his steps. He was tired and just wanted to be home.

Then another thought crossed his mind. He could cut diagonally through the woods. There was an old cow path that led through a hollow and connected with the road just short of his home. The more he thought, the more he liked the idea of this shortcut.

Only one thing made him hesitate. The sky had started clouding up late in the afternoon. There was no moon, and Dusty could see no stars overhead. It would be dark on the footpath. But, he reasoned, it would be no darker than taking the longer way along the roads. He would have to pass Wheaton Cemetery, but he'd done that plenty of times during daylight. What difference would it make if it were night? Weariness made the decision for him. He would take the shortcut through the woods.

XXX

At first, it wasn't difficult to follow the path. But the farther he got from the road, the more the trees crowded in and the murkier the landscape grew. The gloomy environment began to play tricks with his mind. Every shadow looked alien and strange. Somber tree limbs seemed like predatory animals. Branches swaying in the swelling breeze looked like moving appendages. Dark patches of ground appeared to be reptilian creatures lying in wait.

The farther Dusty walked from the road, and the Wilson house the more he questioned his decision to take the time-saving route home. The nearer he came to the cemetery, the more his apprehension rose.

It didn't help that the clouds above had grown steadily thicker and the wind was continuing to rise. Dusty's heart pounded harder and his senses went on alert. He thought he heard stirrings in the brush and trees on either side of him. He was certain he could hear something following him. What could it be?

He concentrated on the staccato noise. It sounded like it was right behind him, walking at the same cadence that he was walking. A faint swish, swish, swish accompanied each step he took.

He tried slowing down. The pulsing sound slowed too. He tried quickening his step. The mysterious murmur accelerated in response. He dared not looked back. He avoided looking to either side. He kept his face pointed straight ahead as the pulsing sound kept pace with his stride.

Dusty was nearing the cemetery now. He could see the granite markers and a few old wooden crosses looming ahead. He was walking briskly now, trying not to break into a full run, afraid that the enigmatic entity behind him would surge forward to overtake him.

Then came a noise that chilled his very soul.

A low, mournful moan rose and fell like a devilish dirge. It definitely came from the cemetery, just ahead. Dusty stopped dead in his tracks, noting that the trailing creature behind him stopped abruptly in his wake. Dusty held his breath, praying the two demons were not working in concert to capture or mutilate him. All was silent for a few tense seconds.

Then the baleful lament repeated louder and longer than before. Whatever fiend made that sound obviously had brought sorrows from deepest hell up into the cemetery this night. Dusty cursed his decision to take the shortcut. He prayed it would not be the end of him. He feared for his life. A chill ran up his spine. His body shook with terror.

Then a third time, the beast bellowed; and this time it was closer. At that instant, Dusty saw a movement from behind a larger monument not 50 feet from where he stood. It revealed itself slowly, coming around the large slab of marble. Suddenly the evil thing appeared, familiar and unexpected.

Dusty recognized the outline of a cow. A white cow. Someone's livestock had gotten out and was trying to find its way home in the dark. Dusty wanted to laugh, but he was still shaking too hard. He had been afraid of a docile, stupid bovine.

But what of the swish, swish, swish that had accompanied him to this place? Dusty concentrated again and tentatively took another step forward. Swish. Another step, another swish. It whispered at him again. Then he took a third step and realized – with equal measures of relief, humiliation and amusement – what had been making the terrifying sound.

After the games that day, he had buttoned his baseball glove to his pants on his left side. With each step, the leather of the mitt had brushed against his denim pants. The glove had been making that mysterious noise all night long, but Dusty hadn't heard it underneath all the noise and commotion of the riotous celebration. Now alone, it was impossible not to hear it. He felt silly, stupid and embarrassed. But the overriding emotion was simply relief.

Dusty unbuttoned the strap of his mitt and put it on his left hand before resuming his walk home. He was breathing much easier. The mitt was refreshingly silent, save when the boy pounded his fist in it and relived again his glorious day on the baseball diamond. Thus, the hero returned home, suitably proud and yet substantially humbled by the events of the day – and the night.

Chapter 10

THE LONG SUMMER

With school out, the summer days began to stream by. The folks of Avery still talked about their team's victory in the baseball tournament. But every week, the victory lost a tiny bit of luster and became a less important topic. Conversations now started with a new topic – the heat.

Temperatures in June had been a bit warmer than usual. As July arrived, thermometers seemed to shoot up a little higher each day. The land was in the midst of a heat wave, like those that had visited nearly every summer since the beginning of the Dust Bowl.

Farmers were desperate for rain. Crops were burning up. Every sweltering day sapped plants of their vitality and took another little bite out of potential yields. Fields that should have been a dark, healthy green were turning pale and yellowish. Oh, what these farmers wouldn't give for a few days of slow, steady rain.

Like all their friends and neighbors, Dusty and his sisters grew lethargic and bored. Playing seemed like a chore. Chores seemed like torture. And an honest day's labor seemed impossible. Even the most industrious adults found it difficult to maintain a conscientious work ethic. Those who were less ambitious didn't even pretend. Hiram had even shut down his still, preferring to hang around the house and take it easy.

In truth, the weather was only one reason Hiram no longer made his way to the little hilltop where he distilled his moonshine. Revenuers were once again active in the county. A new man had been appointed to oversee the district. In his zeal to make a name for himself, he had pushed his men into the hills and hollows of the region, snooping around for illegal liquor factories and hauling their operators off to jail. The smart moonshiners were laying low, waiting for these probes to die down.

Eliza didn't seem particularly pleased to have Hiram hanging around the cabin. The combination of hot weather and Hiram under foot all day accentuated a congenital lazy streak in the young woman. Never the greatest housekeeper to begin with, she curtailed her domestic workload to the bare minimum. She grew indifferent and touchy. Little things irritated her. She seemed impatient for the weather to break so her husband would go back to work in the field, in the woods, at his still: She probably didn't care which.

Dusty and his sisters couldn't understand her grouchy moods. In spite of the heat, she assigned her kids more chores than usual. She mostly weighed them down with the jobs she liked least. The kids predictably balked and complained.

Hiram seldom got involved unless the arguments disturbed his sleeping/drinking/napping/eating/leisure time. Then he might demand the kids keep quiet and obey their mom. After a certain amount of haranguing and direct threats, the kids would sullenly go about finishing their assigned tasks.

Meanwhile, Dusty noticed something else different about his mother. She had stopped walking into Avery as often. In the early days of summer, when Hiram was away more often, she had been more mobile. She often left the house and headed down the dirt road toward the town after telling the kids to keep an eye on the cabin. This happened once, twice or even three times a week. Sometimes she was gone a couple of hours. When she came back, she might have an item or two from the general store, but sometimes she came back empty-handed. Dusty could never figure out quite why.

When the chores were caught up, all three kids tried to find excuses to vacate the cabin. They didn't like being around Hiram when he was drinking or Eliza when she was irritable. They often went to visit their grandma. The next best destination was the creek that ran behind their house and flowed into Dermot's Branch about 200 yards south of their cabin. At the confluence, the water was cool and there was plenty of shade. They'd meet other kids to fish, wade or swim.

Dusty spent many hours fishing, occasionally bringing home enough good-sized catfish, bullhead or carp to provide supper. On some occasions, he would ask to borrow his dad's old .22 rifle and go hunting. He hunted alone or with a couple of other boys who had access to rifles or shotguns. If Dusty was really lucky, he'd come home with a couple of rabbits or a few squirrels. The entrée portion of that evening's menu would be decided. Once he even shot a small deer and came home with meat for the entire week.

Whether off hunting or fishing, Dusty usually stopped by his grandmother's house, often around noon. Grandma Louellen always welcomed the boy. If he'd had any luck fishing or hunting, he would drop off some of the game at her house. She always thanked him and made him feel important. And, as always, she fed him if he was hungry. Grandma's cooking was impossible for Dusty to turn down.

XXX

One day in late June, a day that was relatively cool for that summer, Dusty decided to walk into Avery. He had a nickel and wanted to buy a bottle of pop. The idea of a cold bottle of cola made the two-mile-plus walk into town seem worthwhile. He made sure his sisters weren't watching and took off down the road. He soon wandered into Ivan Reynolds' store and saw Ronnie Schwartz at the counter, hunched over a catalog.

"Whatcha lookin' at," Dusty asked.

Ronnie looked up and smiled. "Hey, Dusty, how are ya? I was just lookin' at these guns in the Sears catalog. They got some nice ones."

"Lemme see," Dusty asked, sidling up to his friend and peering over his shoulder. Ronnie moved over so Dusty could see the pages of the catalog.

"See these shotguns? They got Rangers, Winchesters, even a Browning," Ronnie said pointing at each model.

"Wow, the Browning is $45," Dusty said with his eyes widening. "I could never afford one like that."

"Me neither," Ronnie frowned. "Sure would be nice though."

"What about rifles? Let's look at the .22s," Dusty urged his friend. A couple of pages later, they found Ranger, Winchester and Springfield rifles.

"That Ranger looks fine," Ronnie said. "Only $3.49. But I can't afford that either."

"Nope, I can't either," Dusty said. "Hey, look at this."

His eyes lit on a .22-caliber Winchester single-shot rifle. It was Model 67 bolt-action rifle with a 27-inch barrel.

"Now that's a grownup gun," Dusty said. "See here? 'Ideal for open field shooting. Shoots .22 Cal. short, long and long rifle cartridges, regular or high speed.' That's the one."

"Whaddya mean that's the one?" Ronnie asked.

"If I had the money, that's the one I'd buy," Dusty said.

"Well, fine, but I think you're dreamin'," Ronnie laughed. "It's $4.85. If you can't afford the Ranger, you can't afford this one."

"I know," Dusty said solemnly. "But if I did have the money, that would be the one."

"Well, if I had the money, I'd buy the Browning shotgun," Ronnie said wistfully.

"Be nice, wouldn't it?" Dusty said. "Well, I gotta get going. Hey, Ivan, can I get a Coke? Here's my nickel."

After saying goodbye to Ronnie, Dusty left the store. He relished every sip of the cold cola on the long walk. He couldn't get the Winchester out of his mind. He really wanted that rifle. If only there was some way to get it. He wouldn't have to borrow his dad's old .22. Think of the game he could bring home with the Winchester.

XXX

Instead of heading straight home, Dusty meandered down to Dermot's Branch. He liked to watch the waters rush by in the spring after heavy rains or drift by placidly, as they were starting to do now, during the long dry spells.

Dusty found sitting beside this small river was both peaceful and perplexing. On one hand, the river was pretty much always the same:

Sometimes the water was higher or flowed faster, sometimes – when it was lower – it seemed to move like thin molasses. But it was always there, the banks confining it, keeping its course steady and apparently eternal. It was always familiar, comfortable, like home.

On the other hand, it was always new water running between those enclosing banks. Once the current had moved on, it never returned. A new, slightly different current replaced it. You could see the water whirling, eddying and tumbling in different but parallel pathways as it flowed downstream. Like it had a place to go.

Where did that water go? Eventually to the Gulf of Mexico, Dusty knew that. But what kind of strange journey was it making to get there? Every now and then, the young boy wondered what it would be like to float along with the water, down the stream, into the Eleven Point River, on to the Mighty Mississippi and, finally, to the ocean. That would be some adventure.

But such an odyssey would require leaving behind all he knew: family, friends and the familiar woods that were his home. He figured he'd always want to be close to the native comforts of the Ozarks. He couldn't envision leaving that behind on a lark.

So, for Dusty, trips down America's vast watercourses would be the stuff of daydreams. And that was fine. Daydreams were pleasing. They were fun and harmless. No one could blame you for a daydream. It just wasn't real enough to worry about.

XXX

As July grew hotter, the days gradually started to grow shorter. Dawn came a bit later each morning and sunset came a little earlier each day. Dusty would rest in his bed at night, trying to tolerate the residual heat from the day, which seemed to oppress him most of the night. He impatiently anticipated any faint breeze that might cool his little room on the porch. Some nights it was so warm and stuffy in that confined little room that he'd take his pillow out onto the open porch and lie down on the wooden floor.

During those sweaty nights, Dusty would ponder every little thing going on in his life. Some of the thoughts were small while others were of modest importance. But more and more, heavy topics were invading his brain at night. One issue in particular wore a dreary path through his mind. Too often he found himself recalling his grandma's words about his dad.

"For your father, I see troubles. I see troubles for all my sons. I hope my visions are false."

He wondered what she meant. What troubles did she see? Was something going to happen to his dad? Was something going to happen to his uncles? The more he thought about the possibilities, the more his imagination took off on terrible trajectories. He knew his grandma wouldn't lie to him about her visions. But did she know things she wasn't telling him?

Some nights, Dusty had dreams about his dad and his uncles. They involved all sorts of potential calamities and catastrophes. In most of those dreams, Dusty was there, trying to help extract one or more of them from some crisis. Sometimes, in one of these nightmares, Dusty would be unable to do something or go somewhere to save his relatives from some unknown danger.

This theme repeated in various settings. He was responsible for performing some key task to alleviate a threat, but he always got delayed or distracted by some insignificant detail.

One sweltering night in early August, Dusty dreamed that his sisters had spotted three large, brown bears coming out of the woods toward the cabin. Eliza sent Dusty to the shed to bring his dad back to the house. On the way there, his old dog Bub – who had been dead for more than five years – ran up to him wanting to play. Dusty knew he had to warn his dad about the bears, but Bub was so enthusiastic and insistent. It had been so long since Dusty had run and wrestled with his beloved dog. Dusty grabbed a stick, threw it and watched Bub run to fetch it.

Then Dusty remembered the bears. He had thrown the stick in the direction of the bears. He started to call to Bub and run after him. However, the dog's full attention was on chasing the stick, which landed in the grass not 30 feet from the bears. Dusty hesitated, knowing he should turn back to the shed and get his dad. Instead, something compelled him to run toward the dog … and the bears.

He didn't remember exactly what happened next, but somehow Bub was gone. (Did the bears get him?) Dusty remembered his mission and turned to run back to the shed. He flung open the door and told his dad about the approaching bears. Hiram looked at his son with some annoyance.

"I'll be there soon," he finally said. "I've gotta fix this lamp first." And he went on tinkering with an old, useless kerosene lamp. Dusty froze not knowing what to do. Then Hiram looked up at Dusty and said calmly, "Get back to the house. I'll be along."

Reluctant to leave his dad, but bound to obey, Dusty ran back to the house, past the bears, who were strolling nearer, ambling into a position to block the path from the house to the shed. Dusty made it to the cabin door and turned to look back. At this point, Hiram came out of the shed and walked slowly, carefully toward the bears.

Dusty stood with his sisters and his mom, looking at the scene. For some reason, they didn't close the cabin door, instead standing at the threshold watching the bears. Dusty wanted to go help his father, but his sisters begged him not to leave. His mother said nothing. She was quiet, stoic, almost noncommittal. His sisters were crying. Dusty couldn't leave them. He put his arms around them, and together they watched the continuing spectacle.

At this point, Hiram was among the bears, petting their heads and talking low and gently to them. The bears reared up on their hind legs one after the other and put their paws on his dad's chest and shoulders. Dusty could see Hiram growing more nervous and uncomfortable. His dad had no defense against the huge, toothy, sharp-clawed beasts.

And suddenly Dusty knew his dad would not escape. The bears would inevitably turn vicious. He could see his dad knew this too, but Hiram continued petting and soothing the bears, deferring the outcome as long as he could.

Then Dusty woke up in a cold sweat, gasping for air and shocked at his sudden return to reality. For several confusing minutes, he couldn't acclimate himself to the here and now. Part of him was still somewhere in the dream, searching for a way to save his father. Part of him felt guilty for leaving the dream just when his dad was facing mortal peril.

He slowly regained his senses, and as he did, he wondered what the dream meant. Should he tell his grandma about the nightmare? She had seen many visions. She always seemed to understand their meanings. Pondering such weighty thoughts, the weary boy eventually drifted back to sleep.

XXX

Dusty wasn't the only Brodie suffering bad dreams at this time. A couple of nights later, his grandmother had a nightmare. It didn't involve Hiram. It was about her middle son, Martin.

Louellen's dream took place at night, on top of a tall, barren hill crowned with a level plateau about 75 feet across. The sky was overcast, but a pale, sheepish moon kept trying to peek between the clouds. The wind was blowing, no, gusting. It would howl past then recede before welling up again. The noise of the wind was the soundtrack of her dream, and it played on as she watched the cold, treeless plain.

In her dream, Martin had climbed the hill to stop a fight. There was a tall man clothed in a dark cape or blanket on one side of the hilltop. Another figure in white, pale and smallish, was standing resolutely but forlornly on the opposite side of the plateau.

It was clear to Louellen that the dark man was evil and the smaller person was innocent, perhaps even noble. Martin hurried up the hill and inserted himself between the two would-be combatants. He tried to talk them out of their difference. He was pleading with them to avoid conflict. He was almost begging them to stand down.

The dark figure sneered and ignored his pleas. The pale entity sadly shook its head; it saw no way to avoid the looming battle. Then

Martin ran out of words. He tried to talk but could find nothing to say. All that came out of his mouth was a hoarse whisper, almost a wheezing sound. Words would not prevent the inevitable.

At this point, the wind picked up and roared across the hilltop. Lightning flashed, striking the earth with a terrific blast as a peal of deafening thunder shook the ground and echoed across the landscape. At once, the two adversaries flew toward each other. The moon burst forth from between inky clouds, lighting the grounds. Bright knife blades shown in the belligerents' hands. They went after each other, weaving back and forth in a dangerous dance.

All this time, Martin tried to intervene, to come between and separate the desperate foes. He wasn't quick enough. Louellen tried to will Martin to succeed, but she feared the flashing blades would catch her son and wound him rather than the intended targets.

After a vicious clash, the fighters pulled apart for a moment. Again, lightning blazed the hill and thunder rattled the turf. Martin seized upon the slight pause to station himself directly between the two opponents. At the same instant, they charged again at each other, blades arcing overhead in near perfect symmetry. Both shanks sank to the hilt into Martin's chest. He let out a mournful cry and fell to his knees. Both enemies dissolved and shot like comets into the clouds above. The wind died instantly and the barren hilltop was silent and empty except for the dying form of Martin Brodie.

Louellen tried to run up the hill to his side. But she was swimming in molasses. Her legs would not move. Her feet would not go forward. She was making little progress against the night. She wailed trying to reach her wounded son, but her strength was giving out and she realized she couldn't make it.

Louellen Brodie woke and sat bolt upright in her bed. The night was calm. The stars were out. There was no sound of wind. It had been a dream. But that realization did nothing to calm the old Cherokee woman. She sat for a couple of hours staring straight ahead into the darkness, seeing nothing, but understanding too much. Something bad was on the horizon. Something awful was about to happen.

As Louellen sat and wondered, she knew nothing about Dusty's dream. And she would not learn for a couple of days about the dream Martin was having that same night. A vision that was closer to reality than either of the nightmares Dusty or his grandma experienced.

Chapter 11

THE KENNETH FAIR

The next day happened to be the start of the Kenneth Fair, an annual event that drew people from all the surrounding hills, hollows and towns. For years, the Kenneth Fair had been the highlight of the summer. It was the largest fair in the area outside of the Drury County Fair, which was held in Delphia way over on the far side of the county.

The early August event was a time to gather, socialize and celebrate accomplishments. Families came, saw relatives they hadn't seen for weeks or months and caught up with their neighbors. Occasionally they met a few new folks – regular attendees liked to invite all sorts of visitors.

It was a time to share stories – good and bad. A time to commiserate with those who were facing troubles. A time to rejoice with those blessed with good fortune. Or, if you were of a different bent, you might revel quietly in the struggles of your rivals or bite back your bitterness when they were prosperous.

For many, the fair provided a time for a little showing off. Farmers brought their best wares to the community hall on the north side of the town square for the annual judging. Women entered pies, cakes, jellies, jams, other foods and crafts, including every conceivable form of needlework. These usually reserved folks vied for red, white and blue ribbons and – often more important – the inevitable esteem that came with winning.

More than a little pride went into the creation of each item entered. More than a little envy was felt by the runners-up and losers. More than a little jealousy flared up. On rare occasions, small feuds erupted between contestants.

If Mrs. Samuel Drake's blueberry pie won the competition year after year, Mrs. Jacob Wheeler would invariably leave the community hall in a huff and spread malicious rumors about the judges and their inferior lineages.

If Claude Wilkins produced the largest watermelon this year, Herb Carter might attribute his second-place finish to bad weather in his neighborhood as compared to the Wilkins farm. If Wilkens heard, he might hint that the better farmer usually gets the better weather.

Everybody who won stood a bit taller, some with their noses significantly higher. For the next year, they had bragging rights – whether or not they were the kind to brag out loud. Their rivals temporarily lost face. Some bore their disappointment stoically or even jovially. Others found it difficult to hide their vexation.

The fair was also a time for letting loose. Music was a feature both day and night. And the competition among the amateur entertainers was just as fierce as among the gardeners and housewives. Each fiddle player tried to outperform the previous player. Each banjo player tried to outpick the last. Each singer attempted to outshine the previous participant – sometimes with sheer lung power.

Dancing was condoned by almost everyone except a handful of the most devout Baptists … and perhaps a few fathers who were staunchly protective of their daughters. Those daughters had waited months to flaunt their charms and flirt with the young men of the county. Those young men likewise were keen to impress the pretty and charming young ladies.

Such dances had kindled the sparks of more than a few romances. Some of the embers died before morning. Others led to brief love affairs. Some resulted in longer relationships. In a few cases, inflamed passions led to marriage proposals. Two lives might be forged into harmonious matrimony. The Baptists were right about one thing: You could never tell what dancing might lead to.

It's true that some of the dancers were under the influence of more than their attractive partners. Alcohol was available in ample quantities to those who wanted it. Though technically forbidden on the fairgrounds, strong drink was never hard to find. In fact, the competition among the moonshiners for praise – and sales – was as fierce as it was for the community hall entries.

There were always plenty of hillbillies who would surreptitiously haul his (or her: it wasn't unheard of) latest batch of homemade to Kenneth. They would hide a few jugs or bottles under a tarp in the back of their trucks or under the seat of their car if they owned one. A few graybeard moonshiners would hitch up their teams and ramble into town on wagons carrying concealed jugs of their finest liquor.

As the afternoon wore on, the men and older boys who kept company with the moonshiners began to take on a sort of glow. Some got a tad cheerful. Some exuberant in their joy. Some simply grew muddled as they slowly sank into a peaceful stupor. Unfortunately, there were those who got pretty rambunctious … or downright unruly.

These imbibers accounted for the vast majority of troublemakers at the fair each year. They were the main reason the Sheriff John Lawson always added a couple of temporary deputies to help him and his permanent deputy, Cliff Sanger, patrol the square and nearby streets during the fair. Along with Kenneth's two good ole boy police officers, who were off duty more than on duty, they were the law enforcement squad for the big shindig.

While seldom bothering the moonshiners themselves, Lawson and his constables would keep sharp eyes on the crowd for the few who eventually got out of control. If worse came to worse, one or two deputies would escort an inebriate to the jail, which was located in the back part of the sheriff's office. This usually quelled the rowdiness. Most of the detained ended up sleeping it off before Lawson released them the next morning.

XXX

Naturally, the Brodies were smack dab in the middle of the moonshine enterprise. Several members of the clan, including Hiram, conveyed a few containers of their individual (and highly potent) brands of white lightning into Kenneth every August. They would park along a darker street near the town square, shying away from beaten paths for a measure of privacy. Even the Brodie men who were not peddling jugs themselves could often be found hanging around where the moonshine merchants gathered.

Most customers were regulars, local men who routinely purchased varying amounts of illicit alcohol throughout the year. Others were more moderate drinkers who found the fair a reasonable excuse to have a taste or two. Of course, every year a few outsiders, possessing a well-developed instinct for sniffing out booze, would make their way to "moonshine row."

This year, an unwanted stranger would eventually find his way onto Spruce Street, a short block west of the square. Rafe Manx would appear already well-oiled and rowdy. A tall, dark and decidedly unhandsome fellow, Rafe had a face that only Hollywood could love. He was the archetype of the bad guy, the ideal "heavy."

In fact, almost everything about Rafe Manx was "heavy." He was just over six feet tall, with a bulldog face featuring a cleft chin that might have been attractive on another man. His dark eyes looked almost black, set above heavily sagging bags. A livid scar ran across the left side of his forehead, from above the eye to just short of the ear. Built like a fullback, his solid muscular core was due more to genetics than any physical fitness regimen.

Rafe was dressed in a well-worn white cotton shirt that he had apparently not changed for several days. Over the shirt he wore shabby denim overalls that were even dirtier than his shirt. His heavy brown work boots clomped as he strode across the ground with a wide, confident gait. He was bowlegged and gave the impression of a drunken sailor still trying to find his land legs. In fairness, his wardrobe wasn't really out of place in a small Missouri town in the middle of the Depression, but his sinister visage did nothing to endear him to anyone who crossed his path.

Because of his malignant appearance, no one in Kenneth would have been surprised to find out that Rafe sported a criminal record. His past included arrests for assault, assault with a deadly weapon, public intoxication, disturbing the peace, vagrancy, robbery and theft. He was convicted of only a couple of charges: Eyewitnesses had a mysterious habit of forgetting what they had seen or what they had told authorities they had seen. There were rumors – but only rumors – that he may have committed more grievous crimes.

Another unsavory character had accompanied Rafe to the fair. She was an incessantly annoying chatterbox of a bimbo named Rosie. She was a fleshy woman who featured dyed blond hair, an extravagance of makeup and a too-tight second-hand silk dress that revealed every curve of her stout body. Rosie carried herself with a hard smugness. She possessed an overdeveloped sense of self-importance.

When the Drury County women saw her, they raised at least one eyebrow. Many couldn't help whispering various criticisms behind their hands. All the females in the crowd disliked her immediately. But none would dare start anything with the burly floozy. She had the hard eyes of a bird of prey and arms that looked like she could pull up stumps if she wanted. Her entire being yelled, "Don't mess with me." Other women seldom did.

Her effect on the men of the crowd was generally similar: immediate dislike. Yes, a few men may have eyed her in a salacious manner due to her almost lewd appearance. However, most men were soon overpowered by a rising sense of repugnance.

Rosie rode Rafe's arm as they walked through the town square. It was clear both had started drinking well before appearing at the festivities. Rosie possessed a debauching glow. The odor of cheap booze emanated from Rafe as Rosie led her scruffy thug along the street.

She seemed to exert a tenuous control over her man, but it reminded at least one onlooker of a wildcat riding a bull. If Rafe wanted to pull at the reins, Rosie would have been thrown before she knew what had happened. For now, though, Rafe was content to follow Rosie's lead as they sashayed around the perimeter of the square, sizing up the Kenneth fair for who knew what purpose.

One person who noticed the couple soon after their arrival was Martin Brodie. Dusty's uncle watched the unsavory couple saunter into the square with a distrusting eye. And, though he possessed no hard proof, Martin was dead certain he was watching evil afoot.

Martin Brodie was a quiet, solemn man. Like Hiram, he could cut timber and drink with the best of the Brodie and Jennings men. However, he was very different from his older brother. He was placid, calm. While most people in Drury County had their Christian names abbreviated to a diminutive form or went by a folksy nickname, everyone always referred to this Brodie brother by his formal name: Martin.

Reserved? Yes, but Martin was also straightforward. He rarely spoke without good reason, and he always spoke with good reasoning. He was quicker to settle an argument than to begin one. He was more likely to stop an altercation than start one. But behind the quiet façade, people who knew him well perceived a strong resolve. Martin was the last of the Brodies anyone would expect to pick a fight. But if he got into one, most people figured he make a pretty good showing.

For a few minutes, Martin eyed Rafe and Rosie with a composed contempt. As he watched the audacious pair moving through the crowd, that contempt grew. Rafe began to subtly intimidate any person in his path. Rosie slyly egged him on. Martin felt intense disgust welling up inside.

Seeing all he could stand of the twosome, Martin retreated from the square down Spruce Street. As Martin ambled down the dim street, he saw a neighbor standing alone by his beat-up 1927 Model A Ford.

"Evening, Martin," local farmer and parttime distiller Billy Todd said in greeting as Martin strode up to the Ford.

"Hello, Billy," Martin replied as Todd moved toward the rumble seat of the vehicle.

"You got a thirst?" he asked Martin. Martin nodded silently. "Try this. Just finished this batch last week. It's pretty good. Not my best, but it'll do."

"Thanks," Martin said, taking a tin cup from Billy. He took a slow, careful sip and licked his lips as he looked off in the distance. Then he nodded his head in approval. Billy broke out into a grin.

"Glad you like it," he said. "Boy, it's a warm night. A drink or two sure helps in weather like this."

Martin nodded and took another sip.

"Anything going on up at the square?" Billy asked, leaning back against door of the Ford. The way Martin tightened his lips and narrowed his eyes told Billy more than anything Martin would say. It was a look that made Billy more than a little uncomfortable, but he was hard-pressed to say why.

"Trouble brewing," Martin said simply.

"Trouble? What kind of trouble?" Billy asked growing apprehensive. He'd never seen Martin Brodie look this vexed.

"Bad trouble, I'm afraid," Martin said before draining the contentents of the cup. When he withdrew the cup from his face, his familiar stoic reserve seemed to have returned. "Thanks for the drink. Mighty good shine, Billy."

Billy didn't respond at first. His slightly inebriated mind was trying to decide if what he'd just observed was of any importance. "Come back if you want more," Billy said, deciding whatever it was wasn't worth his personal worry.

Martin was already off, walking away and waving a hand in mute reply. He wandered on down Spruce Street, farther from the square. He was looking for Hiram or Cleve. He wanted to speak to them now and warn them about the unwelcome strangers.

XXX

Meanwhile, as the sun was beginning to set, Rafe and Rosie continued weaving their little trail of terror. They bumped into an old farmer – perhaps accidentally, perhaps not – and Rafe threatened to beat the man senseless.

"You'd better go on home, you old bastard!" Rosie yelled at the cowering man. The farmer went home. It was getting dark anyway, he told himself.

Their next target was Gerty Shanks, who worked for the school district helping with various secretarial and administrative tasks. This occupation allowed her to see plenty of details about various students and their parents, information that provided rich material for gossip. She was in the middle of spilling some new scuttlebutt when Rafe and Rosie approached her from behind. Their attention was drawn to Gerty's ample behind, which no garment could conceal.

"Good Lord, she don't need no cushions on her couch," Rosie hooted loudly, making sure everyone nearby would hear. "I didn't know they made lard tubs so big." Rosie laughed at her own cleverness and elbowed Rafe, enticing him to join in.

He somehow couldn't resist reaching out to give Gerty a hard smack on her rump. That silenced her gossip. The hefty woman lunged forward, spilling a half-full cup of lemonade on the always prim and proper Doris Winger, wife of the mayor. Rosie and Rafe thought that was hilarious. No one else in the crowd did. Whooping and roaring, the inconsiderate couple moved on.

Incidents like this piled up. Finally, James Findlay, an undersized railroad worker who was nearing pension eligibility, stood firmly in the couple's way. It took courage, but it was an indiscreet decision.

"Mister, I don't know who you think you are, but you can't treat people here that way," Findlay said.

Rafe stopped laughing and Rosie frowned.

"You got no right to talk to Rafe like that," she spewed. "Rafe, you show him who's boss."

Rafe looked at Rosie, slowly smiled then suddenly hit Findlay in the nose. Blood spurted from the elder man's face as he staggered backward. Rafe moved in and punched Findlay in the gut, doubling him over. Before Findlay could react, Rafe laced his fingers and brought his fists down on the smaller man's back, knocking him face-first onto the ground.

"Next time, send a man to try to stop me," Rafe Manx growled. He took Rosie's arm and sauntered away as she hurled a string of blue language over her shoulder at the fallen man.

Several people jumped in to help Findlay up. But no one tried to stop Rafe and Rosie.

Chapter 12

THE WINDFALL

While the Brodie men were making themselves at home among the moonshiners, the rest of the family was wondering through the community hall, looking at the many entries. Eliza and her daughters soon settled down to listen to a string of young ladies singing in front of a panel of self-important, stone-faced judges.

Unfortunately, Louellen had been feeling a little under the weather since her disturbing dream about Martin. She had decided to stay home and spent a restless evening, punctuated by waves of chilling apprehension. She wondered if she might have a touch of influenza.

Meanwhile, Dusty had grown tired of the vegetables, pies and crafts. He had wondered around looking at the carnival booths. He had stopped at one of these booths to watch four high school boys knock stuffed dolls off shelves with lopsided baseballs. As twilight approached, they were slowly driving the old carney out of business.

The four boys, led by Percy Jennings and his good friend Henry Franks, would bet on one another. They had to knock the dolls off the shelves with the battered and misshapen balls the carney offered. Though the balls lacked ideal density or dependable aerodynamics, this team of young hurlers weren't bothered. These were rawboned country boys who might even give ol' Dizzy Dean a run for his money in the velocity department. But they weren't just a bunch of scatter-armed hicks. They had control. Control like the old carney had never seen before.

They'd bet their nickels on the first pitcher up and cheer him on as he knocked down doll after doll, adding to their winnings with every delivery. When the hurler started to tire, the second would take over, flinging balls harder and truer than the first. And so it went, slinger after slinger knocking down dolls and increasing the team's payroll.

Finally, the old carney had seen enough. "OK, boys, that's it," he barked. "You've about cleaned me out. Take your money and get out of here."

Percy wasn't about to leave yet. He had the best arm of the bunch, and he had just started his turn at the defenseless dolls. He was just getting warmed up.

"Your sign don't say nothin' 'bout no limits on throws," he challenged. "We wanna keep playing."

"I don't care what the sign says or don't say," the carney countered. "You've had your fun and made your money. Now scram!"

Percy turned to walk away. As he did, he looked at Dusty, who had been standing at the edge of the booth watching. An idea hit him and he grinned … inside. To the carney he showed a sad, disappointed face.

"Say fella, would you go double or nothing on what we've won so far for just one more throw?" Percy pleaded. "It doesn't even have to be me throwing. You get to pick who makes the last toss. Double or nothing. Waddaya say?"

"No dice," the carny said.

"C'mon, pick any us standing right here to make one throw," Percy begged.

The old carney looked around. Suddenly he saw a way to get his money back. He was about to work a hustle on these ignorant rubes.

"OK, if I pick the ball, I pick the thrower and the thrower has to knock a doll off the shelf, not down, but off the shelf, then it's a bet. Double or nothing."

Percy turned his back on the carney and winked at his fellow pitchers. He pretended to discuss it with them. One nodded a hesitant yes, shook his head in a definite no. Henry Franks even blurted out, "Hell, no!"

The old carney figured his chances at recouping his losses were in danger. Then Percy started whispering and gesturing with more emphasis. His pals seem to respond and he got two "yes" nods. Finally,

Henry threw up his arms in disgust and said, "OK, fine. But I'm telling you, it's a bad idea. We should just take what we've won and go."

Percy turned back to the carney and said, "We agree. You pick the ball. You pick the hurler. The doll has to hit the ground. Now, who do you pick?"

The carney smiled. He had them now. As the daylight was fading, he looked over at the skinny kid who'd been standing by the booth all this time, watching the older boys throw. He pointed at Dusty and said, "I pick him."

Percy and his pals looked shocked. They howled and argued, saying that was no fair. They claimed the bet was off. It was supposed to be one of them he picked. They wouldn't go through with it.

The carney smiled contentedly and let them bellow for a while. A small crowd was gathering, drawn by the boys' protests. The onlookers soon figured out what was going on. The old carney let the teens squabble and then spoke in voice loud enough for the whole audience to hear.

"You said I could pick the thrower. You didn't say it had to be one of you. Now, you're gonna honor your bet or I'll get a crew of ruffians the likes of which you ain't never seen. We'll drive you out of the square, out of this town and out of this county. Understand?"

Percy and his gang knew when they were licked. They complained, grumbled and called the carney a thief. But they finally gave in, reluctantly agreeing to the carney's terms. The crowd booed the old hustler and called him a variety of uncomplimentary names. They were nearly unanimous in rooting for the young boy to come through. But the carney was a tough, thick-skinned man who knew he'd be leaving town in the morning. He wasn't going to back down with a day's income on the line.

Percy, still sporting a look of concern, called to the younger boy. "Hey, Dusty, c'mon over here."

Curious, Dusty walked over to Percy, who bent down and whispered to him.

"You got a good arm. How'd you like an even share of our winnings. That'd be 15 percent. Waddaya think, Dusty? Can you do it?"

Dusty was in awe of Percy's strength, guile and guts. But he summoned some guts himself and corrected the older boy. "A fifth is 20 percent. I'll do it for 20 percent."

Percy's eyes widened in amazement. Then he started laughing. He couldn't help it. Dusty had some grit. He admired a kid with some sand. This would be a great story, win or lose.

"All right," Percy said, still laughing. "Knock down a doll."

The old carney still felt the odds were heavily in his favor. He picked the softest, most lopsided ball in his collection and handed it to Dusty.

"Don't get nervous, kid," the old man said. "Just throw it as hard as you can. Good luck." Then he stepped back.

Dusty took the asymmetrical sphere and tossed it up and down a few times to get familiar with the weight and balance. He knew from skipping rocks on the river, tossing stones at squirrels and playing baseball with battered second-hand baseballs that every object had a center of balance. Getting a feel for that balance was critical. After a few tosses, he finally thought he had found it. He tossed the ball once more for confirmation.

Dusty eyed the row of dolls. They seemed smaller now than when he'd watched the older boys throwing. But he had a strange sense of calm. He leaned back, cocked his arm, stepped forward and let fly. The ball shot forward, sweeping a little to the left and dropping a bit. It wasn't a bullet, but it was a nice, firm, confident peg. The ball bent a little more at the end and whacked a doll just under its center point. A soft "plop" sounded as the doll kicked up and backward, off the shelf and onto the ground.

Percy and his pals were all over Dusty. They slapped him on the back, tousled his hair and shook his hand.

The carney, with a bitter expression they all thoroughly enjoyed, started counting out coins to match their bet. With the crowd that had gathered, he had no option. The kids had hustled the hustler. Henry stood beside the carney, counting with him. The crowd stood cheering and applauding in approval.

All but Rafe and Rosie, who were standing near the back sharing a knowing look.

XXX

Near the corner of Spruce and Dogwood streets, Martin found Hiram and Cleve gathered around Riley Schwartz's truck. Riley was telling a story about (what else) fishing and drinking. The event apparently involved more drinking than fishing.

"… And then I said, 'Wade, I think you got a bite on that line of yours.' And Wade opened one eye – just one – and he looked at the line moving back and forth and he said, 'Only place I got to put him is in my jug, and I don't want no catfish drinkin' up my liquor.' Then he went right back to snoring. All the time, that line just a-playin' back and forth in the water," Riley laughed. Hiram and Cleve joined him in laughing. They were glassy-eyed and on their way to tying one on in a big way.

" 'Don't want no catfish drinkin' up my liquor,' " Hiram repeated. "If that don't beat all. Hey Martin, did you hear about the last time Riley went fishin' with Wade?"

"Yeah, I heard it," Martin said without a smile. "Say, Riley I got some business to talk with Hiram and Cleve. Can I steal 'em away from you a minute?"

"Sure thing," Riley said, taking another tug on his jug and setting it on floorboard of his truck.

After the Brodie brothers had move toward Hiram's old Model T truck, Cleve broke the silence.

"What's up, Martin. You look like you just drank vinegar."

"I've got a bad feelin' about a fella who's up on the square. He's with some broad, and he's spoilin' for a fight. And I don't think there's anyone in this town that can take him. Except us."

Hiram shrugged, his eyes coming slightly back into focus.

"I don't see what that's got to do with us," Hiram said. "Let the sheriff or one his deputies take care of it."

"Yeah, why's it our business?" Cleve asked. The potent moonshine obviously was affecting Cleve more than Hiram. They both drank hard, but the Hiram could hold his liquor better.

"This fella up there is out to hurt somebody," Martin said. "I can feel it. I don't say go after him. But if he sticks his nose in OUR business, we need to be ready."

His brothers looked at each other but were quiet. They knew Martin didn't exaggerate. In fact, he tended to play down bad news. Finally, Hiram spoke.

"OK, Martin, but what makes you so sure?" he asked.

"I had a dream last night," Martin said. "I dreamt blood. Right up there in the square. And I saw a man, not his face, just his outline. It was that man up there. In the dream, he's the one that spilt the blood."

Hiram and Cleve were wide-eyed and moved by Martin's words. They knew of only one time Martin had talked about a dream with such emotion. It was a dream Martin had the night his fiancée, Clara Jean Jamison, had died. Early the next morning, Martin told his brothers about his dream.

He had seen Clara Jean at the church in a white dress, a wedding gown. She wore a white veil over her face. When Martin walked up and lifted the veil, Clara Jean's face was under water. The dream ended there. Just before noon, Clara Jean's brother found her body in the Eleven Point River. She had drowned sometime during the night.

Hiram and Cleve had no more questions for Martin. They were ready to work on plans to meet this stranger and make sure it wasn't any Brodie blood that was shed.

XXX

The crowd slowly thinned out at the carnival booth. The bitter carney was closing up his tent. Meanwhile, Percy and Henry counted up the money they'd won. It came to $29.50. This was a substantial pile of cash in 1930s southern Missouri.

"Wow, would ya look at that," Henry exclaimed. "You could work a month and never see that kinda dough."

"So 29.50 divided by five is …" Surprised, Percy and Henry stared at him then, unsure, looked at each other.

"Five ninety each," Dusty said. He was good with numbers. Percy and Henry looked at him, unsure.

"Let me figure it," Henry said. He took out his knife and began carving in the ground. "That's 5.90 times 5 … is 45 … carry the 4 … yep, it comes out to 29.50." They all looked at Dusty like he was from another world. "What are you, some kind of adding machine?" Henry asked.

"No, but sometimes I wouldn't mind being a cash register," Dusty said with a wide smile.

"Well, help me count our five dollars and 90 cents and you can add that to your till," Percy laughed.

A few minutes later, his pockets full of nickels, dimes and quarters, Dusty started out toward Spruce Street to find his dad's truck. He would hide his winnings. He had an ideal place in mind, an old burlap sack that contained a coil of rope, some old tools and other odds and ends. He figured it was a place where neither his dad nor anyone else would find his treasure. Once he got home, he'd wait until late at night then sneak out to the truck, gather up his horde of coins and go hide them in the hollow tree stump about half way to his grandma's place.

The next morning, he would collect the money and walk all the way into Avery to Ivan Reynolds' general store. He would open the Sears Catalog and order his own brand new 22-caliber Winchester bolt action, single shot Model 67 rifle for $4.85.

He made his way carefully through the crowd, hands in the pockets of his overalls, gripping as many of the coins as his fingers could capture, hoping to keep them from jingling as he passed through the throng of fairgoers..

Despite his attempts at being discreet, his efforts to hide his bonanza had failed. He had no way of knowing he was being stalked. Walking quietly for the first time that night, a few measured paces behind the unsuspecting boy, came the vicious Rafe Manx and the very greedy Rosie.

Chapter 13

THE FIERCE FIGHT

Martin, Hiram and Cleve huddled on the passenger side of Hiram's truck, parked on the opposite side of the street and just a few feet closer to the town square than Riley's truck. The brothers tried to keep hidden from Riley's direct gaze, but it didn't really matter. Riley kept nipping at his jug and seemed to be unaware of anything else.

They made a quick inventory of any weapons available. Hiram had a shotgun and a keen-edged axe in the bed of his truck. The axe could inflict a decisive wound, especially when wielded by an expert lumber man. And, as always, he had a hunting knife tucked into his right boot. Martin, like Hiram, carried a hunting knife in his overalls, while Cleve had only a pocket knife.

It wasn't much of an arsenal. Martin usually carried a .22 rifle in his car, but Cleve had offered a ride into Kenneth to a certain Miss Jeannie Allworth. Cleve was attempting to woo the young widow. Knowing Miss Jeannie detested violence, especially firearms, he had argued with Martin to leave the weapon at home.

Cleve had been trying to court and spark Miss Jeannie for nearly a year. Around her, he always tried to be on his best behavior. She had only agreed to accompany Cleve into town because she knew Martin would provide an honorable chaperone. Truth be known, she had as much interest in Martin as in his younger brother.

Something told Martin to take the rifle along. The dream and a few other omens – or at least uncomfortable thoughts – told him danger was near. But Cleve's pleas to "appear civilized" in front of Miss Jeannie won out. For his brother's sake, Martin had reluctantly given in.

This decision left the brothers lightly armed. Hiram kept the shotgun. Cleve took the axe. Martin would have make do with his knife if necessary. With this small armory, the Brodie brothers headed down Spruce Street toward the square to find a place to intercept Rafe and Rosie if the pair chose to invade the street that was lined with moonshiners and their customers.

Spruce Street dropped downward from the square into a small depression perhaps 50 feet west of the square. The street then ascended at a more gradual tilt until reaching the intersection with Dogwood Street – now at the brothers' backs. The area the Brodies were entering was the low ground between the square and Dogwood Street.

At the lowest point sat Billy Todd's Model A, parked under an ancient white oak tree. The old tree towered nearly a hundred feet above the street in the front lawn of a dilapidated house. This huge tree provided additional shadow to conceal any sampling of moonshine near Billy's vehicle. Billy took full advantage of the added darkness to mask his and his visitors' activities.

When they reached the oak tree, Martin stopped his brothers. "This'll do," he said. "This tree forms a natural blind. If he comes this way, we'll see him."

"That'll give us some protection," Cleve agreed.

Hiram looked around. "I'd rather have the high ground, but we can't go much closer to the square armed like this." Hiram sauntered over to the big tree and stood in its deep shadows. Apparently satisfied, he held the shotgun across his chest.

"Martin, you know what this fella looks like," he said. "Sing out if you see him."

"Awright," Martin said. "But don't be shootin' unless the sonofabitch pulls a gun. None of us needs to be going to jail for killin' an unarmed man."

All agreed.

Cleve ambled over to Riley's truck, axe in hand. Billy offered him a drink. Without so much as a glance his way, Cleve said, "No thanks." Billy realized something important was afoot. But he wasn't about to interfere in Brodie business without an invitation.

XXX

On the square, Sheriff Lawson was getting wind of the confrontations between crowd members and the unpleasant duo of Rafe and Rosie. Mayor Winger had caught up with him on Lewis Street, on the far eastern side of the square. Lawson was helping one of the temporary deputies settle a small dustup between one of the Denny boys and Riley Schwartz' son, Ronnie. The peace officers had made the two boys shake hands and go their separate ways. Time would tell whether the hatchet was truly buried.

"Sheriff, there's a man and woman causing trouble," the mayor bellowed as he crossed Lewis Street and hurried toward the sheriff. "He hit Gerty and knocked her into Doris. I've heard other complaints about 'em too."

Before Lawson could reply, Jimmer Cornet came running across the street to join the trio.

"Sheriff, some fellow just attacked old man Findlay," the Cornet boy cried. "I think he broke his nose. Findlay's hurting. He's sitting by the lemonade stand."

"Must be the same fellow," Mayor Winger declared. "Jimmer, was he with a blond woman with a foul mouth?"

"Yes, sir," Jimmer nodded. "I can't repeat some of the things she said, but she sure egged it on."

"All right, I've got to go," Lawson said, narrowing his eyes and gritting his teeth. This was the part of the job he hated. "You three split up and find Cliff. Send him to the west side of the square. And tell him to hurry."

Lawson hustled across the street into the crowded square. With a determined step, he hurried through or around the little knots of people, constantly dodging to avoid colliding with anyone. Meanwhile, the parttime deputy, the mayor and young Jimmer Cornet took off north, south and west in search of Deputy Sanger.

XXX

Dusty was well aware of the drinking going on along Spruce Street. He knew his dad had parked the truck closer to Dogwood than to the square. In general, Spruce Street was a safe area of Kenneth, a quiet neighborhood of older but mostly substantial houses. Tonight, the relative safety of the area depended on the fairgoers populating that street. When men – or women – of a southern Missouri town are drinking "likker," they can get a bit wild. A few get downright mean.

Dusty had no intention of letting some drunk hillbilly catch him with his pockets full of coins. In particular, he feared running into his dad. Hiram could be a mean drunk. Given the chance, Dusty knew his dad would confiscate the little fortune he carried. It would be spent by morning. And his dad would never show any regret.

Dusty was determined to avoid Hiram or any other cash-hungry drunks. He planned to sneak over to his dad's truck, wait until no one was looking and hide the money in the bed of the truck. He figured the gunny sack would keep the coins from jangling too much. His dad would never know they were there. That, at least, was his plan.

Dusty came to the western edge of the square and looked across Clark Street. A small grocery store stood on east side of the street. A drug store was on one side and the post office on the other side of the store. There was a small alley between the store and the post office. Dusty saw a clandestine route back to the truck.

The boy made his way across the street and walked past the drug store to the grocery store. He slowed down and casually looked all around to make sure no one was following. He did his best to be inconspicuous. No one seemed to notice him.

He didn't see Rafe and Rosie, crossing Clark Street just twenty steps behind him toward the far side of the drug store. They stopped, pretending to look in the store window. If Dusty saw them at all, they meant nothing to him. He looked to be in the clear.

The boy edged coolly to the corner of the grocery store. With another quick look around, he sneaked through the narrow gap between the buildings. In back of the store was a sort of narrow alley that ran behind the houses on Spruce Street on the right and those facing Pine Street on the left. Residents used this unimproved lane to get horses and, in more recent years, cars or trucks to backyard stables or sheds. The path was unkempt and littered with odd pieces of junk, trash and plenty of weeds. It was a fairly secluded area, visible only from the back windows or doors of the houses on either side.

It was getting darker, making navigation a bit of a problem, but Dusty thought the shadows were an asset. He carefully made his way past sheds, outhouses and trash cans in back of these houses until he almost reached Dogwood Street.

Soon he reached an abandoned house with the remnants of a back porch in the slow process of falling down. The windows along this side of the house were broken out. Dusty thought this might offer good backup plan. If he found his dad was hanging around the truck, he could sneak back and hide his money inside this house. Satisfied with Plan B, he crept to the far side of the house then cut north toward Spruce Street.

Directly behind him, moving quickly but discreetly through the shadows, were Rafe and Rosie. People who'd heard Rosie in the square just minutes before would have wondered at the way she was keeping her mouth shut for now. Greed can be a great motivator.

As Dusty, followed by his adversaries, was moving along the dim alley, Hiram, Cleve and Martin were well past the old house and looking intently toward the square. They didn't see the boy or his pursuers.

As dusk turned to darkness, the Brodies peered ahead, looking for the big man and his woman. The sounds from the fair filtered down the road to them. The buzz of insects cut through the night air. Tension that had started to rise as Martin told them about his dream continued to ratchet up slowly as the Brodies awaited a pending confrontation.

XXX

Sheriff Lawson soon reached the west side of the square. As he had hurried through the crowd, he had asked several people if they'd seen the bully and his companion and, if so, which way had they gone.

He was talking with a couple who'd been watching Percy and the other boys knocking down dolls. They'd gotten a kick out of young Dusty Brodie and the older boys winning the big pot of money. In answer to the sheriff's question, the man said he'd seen a couple who might have been Rafe and Rosie crossing Clark Street about five minutes ago. His wife thought she had seen Dusty Brodie going that direction at about the same time.

Henry Franks was wandering by, whistling a happy little tune to himself, when he heard someone mention Dusty's name. He turned to look at the trio and saw a tense look on the sheriff's face.

"I bet Dusty's heading to Hiram's rig with his money," Henry told the sheriff. "It's parked up Spruce Street a ways."

Lawson wondered just how this too-young-to-drink teenager knew where Hiram had parked a vehicle almost certain to be carrying moonshine. But he didn't have time to ask. He turned north and crossed the street, heading for the corner of Clark and Spruce. He hoped he wouldn't find the bully trying to intimidate any of the local moonshiners. Things might get out of hand in a hurry.

Just as Lawson neared the intersection of Spruce Street, Deputy Sanger came running across the street to catch him.

"What's going on, John?" Cliff Sanger said, trying to catch his breath. "The mayor said you needed help with a troublemaker."

"A troublemaker and a witch, I think," Lawson responded. "If they're headed down Spruce Street, there may be more trouble than that sonofabitch has bargained for."

Together, the two lawmen turned the corner and headed down the hill on Spruce Street. Lawson took the right side of the road with Sanger on the left.

It was darker than ever between the two houses. Dusty edged along the side of the abandoned house, his right hand tracing a board on the exterior of the building to steady himself as he felt his way through the overgrown grass. The house on his left, also facing Spruce Street, offered a lawn that had been mowed recently, but a full moon was illuminating the ground there. Dusty felt safer in the shadows.

With Rafe and Rosie behind him, he wasn't safe at all. When Rafe saw Dusty turn toward the street – and possibly other people – he knew he had to make his play. The two predators rounded the corner of the house and hurried to catch Dusty before he reached the front of the dwelling.

Dusty was nearing the side of the front porch when he heard a rustling behind him. Moving like a lion attacking a stray antelope, Rafe lunged at Dusty. For a brief moment, the boy froze in surprise and terror. The young Brodie boy was no match for Rafe's strength, but his agility gave him a small chance to escape.

Just like on the baseball field, Dusty's reflexes took over. He faked a move to his left, away from the house. As he felt his attacker react, Dusty juked back toward the wall of the house and tried to jump up on the porch, which sat two feet above the ground. He thought he'd made it, but just as his left foot hit the porch, he felt a sudden tug on his right ankle. Rafe was still to his left but was turning quickly to take another swipe at Dusty. What was holding his right foot?

Rosie was more agile than she appeared. When Rafe had vaulted at the boy and missed, she had sprinted forward to contain their prey. Dusty almost made the porch in time, but Rosie reached out her left hand and grabbed the boy's right ankle. Her grip was tight. She was sure she could hold the boy a couple of seconds until Rafe arrived to subdue their victim.

A real surge of fear rose in Dusty's chest along with a shocking amount of adrenalin. His hands grabbed at the porch floor, while his left foot kicked at the ground. Simultaneously, he wrenched his right knee forward, bumping into the side of the house. It hurt like thunder, but Dusty didn't have time to pay attention. His right shoe came off in Rosie's hand just as Rafe reached for him again. He managed to thrust himself up and onto the porch, scrambling to his feet running toward the street. He kicked off his left shoe, making him barefoot but still very mobile.

Riley Schwartz heard the commotion and looked up with bleary eyes. He watched a few seconds before recognizing Dusty Brodie being chased by a large man and a robust woman. The woman loudly cussed the boy. It appeared Dusty had kicked her wrist in freeing himself. Her howl roused Riley, who then decided Dusty needed help. Rising on wobbling legs, Riley gathered his balance and ran to aid the young boy. He was still carrying his jug of moonshine.

XXX

Despite the general buzz rising from the town square, Rosie's yelp alerted the Brodie brothers. Hiram and Cleve turned around and looked back up Spruce Street to see what was going on behind them. But Martin seemed to realize the urgency in the rear. He took off up the street, running with a speed no one would have guessed he possessed. Maybe he was driven by last night's dream. Whatever the reason, Martin was making tracks, heading with certainty in the direction of Dusty, Rosie and Rafe.

Hiram and Cleve stood agape for a few seconds, watching Martin hurrying toward Hiram's truck. Then the two remaining brothers took off to follow their brother.

Lawson and Sanger also had heard Rosie's yell. And they saw Martin Brodie emerge from the shadows and head up Spruce Street toward Dogwood Street. After quick glance at each other, and they too were sprinting toward the confrontation.

XXX

Dusty had remained a step ahead of Rafe, running like a jackrabbit all over the front yard of the abandoned house. A strange thing was happening. He knew he was quicker than this large man, but he couldn't seem to move with his usual speed and agility. Then he realized his right knee was throbbing. He also was weighed down by the mass of coins in his pockets. He knew he couldn't take the time to rid himself of their weight; Rafe would be on him.

He continued to dodge and dart around the yard, avoiding Rafe while Rosie continued her verbal assault. She occasionally picked up and threw sticks, pieces of a broken flower pot and in one case a loose brick from the corner of the crumbling house. Dusty had to keep an eye out for her mostly errant missiles. This took away from the attention required to stay out of Rafe's grasp.

Suddenly Riley Schwartz appeared in the yard, jug in hand. He started yelling at Rafe to leave Dusty alone. Now Rosie had another target for her off-target volleys. The far-from-sober Riley was a little slow in eluding her peltings. Still, he worked his way toward Rafe, using his jug to ward off a barrage consisting mainly of pottery shards.

Rafe was becoming frustrated with Dusty. He didn't expect this skinny kid to provide such a contest. As his anger rose, he focused solely and fiercely on the boy with the pockets full of money. He didn't see Riley coming in from the left swinging his half empty jug.

"Duck, Rafe!" Rosie yelled. He did. Just in time. Riley's wild swing clipped the top of Rafe's head. The glancing contact left Riley off balance. Rafe recovered more quickly. He turned on Riley and bashed the dizzy moonshiner's jaw. The deep cracking sound likely meant shattered teeth, broken bones or both. Riley moaned and fell, still holding the jug in his hand.

This interlude gave Dusty a chance to head toward his dad's truck. He got on the far side of the truck and tried his best to keep the vehicle between himself and Rafe. The angry thug sneered and pulled a long knife from his pantleg. As he brandished it, enough light gleamed off the blade to warn Dusty that he was now in real danger.

"When I catch you, I'm gonna skin you alive!" Rafe growled, spitting verbal venom at the boy.

Dusty's eyes widened in fear. He felt himself starting to panic. He didn't know how much longer he could hold off this powerful, wild-eyed demon. Rafe began angling to his right around the front of the truck. When Dusty reacted, Rafe hit the brakes and reversed directions. The two repeated this deadly dance two or three times before the tables suddenly turned.

With a swiftness that amazed and stunned Rafe, a man came charging at him with a knife drawn and ready for combat. Martin had heard Rafe threaten his nephew. He wasn't about to let this man harm any of his kin, much less an unarmed boy.

Martin drew up suddenly between Rafe and Dusty. His eyes were daggers that glared at Rafe.

"Drop that knife or sure as hell, I'll kill you," Martin said in a surprisingly soft, even voice. "Dusty, stay behind me."

Rafe was shaken by this sudden appearance, but he wasn't about to back down. He scowled and returned Martin's glare.

"I'll send *you* straight to hell," the brute hissed.

Then he lunged at Martin, who merely moved one foot back, leaned away from Rafe's slicing blade and stuck his own knife into the big man's side just below the right armpit. Rafe grunted and staggered to his left, but somehow kept his feet. He turned and readied to make another rush at Martin.

Dusty saw all this happen in a flash, as if time had somehow speeded up. He didn't know his uncle possessed such dexterity. Caught in the awe of the moment, he almost didn't see the shape moving up behind Martin, who was now facing the street and Rafe. It was Rosie, a large chunk of brick held overhead, racing toward his uncle.

"Behind you," Dusty shouted. It was barely warning enough. Martin turned to see Rosie swinging the object down toward his head. He stepped again, pivoting away while bringing his knife across Rosie's face. A thin line of blood appeared on her left cheek and chin. It quickly began welling into a significant current of blood.

A shocked Dusty didn't see Rafe swooping in on Martin, taking advantage Rosie's interference to renew his attack. If the first foray between the two men looked abrupt and brutal, the second was almost explosive. Rafe tried thrusting his knife into Martin's midsection.

In a reaction that grew into legend during subsequent retellings, Martin somehow thwarted the blow with his left arm and plunged his own knife deep into Rafe's chest just under the sternum. The noise

Rafe let out was like a grunt accompanied by a gush of air followed by a doleful low whimper. Within seconds, Rafe was dead on the ground.

Chapter 14

THE FALLOUT

Hiram and Cleve were at Martin's side almost instantly. They had hurried up the hill but arrived too late to affect the struggle. Hiram later said he had aimed his shotgun at Rafe twice, but he had not fired for fear of hitting first Dusty and then Martin. Cleve, with the axe, was never in position to wield his weapon.

The sheriff and deputy were on the scene in short order. Sanger began giving first aid to Rosie, who was still bleeding freely and cursing just as freely. The deputy quickly determined that she would live. But Rosie's face would always carry the mark of Martin's blade.

Cleve, meanwhile, was attending Riley Schwartz, who remained unconscious for several minutes. It was impossible to tell whether he had collapsed from the blow to his jaw or from the alcohol in his veins. Riley ultimately would lose a tooth. His bruised jaw turned purple overnight and troubled him for several weeks. On the plus side, he had a pretty good story to tell. Each time he told it, he naturally embellished his role in saving "that poor Brodie boy's life."

As a crowd of moonshiners and their customers gathered around the scene, Sheriff Lawson bent over Rafe's bloody body, checking for vital signs. He found none. He noted two stab wounds. He then looked up at Martin's face … and at his hand.

"I need that knife, Martin," Lawson said, reaching a hand out to the newly minted killer.

Without a word, Martin offered the weapon to the sheriff, handle first. Lawson let out a sigh. He was very glad he hadn't needed to argue with Martin, especially with two other Brodies standing nearby with gun and axe.

"How did this get started?" the sheriff asked no one in particular. Dusty found himself talking. Words slipped out and started tumbling one after another. He didn't have any control over what he was saying. He was staring at Rafe's body.

"Him and that woman jumped me in the dark," the boy said. Words flooded out faster and faster. "He lunged at me, but I got away. Then she grabbed my foot. I shook free, but this man started chasing me all over the place. I was just trying to get away. I thought he was gonna catch me. Then Riley came over and tried to hit the guy. But the big man ducked and then he slugged Riley upside his head. Riley fell over, and the guy started chasing me around the truck. Then he pulled a knife."

Suddenly, Dusty didn't know how to describe the rest.

"Go on, boy," Lawson said.

Dusty looked at Martin then at his dad. Their faces were blank. Dusty kept looking for a signal to stop or go on talking. None came. Tears began welling up in the boy's eyes. He started shaking. He didn't know why he was so scared now, now that it was all over.

"Take your time," Sheriff Lawson said gently.

Dusty swallowed hard and the words came again, a little slower and more controlled now.

"All at once Uncle Martin came up and jumped in between me and that man with the knife," he said. "The big guy tried to stab my uncle, but Martin ducked out of the way. I saw Martin had a knife and he swung it up and stabbed that man in the side as he went by. It happened so fast.

"Then she," he said pointing at the moaning and muttering Rosie, "she ran up and tried to hit Martin over the head with a brick. He ducked again and cut her face. She started howling. And the next thing I knew, that man came at Martin from behind. He was moving like a tiger, but somehow he missed. Martin got away and stabbed the man again. He went down real quick. Just where he is now."

"Okay, Dusty," Lawson said. "You did just fine. Just one more question. Think before you answer it. Who stabbed at who first?"

Again Dusty looked at the faces of Martin, Hiram and Cleve.

No expressions. No suggestions. No clues. It seemed like the faces on Mount Rushmore might change expression before any the Brodie brothers.

"Well," Dusty finally said, "the stranger swung his knife first … but Martin was the first one to draw blood."

The sheriff nodded soberly. He looked at the dead man, then at Martin.

"That how it happened, Martin?" Lawson asked.

"That's just about it. He said he was gonna gut the boy, so I killed him," Martin said calmly.

Lawson looked at Sanger, still tended a moaning Rosie. "Waddaya think, Cliff? Sound like a justifiable homicide to you?"

"If ever there was one," Sanger said decidedly. Hearing this, Rosie took a swing a Sanger, her now-bloody fist glancing off his ear. Sanger responded with a backhand slap to the uninjured side of Rosie's face. She let out another loud string of curses. Sanger continued holding his bloody handkerchief to cut on Rosie's cheek, but he may have added a little extra pressure because Rosie stopped cursing long enough to let out a painful gasp.

Lawson turned back to Dusty. "Why were they after you, Dusty?"

A flash of fear rose in Dusty. He didn't want to tell anyone about his little fortune. He especially didn't want his dad to know.

"I-I don't know. They just followed me. For no reason, I guess."

"Liar!" Rosie yelled, pushing Sanger's hand from her face. "You got your pockets full of money. We aimed to get that money. Now Rafe is dead, and it's all because of you!"

Dusty's eyes widened with alarm. He looked at Rosie. He looked at Lawson. He glanced at Martin. At the dead man. Finally, he looked at his dad.

"You got some money on you," Hiram said, more a statement than a question. "You better give it to me." He eyed the sheriff. "For safe keeping."

Although the sheriff knew what was likely to happen to the money, he had to intention of interfering. That was a family matter.

"Better give that money to your daddy," he told Dusty. The poor boy cast his head down and dug into his pockets, first emptying the right pocket, then the left. His dad took the hoard of coins and began filling his own pockets. There would be no hiding them in a gunny sack, no trip to Avery, no .22-caliber Winchester bolt action, single shot Model 67 rifle. Dusty never saw a nickel of his winnings again.

The sheriff turned back to Martin, who – like everyone else – realized Dusty's money was now Hiram's.

"Martin, I need you to come with me," Lawson said. "It looks like self-defense, but I'm gonna need your statement."

Riley was conscious now. He was mumbling some jibberish as Cleve attended to him. The sheriff pointed at Hiram and Cleve. "I'll need your statements, too," Lawson said. "Can you two manage to get Riley to my office?"

They nodded yes.

"Cliff, get the woman to Doc Tebbetts, but don't let her out of your sight," he said. "Then bring her directly to the jail. And bring the doc with you to take a look at Riley."

Lawson spotted Billy Todd in the crowd and said, "Billy, can you get a few fellas together and carry this body up to Doc's office? We can leave him there until we figure this all out." Billy nodded.

The sheriff looked down at Dusty. "Okay, son, come with me." Then he led a solemn, quiet parade to his office/jailhouse.

As the sheriff led Martin and Dusty back up Spruce Street, he spoke softly to his prisoner.

"Martin, I'm sorry things happened this way," sheriff said. "You're in a bit of trouble. I don't think a jury would convict you, so if it comes to trial, demand a jury. Don't let a judge decide the case. I'm gonna have to hold you in jail awhile to sort this out, make a report."

"All right," Martin said stoically. He'd hardly spoken since the fight ended.

After walking in silence for several seconds, Lawson let out a heavy sigh. "Are you sorry about how any of this turned out, Martin?" The sheriff may have been referring to the dead man, the arrest or even to Dusty's financial losses. Martin wasn't sure.

But his reply didn't weigh in on any of those issues. Looking straight ahead, he simply said, "The only thing I'm sorry about is that I missed that bitch's throat."

XXX

At the sheriff's office, Riley gradually regained his senses. Because he was full of moonshine, the full, painful effect of his injury wouldn't be apparent until the next morning. For now, he sat in a chair holding his jaw in his hand and trying to follow the tense proceedings.

Lawson took Martin's official statement. Then he took statements from Hiram and Cleve. Finally, as the sheriff was talking to Dusty, Cliff Sanger led a patched-up Rosie into the jail. Behind them came Doc Tebbetts, his black medical bag in hand. Rosie was strangely quiet now, but she still wore a nasty scowl.

"Doc gave her a sedative," Sanger told Lawson.

"For pain?" Lawson asked, somewhat confused.

"No," the doc said. "To calm her down and shut her up."

Sanger added, "She was raising Cain so much Doc had to settle her down to sew her up."

Lawson shook his head, a little smile appearing momentarily. Sanger guided Rosie back to the jail cells to lock her away. Doc Tebbetts went over to check on Riley, who was slumped in a chair. Meanwhile, the sheriff slowly turned back to Dusty and resumed questioning the boy.

Dusty repeated his story in much the same terms as he'd used at the scene of the killing. After a while, Lawson patted him on the shoulder, looked him in the eye and said, "Dusty, you did good. You kept your cool pretty well considering. You can go now." He paused a moment then added. "Try to forget what happened and get some rest. It'll all be better in the morning."

Again, he may have been referring to the chase, the killing, the interrogation or the loss of all his money. The sheriff wasn't specific — probably intentionally.

Lawson then went over to Doc Tebbetts, who was still looking at the injured man's jaw. The doc was in his fifties, a little overweight, but spry enough. He was pretty well liked in Kenneth and the surrounding area, despite his crusty edge and a dry – some would say mean-spirited – sense of humor.

Doc Tebbetts was thorough enough, but he worked among people who often couldn't – or wouldn't – pay for his services. Some were so poor they didn't even bother seeking his help. The doctor was known to dispense free treatment from time to time … if he really thought the patient deserved it. But he would also freely dispense reproach for patients who failed to pay their bills.

"What's the damage?" the sheriff asked.

"Well, he's got a loose tooth that may need to come out," the elderly doctor said. "Or it may come out on it's own. Doesn't appear the jaw is broken, but he's got a good bruise developing. I'd give him something to kill the pain, but I think he's already medicated himself."

Lawson nodded. "What should we do about him tonight?"

The doc sighed and thought for a moment. "Well, I wouldn't send him home. When the booze wears off, he'll be in a good deal of pain. I would ask you to hold him in a cell overnight, but I don't see him and that tramp sharing a room, do you?"

"I'd prefer that didn't happen," Lawson said.

"All right, I'll keep Riley in my office tonight," the resigned doctor said. "Give me a chance to check on him in the morning. Then I'll just send him home."

"Sounds good," Lawson said. "Thanks a lot, Doc."

"Oh, yes, once again old doc's gotta be the good Samaritan," the physician complained.

Lawson then turned to Hiram and Cleve.

"I think you should take the boy home right away. I'll be in touch if I need anything else from you," the sheriff said. "A word of advice: I wouldn't talk too much about what happened until the district attorney decides on charges. I don't think Martin will be convicted of anything, but you may need to testify. I wouldn't want some lawyer to twist anything you said before the hearing into something he could use against your brother."

Hiram and Cleve looked at each other. Hiram spoke.

"So Martin's staying here?"

"For tonight," Lawson said. "I expect we can release him tomorrow. But I can't make that decision until I talk to the prosecutor."

Hiram and Cleve again exchanged looks. Hiram spoke again.

"Awright. For now," he said. "Martin, you take care. We'll have you out tomorrow … one way or another."

With that, he pulled Dusty to his side. The three free Brodies went out the door. Hiram found Eliza and the girls, explaining what had happened as he drove them all home. Meanwhile, Cleve located Jeannie Allworth and fetched Martin's car to drive her home.

XXX

Martin ended up being released a day later than Lawson expected. The prosecutor indeed made noises about charging Dusty's uncle with murder or manslaughter. Hiram and Cleve did go into Kenneth the next morning to take Martin home. They were hardly satisfied with the news the sheriff gave them. It was Martin who calmed them down. He told them Lawson was just doing his job. The confined brother promised them he'd be out before the week was up.

Lawson was eventually able to convince the district attorney not to indict Martin Brodie. Enquiries to several law enforcement offices in Missouri revealed a long list of crimes and suspected crimes in Rafe's past. He was still wanted in one town as a suspect in a shooting fatality. Rafe Manx's death was, to the law, a case of good riddance.

Rosie, likewise, turned out to have a record. Not as lengthy or violent as Rafe's, but she was guilty of enough misconduct that her testimony wouldn't hold water in Kenneth. Not if Martin and other local citizens contradicted her account. After being held a week on charges of assault and attempted robbery, she was released. Lawson and Sanger had the pleasure of running her out of town and giving her a stern warning that she would be jailed on sight – and formally charged – if she ever returned to the county.

Because Martin was being held in the Kenneth jail, Dusty spent the two nights after the killing with his grandma. She had been shaken by the news of the fight. But she was thankful her son had not been hurt. It seemed her forebodings had been correct. But Martin had not come to any harm. He was going to be released and his actions would be justified.

When Dusty told her of his winnings at the carnival booth, she had been delighted with his success. She felt sad that he had lost the money, but she knew she could never make Hiram return it. Truth be known, most of it had already been spent. Hiram had bought supplies to restart the still. He was planning to head up the hill as soon as Martin's situation cleared up.

Dusty spent more time with his grandma that month, partly because his family thought she needed someone to keep an eye on her and help out. But Dusty was also glad to be away from his father. Hiram had taken the money, but for some reason he was holding a grudge against his son. In Hiram's mind, Dusty had gotten Martin in trouble; in fact, he had almost gotten Martin killed. What if Rafe Manx had been carrying a gun?

Even when Martin returned home and could watch over Louellen – at least in the evenings after working at the post office – Dusty continued to visit frequently. He noticed his grandmother seeming to grow more anxious, more introspective day by day. Evaporating was the sense of relief she had experienced after hearing Martin was uninjured during the knife fight.

Louellen thought the fight had been the ominous event she had been dreading. But the feelings of apprehension continued to visit her in waves, most often at night. She had many dreams of her sons in various situations of crisis or danger. She could do nothing in these dreams to help them. One nightmare might concern Hiram. Another might concern Cleve. Still another would involve all three. No matter who was threatened, Louellen felt powerless to protect them.

She began to think another possible tragedy lay on the horizon. As she worried for her sons, she unknowingly pushed Dusty away. She was never mean or unsympathetic toward her grandson, but she was more distant and impersonal than she intended.

As the last days of August approached, Louellen's feelings of concern increased. The old woman found it difficult to eat. Chores were more burdensome. Sleep was fitful if not impossible. The lean Cherokee woman began to grow thinner and frailer.

She yearned for a respite. She sought positive omens. She hoped all her premonitions were overblown or simply fabricated. She walked alone in the woods to commune with nature and glean portents of good fortune. She sang old prayers for peace, protection and plenty. She asked the spirits to watch over her family.

Would the gods listen to her? Would they grant her desires? Would they protect her family from the evil things lurking just beyond her perception?

Chapter 15

THE SUDDEN ILLNESS

While Louellen pondered her persistent feelings of dread, the rest of the Brodie brood returned to a more normal pattern of life. August was winding down. It was only a couple of weeks before school started up again. Dusty and his sisters found they were spending more time than usual at their grandma's place.

Eliza encouraged these more-frequent visits. On several occasions, she even suggested Dusty take his sisters to visit their grandma. Nancy and Jenny were eager to go: They knew once school started again, they would see their grandma less often. Dusty began to expect them to tag along almost every time he went to visit Louellen.

The company of her grandchildren was usually good for the old woman. But recently she hadn't quite been herself. Only Dusty seemed to notice that at times she was quieter than usual, almost distant.

One day, Nancy realized her grandma wasn't paying attention to her as she described an early-morning visit by a group of seven deer of various sizes. The Brodie kids had watched them for several minutes that morning before heading to the old woman's house. Louellen seemed unamazed by this remarkable event. She simply said, "That's nice, my child."

Later, Nancy asked Dusty why her grandma didn't care about the deer sightings.

"She isn't feeling very good today," Dusty said, trying to placate his sister. "She didn't mean anything by it. Doesn't she always listen when we tell her about the things we see?"

"Yes," Nancy said, screwing her face up. "You mean she's too sick to listen to me?"

"That's not it," Dusty replied. "I think she's got more on her mind than usual. I'm betting she's still worried about Uncle Martin and that man he killed."

"You think she's mad at Uncle Martin?" Jenny chimed in.

"No, not mad," Dusty told her. "She just knows that our uncle could have been hurt. Heck, I could have been hurt. I think she's worrying more than usual. She'll be her same old self soon."

That seemed to explain the situation to the girls. They promised they would not bother their grandma with stories if she looked like she was thinking about something important.

XXX

Meanwhile, Martin's job at the post office made it difficult to avoid people, most of whom only wanted to talk to him about the killing. If someone brought it up, Martin would frown at them and either change the subject or just refuse to answer. He wanted the event to fade from memory – the town's and his own – as quickly as possible.

As for Cleve, the evening he had planned with Miss Jeannie Allworth had been ruined. He tried to make up for the lost opportunity by visiting her on any excuse he could devise. He wanted to court her seriously. She demurred, but not too much. He thought her polite rejections were just playing hard to get. He never suspected she might have another potential beau in mind.

When Cleve was not pursuing the attractive widow, he was helping Hiram. Since confiscating Dusty's riches, his dad had revved up the still again. It was a gamble because the revenuers were still prowling around here and there. Throughout that summer, they'd busted up a handful of stills and arrested Willie Packert, an old man whose sight and hearing weren't what they used to be. They'd been able to creep up on Willie and take him before he knew they were on his land.

Early that summer, they'd nabbed the Lindsay brothers, Pete and Darryl, who had a substantial operation over near the Simmons County line. They'd already been tried and sentenced to three years in federal prison. After the verdict was announced, moonshining activities had, predictably, slowed to a trickle.

Riley Schwartz had spent the month of August nursing his sore jaw. Instead of making shine, he was drinking more of it than usual – purely for medicinal purposes.

Billy Todd had also ceased production after the batch he'd made to take to the fair. One day in mid-July, Billy had seen a couple of government men snooping around his place. He thought they might be getting close to finding his still, so he had closed up shop.

By early August, the revenuers seemed to have slowed their meddling and probing in the immediate area. Hiram reckoned the coast was clear for now. His place was well-hidden, and demand for white lightning was brisk because so many local producers were temporarily underground.

The only other major supplier still operating in that neck of the woods was the Jennings family. Brothers Jake and Kyle, helped by their father, known to most simply as Pop Jennings, had brazenly continued making moonshine despite the presence of the agents in the surrounding hills. Jake – Hiram's one-time rival for Eliza's affections – was the ringleader of the operation. He was not the most scrupulous liquor maker in the Ozarks.

The Jennings liquor was often inferior, but they made gallons of it and sold it cheap. They'd been accused of selling "red" moonshine: If you lit a small amount and the flame was reddish, it was a possible indicator of high levels of lead. Drinking such alcohol could cause blindness, death or (even worse) a terrific hangover. With much of the competition dormant, the Jennings family had raised prices. Desperate drinkers – even those who preferred other recipes – were forking over their scarce cash for a jug or two of the dubious Jennings product.

XXX

One morning, after a few days back home, waiting for his mash to ferment, Hiram had set off to the still. It was too hot a day to work, but it was time to strain the mash and prepare for the distillation process. If all went well, he'd be gone for a couple of days, perhaps longer.

Eliza told the kids she would likely be gone part of the morning. Something about getting material to make a couple of dresses for the girls before school started. Nancy and Jenny had wanted to go with her to pick out material, but their mother had sternly told them she would pick it out herself. She wanted it to be a surprise.

So, as the morning continued to grow warmer, Dusty and his sisters headed over to keep their grandma company. It was already getting hot, and promised to be one of most oppressive days of summer. When Dusty and the girls arrived at their grandma's, they called out to her as they always did. She did not respond. They went into the house, but it was empty. Louellen was nowhere to be seen.

Dusty suggested they look outside. He went around the south side of the cabin, while Nancy and Jenny went around the north side. Soon, Dusty heard both girls yelling.

"We found her!" Jenny called.

"Dusty, come quick!" Nancy shrieked. "She's not moving!"

Dusty ran to the north side of the house and saw his sisters standing over their grandma at the edge of her garden. A hoe lay on the ground beside her. Dusty slid in and felt his grandma's forehead. It was hot. He felt her wrist for a pulse. It was there, but it was too fast.

"She's alive," Dusty said, trying to think. He was almost in a panic. "We need to get her in out of the sun. Maybe she just got too hot."

He lifted the frail woman's shoulders and directed each sister to carry a leg. Slowly, but steadily, they carried their ailing grandmother into the house and laid her on the kitchen floor.

"What do we do?" Nancy cried.

"I don't know," Dusty said. Anxiety was making it hard to think straight.

"Is she going to die?" Jenny asked, tears starting to run down her flushed cheeks.

"Not if I can help it," Dusty said. "We need to get her a doctor. And fast."

He didn't know exactly what to do though. How could he and his sisters help their grandmother?

"Nancy, wet a cloth and put it on her forehead," Dusty said. "Then get another one and gently wash her hands and wrists. Jenny, take a pitcher and go down to the springhouse and get some more water. Only fill it half full so it's easy to carry. Bring it back and put it in this here basin. Go back and get one more half a pitcher. Then help Nancy keep cool rags on grandma's face and hands and arms."

"What are you gonna do?" Nancy asked Dusty, her eyes wide with fear.

"I'm gonna run for help," he said. "I'm the fastest, and I can get there soonest. Just keep at it. I'll send mom back to help you."

With that, Dusty was out the door and into the sweltering daylight. He sprinted as fast as he could back to his home. At first, he didn't even feel the heat, even as it slowly sapped his energy.

It only took a few minutes for him to reach the cabin. He ran in calling to his mom. She didn't answer. He went out back and called again. No response. He looked around and tried to decide what he should do next. He couldn't wait for his mother. He had to do something now.

Dusty came up with two options. Neither plan was perfect. One was to run to the hill where his dad was tending the still. His dad would know what to do. The other was to run all the way to Avery, to the post office to alert Uncle Martin. That would take longer, but the upside was that Martin could call a doctor to come at once. The choice might literally be the difference between life and death.

He pondered the alternatives for only a minute. Then he made up his mind and took off as fast as his feet could carry him.

Chapter 16

THE STILL REVISITED

Hiram had gotten to his still early to finish preparations for the distilling process. It was just approaching midmorning, but the day was heating up rapidly. He was ready to take an extended break and avoid working during the hottest part of the day. He planned to eat a late breakfast and take long nap before starting up the still at about sundown.

At that time, he expected Cleve to join him. Once the sun sank and darkness began to gather, they could start. They'd work all night long drawing off the alcohol from the 40-gallon still.

First came the foreshots, which contained dangerous – often deadly – methanol. The next 25-35 percent of production was the "heads," potent and volatile alcohols not fit for consumption. Never mind that the Jennings family tended to collect the last ounces from this stage to sell as cheap whisky. Hiram faithfully discarded both the foreshots and heads.

The next 30 percent or so was called the "hearts," the good stuff. An experienced moonshiner could fine-tune the still to produce a greater percent of this sweet, smooth, flavorful liquor. This product could sell for $10 to $15 per gallon, depending on quality and demand. The remaining portion coming out of the still was the "tails," which lacked the flavor and smoothness of the hearts. Hiram generally tossed this portion of the run as well.

It would be a long night of work. But for now, Hiram had a full jug from a previous batch to keep him company. He sat on a log by the still to eat his meal. He broke a biscuit in half and started carving a generous slice off a ham – one of the treats he had bought with his son's carnival winnings. A little bit to eat, a little bit to drink and a long peaceful nap lay in front of him.

As always, he was listening for any unusual noises. In the middle of making his sandwich, he thought he heard something moving down near the base of the hill. It appeared to come from the southern slope of the hill, the same direction Dusty had climbed during his unwelcomed visit a few months before.

Hiram froze. He bent his attention toward the slope and listened carefully, barely breathing as he tried to hone in on any strange sound. Soon, he heard something again. Something was definitely on the slope. And it was coming nearer.

Hiram thought to himself, "If it's that danged son of mine, I'll tan his backside. He knows better than come up here." As the sound grew nearer, he realized whoever was coming was in a hurry. They weren't bothering to try to keep quiet.

Putting down the ham sandwich, Hiram crept stealthily to the base of the big pine where his .20-gauge shotgun stood. He didn't want to shoot his son or some careless friend accidentally, but what if the intruder were anyone else? A revenuer? Or a lawman? He had to be prepared.

The noise was getting louder. The trespasser was getting closer. The way it thundered carelessly up the hill made Hiram think it might be a deer or a wild boar or some other large animal. A dog maybe?

The intruder, whatever it was, was near the top of the slope. Soon Hiram heard it coming through the undergrowth exactly where Dusty had appeared in the springtime. This time, however, the dogwood was not in bloom. Hiram had a better view of the edge of the woods.

As the creature drew closer, Hiram raised his gun and aimed. He kept his finger near the trigger, prepared to fire if needed. He watched the brush begin to part. It was a person, but at first glimpse, it didn't look quite like Dusty. It seemed taller ... and wider. Hiram moved his finger to the trigger and waited for the person to come into full view. Hiram was ready: He couldn't miss.

Hiram heard it too late, another sound from behind him. A footstep. Then a cold, level voice.

"Drop the shotgun slowly and put your hands up," a deep male voice said in a controlled monotone. "You're surrounded. There's nowhere to go. Don't make me shoot you."

Hiram felt an immediate sense of rage accompanied by an even stronger sense of embarrassment. He'd been duped. Surprised by from behind. The man in back of him had come up the north side of the hill. And he had done it silently.

Hiram knew the game was up. No sense getting shot, especially with two of them on the scene. The man coming up the southern slope was a federal agent carrying a rifle. Damn! Hiram slowly put the gun down with his right hand, keeping his left raised. He turned around slowly to see another agent with a rifle pointed directly at his midsection. A third agent then came thrashing through the brush up the eastern side of the hill. This one wore a holstered pistol, but he carried an ominous-looking axe.

The revenuers handcuffed Hiram, searched him and charged him with illegal production of alcohol. The lead agent, the one who had gotten the drop on Hiram, noted the time. It was 9:55 a.m. Then the federal agents did the unthinkable. The man with the axe began chopping and smashing the still. The other two agents looked on as the man worked with zeal in the late morning heat, destroying Hiram's prize possession.

To make matters worse, the agent bashed and broke all the jugs Hiram had assembled to transport his never-to-be-finished liquor down the hill. The only thing tangible left unscathed was the length of copper tubing, the tubing that had carried so many gallons of fine, pure moonshine into so many joyful jugs.

XXX

Since leaving the empty cabin, Dusty had been running as fast as he could. It was almost two and a half miles to the post office. The heat was starting to get to the boy, but he had good stamina and enough adrenaline pumping through him to keep up a quick pace. The dirt road to Avery was bumpy and uneven, but Dusty stuck pretty much to it the whole route. He finally came around the last corner and was soon on the main street of Avery.

Dusty had made the run in just about 20 minutes, a real feat for an adult athlete. As he came nearer the post office, he tried to put his thoughts into some order so he could convey the seriousness of the situation to Uncle Martin as quickly and clearly as he could.

Rushing through the door, Dusty saw Martin at the counter waiting on Doris Winger, the mayor's wife. The boy knew he had to dispense with manors and interrupt their transaction.

"Uncle Martin, Grandma passed out in the garden," he said rapidly. "Her skin was hot and she wasn't sweating. Her pulse was really fast. She needs help."

"She's at home?" Martin said coming quickly around the counter.

"Yeah, Nancy and Jenny and I carried her into the kitchen to get her out of the sun," Dusty said. "We laid her on the floor. Nancy and Jenny are with her."

Martin glanced at the clock. It was five minutes after 10.

"Doris, I've gotta go," Martin called over his shoulder to the mayor's wife.

"Don't apologize," she said. "Should I send Doc Tebbetts out to you?"

He thought for maybe one second before saying, "Yes, please."

Then he hurried Dusty to his Ford and started it up, driving fast and just a bit recklessly toward home. On the way, he asked Dusty a string of questions. Why hadn't he gone to get his mom? Where was Hiram? What if anything were the girls doing to nurse their grandmother?

Martin nodded after all of Dusty's answers. When his nephew told him about the cool, wet rags that his nieces were applying, he said, "That's good. Yeah, I think, that's good." It was just about at this point that Dusty suddenly realized how hot and tired he was. It had been a rough morning for a long, desperate run.

About five minutes later, Martin pulled up at the house and ran in with Dusty just behind. The girls were glad to see their uncle. He gently shooed them aside and began checking his mother. She was still hot, but the cool water had brought her temperature down some. Her pulse was still a little quick, but it seemed fairly strong.

Martin gently slapped his mother's face and tried to revive her.

"Mother! Mother! Can you hear me?" he said gently but urgently. "Mother, it's me, Martin. Can you wake up now?"

After another gentle tap, the old woman groaned. She looked up to see her son bent over her. She looked around to see her grandchildren standing around her. She didn't understand why she was on the kitchen floor. How did she get here?

Louellen had a throbbing headache. She also felt slightly sick to her stomach. Something was wrong, but she couldn't make out what it was.

"Are you awake, Mother?" Martin asked, holding her hand and touching her brow.

"Martin," she said. Knowing she recognized him made Martin feel hopeful. "What happened? Why am I on the floor?"

"You collapsed in the garden," Martin told her. "The kids found you. Your granddaughters have been nursing you while Dusty ran into town to get me."

Louellen looked at her granddaughters first and then at Dusty.

"You ran all the way to town in this heat?" she asked.

"Yes, Grandma," Dusty said solemnly.

"Oh, my child, it's too hot for that," she said closing her eyes and trying to remember.

"I don't understand what happened," she whispered. "I was outside … the garden … weeds."

"That's enough, Mother," Martin said softly. "No more talking. Doc's on the way."

When Doc Tebbetts arrived less than half an hour later, he checked Louellen over. Martin sat in a kitchen chair watching. He sent Nancy and Jenny to the springhouse to get some fresh water. When they got back, he insisted they, and especially Dusty, drink to stay hydrated. It was a brutal day, and it was just now approaching noon. Martin himself took a generous draft of water.

After taking Louellen's temperature, checking her pulse several times and questioning the woozy woman, Doc Tebbetts arose.

"Looks like heat exhaustion or a heat stroke, probably a stroke," he said, taking off his wire-rimmed glasses. "Let's get her on the bed. She'll rest better there."

After he and Martin had moved Louellen, the doc took Martin aside.

"I think she'll be OK soon," he said. "But the symptoms of heat stroke and meningitis are pretty much the same. There've been a few of cases of meningitis in Kenneth and up near Richfield, maybe half a dozen. So we can't count that out yet."

"What do we do?" Martin asked.

"Same thing those kids were doing when you got here," the doc said. "Keep her skin moist and cool. Not too moist, now. Make her drink water. She needs to avoid dehydration. Don't let her exert herself for a week or so."

Doc Tebbetts paused a minute.

"By God, those kids did just about everything right. Got her out of the sun. Cooled her off. Kept her still. Just about everything right."

Martin nodded. "They're good kids," he said simply.

The doc nodded.

"Well, I'll come back to check on her tomorrow and then, if all's well, a couple of days later. If it's not meningitis, she'll probably be fine in a few days."

Again, the doc paused.

"One more thing: If it IS meningitis, we can't let it spread. You might want to keep those kids here for a few days. In fact, I insist. And no other visitors. You probably shouldn't go back to the post office either. I'll see you tomorrow."

"Thanks, Doc. What do I owe you?" Martin said.

Doc Tebbetts looked over at Louellen on her bed. "We'll wait about that for now, Martin. No hurry."

XXX

Eliza dropped by the general store in Avery at about 10:30 in the morning. She hurried over to a table of cheap fabrics. She quickly selected two prints, a light blue pattern and a darker green material adorned with small flowers. She strode over to the counter, where Ivan was adding up some figures on a piece of paper.

"Good morning, Ivan. I'll take these please," she said trying to sound carefree and cheery.

"Hello, Eliza. Doing some sewing?" the merchant said in his upbeat the-customer-is-always-right voice.

"School's starting soon, and the girls need new dresses," she replied cooly.

"Well, they don't stop growing, do they?" Ivan said.

"No, they don't," Eliza replied a little impatiently.

"Need any material for a boy? I've got some things on sale that might make a nice shirt for Dusty."

"Dusty doesn't need anything right now," Eliza said coldly. "This here's all I want."

"OK, Eliza," Ivan said, wondering if he'd said anything wrong. Or was the Brodie woman just in a foul mood for some reason? He started ringing up the material on the ancient cash register.

At that point, Doris Winger came in the door.

"Oh, Eliza, it IS you," she said. "I was down the street, and I thought I saw you come in here."

"Good morning, Doris," Eliza said hastily. "I'm just picking up some material, and I'm in a bit of a hurry today."

"Wait," Doris said staring at the impatient woman. "I have some important news. Dusty came into town not half an hour ago. He said Louellen had passed out and was very flushed. Martin and Dusty took off to look after her."

"Oh!" Eliza said. She didn't seem to know what to do. "What did they ... where did they go?"

It was Doris' turn to be puzzled. It took her a couple of seconds to voice the obvious. "They went to Martin's house. Louellen passed out in the garden, apparently boiling in the sun."

"Well … I suppose I oughta go over there," Eliza said as if the idea held absolutely no appeal at all.

"Yes, I think you should," Doris said. She was about to say more when the Mayor Winger himself came bursting through the door.

"Doris, you'll never guess – Oh, Eliza, I didn't see you there," Tom Winger said, suddenly less animated. 'Uh, Ivan, hello. Umm. Eliza, this is hard to say, but have you talked to Hiram this morning?

"Not since this morning when he left to up to … out in the hills to hunt," Eliza said. She was trying to be very careful about what she divulged to these neighbors, well-meaning or not.

"Eliza, did he go up to the still this morning?" Winger asked.

"Well … I really can't say …" Eliza didn't know what was going on, but she felt like walls were closing in on her.

"Dammit, Eliza, I think Hiram's been arrested," the mayor said bluntly. "I saw him in the back of the revenuers' Ford. They drove right past me not 10 minutes ago!"

"Where were they headed?" Ivan butted in.

"Toward Kenneth," Winger said. "I think they found his still."

"Oh God," Doris said, clapping her hand over her mouth. "Louellen is in a poor way. Tom, she passed out sometime this morning. Martin and Dusty went down to take care of her. I called Doc Tebbetts, and he should be there about now. Somebody's got to go down and take care of that woman."

Eliza grew lightheaded. First Louellen had fallen ill. Now Hiram was headed to jail. It was more than she could take. She began heaving, having trouble catching her breath. She thought she was having a heart attack.

Doris and her husband hurried to support Eliza. Ivan watched the stricken woman for just a few seconds then grabbed some bromide salts and rushed over. He held the salts under Eliza's nose and she jerked away. But her eyes were clearer and she was more alert.

"Might be a nervous fit," Ivan said. "Eliza, are you OK now? You almost fainted."

"I'm fine," Eliza said. "Yes, I'm fine now. Can someone take me to see my girls?"

Tom Winger looked at his wife before turning to Eliza. "I'll take you to Louellen's place."

Chapter 17

THE CONFINEMENTS

Early that afternoon, Sheriff Lawson entered his office and walked through, back to the jail cells. Sitting on the tattered cot in one of cells was an angry and impatient Hiram Brodie. Lawson felt some sympathy for the belligerent moonshiner, but there was nothing he could do. Hiram had been caught red-handed. The evidence against him was strong. It would take a legal miracle to keep Hiram out of prison.

"How you doin', Hiram?" Lawson said softly.

"I'm about ready to strangle a couple of federal agents, that's how I'm doin'," the dark-eyed hillbilly said. "How did they know where my still was? And how did they come up the hill without me hearing them? I must be goin' deaf. Of all the stupid …"

Hiram stopped and sighed, realizing talking about it wasn't going to change anything.

"Well, don't waste time worrying about your ears," the sheriff said. "If they had scoped out the place, they might have known how to get up there without making much sound at all."

"I should have heard 'em coming," Hiram said, shaking his head. "You'd have had to make a path up there ahead of time to hike up there without makin' some sound."

"Well, maybe that's just what they did," Lawson said. "Those agents were talking to me after I locked you up. And they were full of themselves. Braggin' about baggin' you so easy."

Hiram rolled his eyes and huffed.

"But they let one thing slip," the sheriff continued. "They said they knew exactly where your still was and … that you would be there this morning."

Hiram looked up surprised. He was trying to add these bits of information to reach a logical conclusion. He looked hard at the sheriff.

"I'm bettin' you're thinkin' just what I've been thinkin'," Lawson said. "Somebody must have tipped 'em off. Somebody helped them find, not just the still, but you at the still."

Hiram leaned forward on the creaking cot.

"That must be it," he mumbled. His mind began searching for a person who disliked him so much they'd turn him over to the revenuers. His mind quickly settled on one name: Jennings.

"You have an idea who it might be, don't you?" Lawson said, watching Hiram carefully.

Hiram looked directly at the sheriff. A couple of seconds later, he answered, "I might."

Lawson nodded slowly. He thought for a bit and then decided to give Hiram some advice that his prisoner likely would not heed.

"Hiram, if I were you … I'd think about getting out of this mess with the easiest sentence I could before I'd consider trying to get even with anyone."

The trapped man continued to look at the sheriff, not speaking. A long silence drifted over the two men for the next few moments. The only sound was a buzzing fly that couldn't decide when or where to land. Finally, Hiram spoke.

"Thanks, John," he said "I appreciate what you're trying to do. But a man can only take so much and still be a man. Someday someone will pay for this. I promise you that."

The sheriff didn't respond. He slowly turned, hands on hips, and walked out of the jail and back into his office.

XXX

It was several minutes past 11 a.m. when the mayor dropped Eliza off at Louellen's house. Doc Tebbetts was just getting in his car to return to his office in Kenneth. As Tom Winger pulled up, the doctor went over to the driver-side door, stopping about six feet away.

"How is she, Doc?" Winger asked.

"Morning, Tom," Doc said. "She's resting in bed. I can't let you go in there. Nothing definite, but I can't rule out meningitis yet, so we have to quarantine the family."

"Who all's in there now?" Eliza asked.

"Louellen," Doc replied. "Martin is taking care of her. Your kids are in there too, helping out."

"I gotta go in," Eliza said, unsteady as she got out of the vehicle. "I need to see my girls."

"You can go in, but once you do, you can't leave until we know it's not contagious meningitis," the doctor said sternly. "Are you prepared to stay here until then? You won't be able to go home. You might expose Hiram or other folks."

"Yes, I'll stay," Eliza said. "I won't expose Hiram. He's in jail." She hurried up to the door and burst in."

Surprised, Doc watched her go, then looked back at the mayor.

"Revenuers," Winger said. "They caught Hiram this morning up at his still. He's probably in jail in Kenneth by now. I don't know what more can happen to this family."

"They've been in the middle of some peculiar dramas this year, that's for sure," Doc said. "Well, I've got to get back to the office. I have a few cases in town and a couple more near Richfield this afternoon. Say, remind folks not to come out here. Don't panic them. It may not be meningitis, but I don't want to take any chances concerning an outbreak."

"Will do, Doc," the mayor said. "Take care."

"You too, Tom … And lay off that moonshine. Those revenuers may pick you up next."

On the way back to town, Mayor Winger stopped at Cleve's place. He found the third Brodie brother in the shed, cleaning off some gardening tools. He quickly told Cleve about Louellen, and repeated the doctor's orders to stay clear of the place. The mayor said only that the doc thought it might be something contagious. He didn't mention meningitis.

Then he told Cleve he had more bad news. Winger explained what he knew about Hiram's arrest. He suggested Cleve get himself up to Kenneth to see what he could do for Hiram. And he provided the name of a West Plains lawyer he thought might be worth contacting.

With that, the mayor returned to town and went about the rest of his day. His last thought before reaching Avery was how worthless the federal agents were. They didn't stop moonshining, they just ruined families. They chopped off income streams for destitute people, and they separated family members. And crime – real criminal activity – was just as big a threat as ever.

XXX

Martin was sitting in a chair beside Louellen's bed when Eliza flew through the front door. She was looking around, a strange wild-eyed expression on her face.

"Martin, where are my girls?" she said. "I need to see them."

Martin frowned. Not a word of hello? Not a question about her mother-in-law? Why the great need to see her daughters just now?

"They're on the back porch with Dusty," he replied. "I sent them out there so mother could get some quiet."

Eliza didn't even glance at Martin or Louellen. She headed through the house and out the back, letting the screen door slam shut behind her. Martin's frown deepened. He looked at Louellen, who was breathing soft and easy, apparently unbothered by the sudden noise.

Eliza rushed out onto the porch and grabbed Nancy and Jenny by the hands, pulling them close to her. She bent down and embraced them both tightly. It was as if she feared she'd never see them again.

"Momma, not so tight," Jenny complained. "You're choking me!"

Nancy, shocked by the sudden and unusual display of affection, stood stiffly. She wondered why her mom was smothering them like this. It felt strange.

Eliza relaxed her grip just a little and looked at her daughters. A few tears welled up in her face, but she was smiling.

Dusty took it all in, feeling a strange feeling. He didn't envy his sisters for being hugged. But he did feel somehow left out. His mom had barely looked at him.

After a couple of minutes, Eliza loosened her grasp.

"What happened here?" she asked no one in particular. Dusty spoke up.

"We found Grandma in the garden," he told her. "She was hot and unconscious. We got her inside. I ran to our house to get you, but you were gone. Then I thought about running to the still to get Dad, but I figured going to the post office to get Martin would be as fast and get the doctor here sooner."

Eliza nodded. It was a noncommittal nod. Dusty couldn't tell if she thought he done the right things or the wrong things.

"Is Grandma gonna be OK?" Nancy asked her mother.

"She's not gonna die, is she?" Jenny added.

"Oh, I don't know about that," Eliza said. Then she looked again at her daughters, who she sensed needed encouragement. "I suppose she'll be just fine. We have to stay here and help Martin take care of her. That's what the doctor said. We can't go nowhere for now. Not even back home."

The last sentence seemed to make Eliza sad for some reason.

"What's wrong, Momma?" Dusty asked. It seemed like his mother was hiding something, something she didn't want him and his sisters to know. Eliza looked at Dusty as if trying to make some decision. Then she looked at the girls. Finally, she looked back toward the door.

"There's something I have to tell Martin," Eliza said coldly. "You might as well hear it, too. Let's go back in the house now. Come on."

When Eliza got inside with the kids, she called Martin to join them in the kitchen. She quickly and stoically told them about Hiram's arrest. The girls cried. Martin swore softly and tried hard to think what should be done. Dusty just stared. He didn't know what to make of it: His dad in jail? They couldn't hold him, could they? He'd be out soon, right?

Then Dusty realized it. The quarantine would keep all five Brodies here in the house, unable to visit his dad. They were trapped here with Grandma. Doctor's orders. Who would go get his dad out of jail?

Martin was puzzling about the same thing.

"Can't do nothing 'til Doc comes tomorrow," he muttered. "Cleve needs to know. Cleve can go. How can we get word to Cleve?"

XXX

It was nearly 1 p.m. when Hiram's truck came tearing up to the quarantined house. Cleve was driving and honking the horn. He had hurried to Hiram's place, borrowed the vehicle and made a mad dash over to his mother's home.

When Martin heard the car horn, he jumped up and ran out to meet his brother. Cleve leaned out the open window.

"How's mother?" he yelled.

"She's doing fine for now," Martin called back. "Cleve, you can't come in here."

"I know," the younger brother said. "Doc Tebbetts told me you was under a quarantine. I just dropped by to tell you I'm goin' up to the jail to see about Hiram."

"You do that," Martin agreed. "See if we can get him out. Come back and tell me what you learn."

"Will do," Cleve said. "You take care of mother."

"We will," Martin said simply.

With that, Cleve put the truck in gear, hit the accelerator and was off, leaving a nebula of hot and thick brown dust in his wake.

Dusty had been watching from the front door. He stood there while Martin stood in the yard just beyond the porch, both watching the truck until Cleve was out of sight and the cloud of dust began to settle. Martin sighed and moved slowly back to the house. The heat seemed to be increasing minute by minute. The few steps to the house seemed to drain the energy from Martin. When he got to the front door, Dusty thought his uncle looked worn and weary.

"Go on in, boy," Martin said. "Nothing we can do for now but take care of your grandma."

Dusty had hoped for some encouraging words. He wanted his uncle to tell him everything would be all right. He wanted Martin to say that grandma would soon be better. He wanted to hear that his dad would be out of jail in a short time. He wanted to know his family would be together again soon.

Martin said nothing more. Dusty followed him into the somber house and felt paralyzed. Was there nothing he could do? He felt helpless and alone. Even with five family members around him, he felt so alone.

XXX

During the afternoon, Martin, Eliza and the kids had worked in shifts to bring cool water from the creek and bathe Louellen's skin to keep her temperature down. The oppressive heat had made their job harder, but Louellen had tolerated it well. By evening, she was not only alert, but trying to talk.

Martin limited her movement and her conversation, constantly telling his mother to save her strength, get more rest and generally lay still in her bed. The old woman grudgingly complied, though she insisted on having her grandkids near her most of the evening.

Louellen actually slept well that night. So did Nancy and Jenny. However, Martin, Eliza and Dusty got little sleep. Martin and Eliza because they were watching over Louellen, Dusty because he had too much to think about.

His primary worries were about his grandma and his dad. He wanted grandma to recover immediately. He also wanted his dad out of jail and back home. Those two issues dominated his thoughts, pushing aside his mother's odd behavior.

The next morning, Louellen woke up brighter and more alert. She even argued with Martin about getting out of bed to make breakfast. They compromised: She could get up to eat breakfast, but Eliza would do the cooking.

About mid-morning, Doc Tebbetts returned to check on Louellen. He was pleased with her progress. His worries about meningitis were mitigated, but he still wanted the family to stay isolated at least another day. Martin cornered him on the porch and pleaded with the doctor to let him, at least, go to Kenneth to check on Hiram.

While Doc Tebbetts was considering his request, Hiram's truck came bouncing up to Doc's car. Cleve got out and hailed Martin and the physician to come nearer. They stopped within about six feet, maintaining what the doctor considered a safe distance.

"I talked to Hiram," Cleve said without preamble. "He's OK. He don't like being locked up, but he says the sheriff and deputy are treatin' him fine."

"Did he give you any kind of message?" Martin asked.

"I'll get to that in a minute," the younger brother said. "First, I need to tell you what Lawson said. He thinks Hiram's in deep trouble. The feds are going to ask for a stiff prison term … like they got for those fellas on the other side of the county."

"Go on," Martin said evenly.

Doc Tebbetts was feeling like a third wheel. He was looking to politely bow out of the conversation when Cleve continued.

"Well, the mayor gave me a phone number for a West Plains lawyer; said he'd had success getting moonshining charges dropped or sentences shortened," Cleve said. "I asked Hiram, and he don't want to spend the money for a fancy lawyer, but I think it's worth the cost if he can get Hiram off."

"If …," Martin said, pondering.

Doc paused a moment then weighed in.

"Look, now, this is a family matter, and I don't want to butt in, but Hiram needs a good lawyer. If what I've been hearing around town is right, they've got him dead to rights. He'll need any and all help he can get to stay out of prison. If it was me, I'd work on keeping Hiram out of the state pen and worry about the money later."

Both Brodies were silent.

"That's my two cents, and you can do what you think's best," the doctor said, walking off toward his car.

Cleve looked at Martin and said, "He's right."

"Let's call this lawyer." Martin slowly nodded.

Chapter 18

THE TRIAL

Over the next couple of days, Louellen recovered quickly if not completely. She was still a little shaky on her feet. She got tired easily. But clearly, she was much better. While admonishing her to continue taking it easy, the doctor was able to rule out meningitis. The quarantined family members were free to go wherever they needed.

In the meantime, Cleve, funded largely by Martin, had posted bail for Hiram. He got to come home, at least until the trial, which was scheduled for Sept. 26. He would spend most of the next month at home or in Kenneth, working with his lawyer to plan a defense.

With her husband back home, Eliza grew increasingly distant and reserved. She barely spoke to Hiram. Not that he seemed to notice: His mind was occupied with the upcoming trial. For some reason, Eliza almost completely ignored Dusty. She showed no warmth, barely speaking to her son most days.

Eliza seemed to have time only for her daughters. She continued to shower them with kind words, frequent hugs and endearing looks. They had no idea why their mother was suddenly doting on them like this. Nancy confided in Dusty that it was beginning to make her feel strange. Why had her mother changed?

Dusty had no explanation. He suggested his sisters just enjoy the attention. He didn't tell Nancy or Jenny, but at times he wondered why he wasn't getting any of this unusual affection.

Dusty, however, was more concerned about what might happen to his dad. His sisters didn't seem to understand the gravity of the arrest. Dusty was careful not to give them the impression that he was worried. But he couldn't help thinking about the possibility that his dad might go to prison.

Dusty continued to visit his grandma, spending lots of time with her. It was partly to help her as she recovered from her illness. It was partly to get away from his angry and anxious father. Perhaps a little of it was to get from his grandma the affection his mother refused to give him.

Louellen didn't consider her grandson's motives for visiting. She was simply glad to have Dusty there to help her around the house. With Martin gone during the days, she felt relieved to have the boy on hand. She wouldn't have admitted it, but she needed his company.

Like Dusty, Louellen worried constantly about Hiram's arrest and the coming trial. She knew the federal agents were bent on making examples of the moonshiners they apprehended. Each arrest was another feather in their caps. Each conviction was a small jump in status. Each broken, distressed family was merely insignificant collateral damage. The revenuers, she concluded, just didn't give a damn about people.

XXX

The last days of summer wound down. September arrived. It was time for the new school year to start. Eliza had hurried to make two simple dresses, one for each of her daughters. Dusty, however, got no new clothes for the school year. As for footwear, he only had a pair of worn and battered brown boots that had gotten him through the previous winter. They were now a bit too small, but at least the wear and tear had loosened them up some. Dusty found they were bearable.

Not that it mattered just yet: September began warm and dry, so he had the option of walking to school barefoot. He wasn't the only student who entered the classroom unshod. He wasn't embarrassed to be barefoot; he was ashamed he didn't have a choice in the matter.

In addition to his shabby wardrobe, Dusty carried another burden to the schoolhouse. Before the first day of school, Eliza made clear that he should watch out for his sisters. He was to be responsible for their safety from the time they left for school until the time they returned home. Dusty intensely disliked the idea that of playing nursemaid to the young girls. He had friends to talk to and play with. Who wanted two little girls tagging along?

For their part, Nancy and Jenny rejected the idea of Dusty as mother hen. They were now another year older. They were too big to need any oversight from their brother. Nancy and Jenny tried to shake free of Dusty's watchful eye. They felt inclined – maybe even obligated – to take advantage of any chance to get away from him. Dusty soon saw that he wouldn't be able to herd his sisters to and from school even if he wanted to.

But the Brodie children faced another challenge. On the first day of school, they found that news of their father's incarceration had spread through the community. Some of their schoolmates, especially the younger ones, gawked at the Brodies as if they were freaks. They whispered behind their hands and generally avoided the trio.

The older kids, most of whom knew the Brodies better, were a bit more welcoming. Still, there was an awkwardness to conversations, even with their closest friends. Though they weren't being shunned or ostracized, Dusty and his sisters were being treated differently than before. It took more than a week for the Brodies and their classmates began to break down the invisible walls separating them.

The new teacher didn't help. During the summer, Knox Cameron's mother had died. He and his aunt had worked together to settle her affairs. Once that was done, Cameron had no reason to stay in Avery. He headed back to college for the fall semester to continue work on his degree.

Once again, the school board was left scrambling for a replacement. The choice, but certainly not a unanimous one, was Sarah Jane Rice. She was, the majority of the board decided, the best of an unimpressive lot of candidates. Mrs. Rice was a relatively well-educated widow of a slightly successful feed salesman. He had left her with skimpy financial resources. Mrs. Rice owned her house, but she had sold the feed business to help fund her golden years.

Unfortunately, the widow had a few luxurious tastes – luxurious at least for Drury County. She knew better than to live beyond her means, yet she was certainly determined to make those means as plentiful as possible. One of her passions was music, particularly classical music. She had spoiled herself by buying mountains of 78 rpm recordings. When she had any spare time, Mrs. Rice would play her 78s on her prized possession – a superbly maintained 1928 Orthophonic Victrola Record Player.

To help pay for a stream of new recordings, Mrs. Rice had sought the teaching position – and had won it. Unfortunately, she was a novice in the classroom. She was robust and confident enough to keep discipline among her students. Her fine singing voice could morph nicely into a stern, commanding roar. While this made governing the students easier, it did nothing to improve her teaching skills. These were rusty and, frankly, very limited. It would be a long school year for both the pupils and their aging schoolmarm.

So, with Mrs. Rice in charge and with their father's trial looming, the Brodies began their studies at Avery's one-room schoolhouse with little enthusiasm.

XXX

In early September, Martin and Cleve were constant visitors at Hiram's cabin. They would come over in the evening to discuss preparations for the trial. At first, Hiram didn't like his West Plains lawyer. However, the more time he spent with the attorney, the more he came to respect the man's abilities.

Oscar Flannery was the son of immigrants from Europe, his father Irish and his mother German. He had the pugnacious personality that was stereotypically associated with his Irish kin. He had a strict, by-the-book discipline that many attributed to his German blood. He had a sharp intellect, inherited probably in part from both of his parents. He could boast of some accomplished near and distant relatives who had established successful careers in Europe. In addition, he had his own special gift: an incredible manner of reading people quickly and accurately.

Flannery rarely misjudged a person he set about studying. He was a Sherlock Holmes of personalities. He diagnosed their strengths, weaknesses, prejudices and soft spots. This, along with his innate intellect, made Flannery a formidable foe in the courtroom.

A large man, he enjoyed his meals and didn't miss many of them. Upon this burly body sat an oval head crowned with a shock of curly brownish-auburn hair. No matter how he combed it or slicked it down, it tended to pop up in little tufts here and there. He made frequent and regular visits to the barber to keep his hair under control, but results were hit and miss.

Flannery featured clear blue eyes that could cut like lightning through a rival, a witness or even a judge. He had a sharp nose, which at times it seemed to point at the soul of whomever he was addressing. His lips were thin and pale: From them he could spew strings of impressive words with machine-gun speed and accuracy.

Still, Hiram's defense was a difficult puzzle for the cunning lawyer. His client had been caught red-handed tending his still. Hiram could show no valid cause for producing illegal liquor. In addition, the prosecutor had strong-armed a couple of former customers into testifying against the hillbilly moonshiner. It looked like an open-and-shut case.

"Hiram, I won't lie to you," Flannery told his endangered client as they sat across from each other in Hiram's cell. "They've got the goods on you. I don't see an easy way to get an innocent verdict."

"So. I'm going to jail," Hiram said.

"Maybe," the lawyer responded. He waited a bit before continuing. "Or maybe not."

Hiram looked hard at Flannery. He had no idea what the man was saying.

"We have one thing going for us," the legal expert said, leaning away from Hiram and musing, looking up at something beyond the ceiling. "We have the judge."

"We do?" Hiram asked. Where was this fellow going?

"We're not asking for a jury trial, so the judge will have to decide the case. And he'll likely have to rule you guilty," Flannery said, glancing at Hiram for a couple of seconds before resuming his examination of whatever he saw above them. "But he doesn't have to sentence you to prison."

Hiram began to understand … at least a little bit.

"What else can he do?" the accused criminal asked.

Without looking at Hiram, Flannery said one word. "Probation."

"Probation?"

"Yes," Flannery turned and leaned in to face Hiram again. "Probation. He could give you a couple of years on probation. If you keep your nose clean, you won't have to go to prison. But … if you screw up and get caught breaking the law – and I mean any law – they'll pick you up and make you serve your time."

"And if they don't arrest me again …?"

"You're free," Flannery smiled. "We need the judge to realize you're the sole support for your family. Without you, they'd be destitute. Without you, they'd be cold, hungry, frightened. Without you, they might not survive."

"Well, I think they could get along," Hiram said, not wanting to entertain the idea that his actions could cause such a disaster for his family. "My brothers and my mother –"

"The judge can't know that," Flannery asserted firmly, shutting his client up. "We have to make the judge believe they can't help your family enough to make a difference in their lives."

"How do we do that?" Hiram wondered.

"Leave that up to me," Flannery smiled, again looking up at the ceiling. "Just leave that to me."

XXX

The trial began on a Monday. Dusty and his sisters wanted to attend, but Hiram and Eliza both nixed the idea. They would go to school. They would come straight home. They would stay there until the rest of the family returned.

Martin and Cleve were bringing Louellen, who – despite still being far from well – insisted on being present to support her eldest son. The old woman was eating too little, sleeping too little and worrying too much, but she would not hear of staying home with Hiram on trial. The trio travelled to Kenneth in Martin's car. Hiram and Eliza took Hiram's truck. At his lawyer's insistence, Hiram was wearing his only suit coat, which was old and shabby. Hiram hated dressing up. Eliza, meanwhile, wore her best dress.

The weather that day was fairly pleasant, a relief after a long string of 90- and 100-degree days over the past two months. The sun was shining. Birds were singing. It had all the appearances of an ideal fall day. But the fine weather was lost on the Brodies. They were not in pleasant moods. In the truck, Hiram kept his thoughts to himself. Eliza didn't contribute much, just an occasional bit of small talk. Neither mentioned the trial or its potential outcomes. Neither expressed any love or affection.

In the other vehicle, the always tight-lipped Martin and the more outgoing Cleve were equally silent during the drive. Louellen also remained quiet, her sons assuming she was being her usual stoic self. The truth? She wasn't feeling her best that morning. She had not eaten any breakfast and had barely sipped at her cup of coffee. In recent days, her thoughts were dominated by the looming trial.

Last night, she had expected some dream or vision to appear. She had expected an omen or a premonition. But no spirits, good or evil, had visited her. Perhaps she didn't sleep long enough to dream. She felt weary, drained as she rode toward the courthouse.

Once in Kenneth, both vehicles found parking spots on the city square. The five Brodies gathered on the steps of the courthouse. Their faces were grim as they went up the steps to the front door and walked in. Cleve asked a uniformed official where the courtroom was. Told it was on the second floor, he took the lead. Hiram and Eliza followed up him up the stairs. Martin led his unwell mother up behind them.

Just outside the courtroom, Sheriff John Lawson spotted the Brodies. He walked up, shook Hiram's hand and told him good luck.

"Thanks for treating me good at the jail," Hiram said. "But I don't ever want to go back there."

"I hope you don't," Lawson said. "I just want you to know I plan to be here all day. If you or your family need anything, let me know."

Martin and Cleve also shook hands with Lawson as they entered the courtroom. Once inside, Hiram saw Oscar Flannery near the front, standing near a table with three chairs. The lawyer, wearing a spiffy suit, was talking to another well-groomed man in a suit. Hiram turned and addressed his family.

"There's Flannery up at that table," he said, fidgeting a bit. "I guess I oughta head on up there."

"We'll be in the row right behind you Hiram," Cleve told his brother. "Don't you worry, now."

Martin shook Hiram's hand firmly and quietly said, "Good luck, brother."

Louellen stepped forward to give Hiram a quick, tight embrace. "You're a good son," she said.

Eliza then offered a quick but passionless hug. Hiram didn't seem to notice the vanilla nature of her gesture. He turned his back on his family and headed up the aisle to meet his legal counsel.

At this point, Flannery saw Hiram approaching and politely but quickly broke off his conversation with the other well-dressed gentleman. The lawyer shook Hiram's hand, showed him to a chair and sat next to his client. They bowed their heads together as Flannery quickly and succinctly reviewed some of the things they'd discussed over the past month: courtroom etiquette, a review of trial procedure and what Hiram should do during the proceedings.

Not long after, the prosecution team entered and moved to its own table. The team consisted of the district attorney and a second, younger man – obviously an aide, Martin surmised.

A few witnesses gathered in the row behind the prosecution. Some spectators had already staked out seats, while others were milling about, talking in mostly hushed tones. Gradually, as 10 a.m. drew near, the Brodies made their ways to the seats behind Hiram. The chatter began to die down. Then the bailiff entered the room and everything grew silent.

"All rise, for Judge Franklin Robinson," the bailiff called out. The audience rose, and in walked an old man ensconced in a massive black robe. Only his head, topped with sparse and wispy white hair, and his impossibly pale hands were visible against the dark cloth of his gown.

Martin's first impression was of a worn-out, half-dead great-grand-father who had seen too much of life and did not particularly relish seeing any more.

Franklin Robinson had been on the bench for 48 of his 77 years. He was regarded by most attorneys as essentially fair but a stickler for protocol. He did not like longwinded counsellors. He did not like unprepared attorneys. He had little patience with frivolous motions and even less patience for frivolous people … be they defense lawyers, prosecutors, witnesses or defendants.

Judge Robinson was not soft on crime: He had no history of providing guilty folks with second or third chances. Still, he was not considered a "hanging judge." Throughout his lengthy career, he had aimed to balance his sentences so he neither abandoned justice for victims nor imposed excessive punishment on the guilty. Considering the alternatives, Hiram could have found himself in a much more hostile courtroom.

At the start of the trial, Oscar Flannery let the prosecution lead the dance. When the district attorney called the federal agents to the stand, Flannery did little to contest their testimony about finding the clandestine still and arresting Hiram in the process of operating it.

Flannery allowed the prosecution to submit its evidence. He only questioned little things about the agents' procedures. He asked about means of locating the still. He also asked why they chose the specific time and date to raid the still.

To Martin, none of this appeared to help Hiram's cause. Their testimony clearly was harming his brother's case. Wasn't this lawyer going to fight back? Everything seemed to be moving too fast with no effort to absolve his brother.

Meanwhile, Louellen was trying to follow the prosecution's case. Her mind felt cloudy and confused. Was she understanding this all accurately? They were making her son seem evil. And Hiram's fancy lawyer seemed to be letting them get by with it. Why wasn't he protesting? She could make no sense of it all.

Even Judge Robinson, had the spectators been able to read his mind, was wondering what the counsel for the defense was up to. Would he be so passive throughout the trial? The judge, for now, was not tremendously impressed.

With few objections or interruptions from Flannery – and because the prosecutors knew Judge Robinson valued brevity – the trial was moving uncommonly swiftly. By noon, the prosecution had all but wrapped up its case.

The judge looked at the clock. He asked the district attorney how many more witnesses he intended to call. The prosecutor said just two more. With another glance at the clock, the judge decided to recess for lunch. The trial would resume at 2 p.m.

When the gavel hit the bench, Flannery turned to confer with Hiram for a few minutes. The family waited quietly at the back of the courtroom. When his conversation with the lawyer was over, Hiram joined them.

"I'm gonna spend the lunch hour with Flannery," he told them. "You all go on and get something to eat."

Martin furrowed his brow. "What's he want to talk about?"

Hiram stared at his brother then looked at the others, one by one, before turning back to Martin. "We're going to discuss my testimony," he said. "The way things are goin', he thinks it may be best if I take the stand."

Cleve and Martin shared a look that asked, "Is that a good thing or a bad thing?" But they kept their silence, not wanting to worry their mother or Eliza.

Hiram departed, and the two brothers led the women out of the courthouse and to a small diner across the street. No one was hungry, but the brothers and Eliza forced themselves to eat, ordering sandwiches and coffee and glasses of sweet tea. Louellen had nothing but a sip or two of coffee.

They stayed for nearly an hour, but everyone was too anxious to sit there any longer. They walked back across the street and up the courthouse steps. The ascent was more difficult for Louellen than it had been that morning. Sheriff Lawson happened to be returning to the courtroom. He saw Louellen walking unsteadily and came over to help Martin escort her. They had to stop and let the laboring woman rest half way up the stairs.

Outside the courtroom, the Brodies sat down on a bench. The sheriff wandered down the hall, leaving the family alone. Cleve tried to make small talk, but no one joined in. Finally, Louellen asked if they could go on inside. She didn't feel comfortable in the hallway.

The family sat in the front row behind the defense table and waited. Time seemed to crawl: The clock crept torturously from 1:20 to 1:50. Then Hiram and Flannery, accompanied by the lawyer's well-dressed companion, walked briskly into the room and to the defense table. The Brodies could read nothing into Hiram's expression. Was everything going accordingly to a plan? Were Hiram and his gaudy attorney at all worried?

XXX

The prosecution team came into the courtroom just before 2 p.m. In short order, the bailiff returned and repeated the order to rise. Judge Robinson came in, looking perhaps even more worn and disinterested than earlier that day. When the judge was seated, he asked the prosecution to call its next witness. To the surprise of all the Brodies, it was Jake Jennings.

All three Brodie brothers were thinking the same thing: This might answer a few questions about the raid on Hiram's still.

The prosecutor essentially elicited this story from Jennings: He had been aware of Hiram's still for a long time. He had been asked to help the federal agents locate area stills. Against his will, he had revealed the location of Hiram's still. The agents had made him lead them to that still. Then the agents had pried from Jennings the names of a couple of Hiram's customers. Those men had become two of the morning's witnesses.

The prosecutor used Jennings to paint Hiram as a long-time, repeated and unrepentant producer of illicit liquor. The DA and the witness conveniently dodged the fact that Jennings had produced as much illegal hooch as Hiram or any other moonshiner in the county. Hiram at once mumbled this information into his lawyer's ear. Flannery merely nodded at his client ... and winked.

When the prosecutor finished with Jennings, he smugly said to Flannery, "Your witness."

Flannery took a few seconds before rising slowly and politely said, "Thank you, sir, so very much."

For the next 20 minutes, Flannery steadily tore away the innocent façade the DA had created to cover the many flaws of Mr. Jake Jennings. He asked why the prosecution's star witness had turned in Mr. Brodie instead of any of the many other moonshiners with whom he was surely acquainted.

When Jennings denied knowing any other distillers, rumrunners or whisky peddlers, Flannery turned and nodded at his well-heeled associate. The man got up discreetly and walked calmly to the back of the courtroom. He opened the door and beckoned. In walked four area moonshiners and several of their customers. Some of the customers had make substantial and frequent purchases from the Jennings enterprise. Jake Jennings recognized all of the men.

Flannery paused to give the witness a chance to look over this collection of potential rebuttal witnesses. Then he turned to Jake and said quietly, "Would you care to alter your last statement in any way?"

From that moment on, Jennings was on the defensive. Flannery nailed him for one lie after another. Perjury charges were just a formality now. But Flannery wasn't ready to let up. He cleverly – even politely – attacked the witness, asking why Hiram was the sacrificial lamb. Eventually, he got Jennings to admit that they were rivals, had always been rivals. And, yes, it was he, Jake Jennings, who had approached the revenuers, offering to lead them to the "biggest and most dangerous moonshiner" in the county.

Oscar Flannery had blown up a key prosecution witness. He had cast a foul shadow over the federal agents, making them look like dupes who had been pulled into a longstanding family feud. But Flannery had done so without greatly besmirching the agents' truthfulness under oath. He was not so discreet with Jennings. When he finally finished with the witness, about 90 percent of those in the courtroom had developed a good level of sympathy for the defendant.

The DA was so shaken by this reversal that he made a knee-jerk decision. He declined the option to redirect questions to Jennings. He didn't want the judge to hear another word from that man. The prosecutor also elected not to call his final witness: He didn't want to give Flannery a chance to destroy the credibility of any more testimony. He instead rested his case, feeling he had at least proved the defendant guilty of the charges against him.

It would be a long time before Hiram learned the identify of the last potential witness. It was his wife, Eliza.

XXX

The trial wasn't over yet. Flannery was about to begin his case for the defense. He had planned to call only one witness. Hiram would explain why he was making moonshine, what the income meant for his family and – most important – how that family might fare with Hiram in prison.

As Flannery rose to address the judge, a disturbance in the courtroom stopped him in his tracks.

Louellen had been feeling light-headed for a couple of minutes. She swayed toward Martin, who caught her.

"Are you okay?" he whispered.

"Dizzy," she muttered.

"You need some air," Martin suggested.

The old woman nodded and started to get up. The room began to spin slowly and then to whirl rapidly around her head. She saw the wooden floor rushing up to hit her face. She had collapsed before Martin could grasp her. The thump of her body hitting the floor caused everyone in the courthouse to turn and look.

As Martin and Cleve dropped to attend her, the judge looked toward the disruption. He was about to reach for his gavel when something held him back.

Hiram, hearing the noise and seeing his brothers bending over their mother, was up in a flash. With astonishing speed for a big man, he rushed to his fallen mother. The three brothers pulled Louellen upright. She was mumbling something incoherent.

The judge sat at the bench watching as the bailiff and others hurried to help out. Sheriff Lawson told a court officer to phone Doc Tebbetts, who – luckily – happened to be in his office. He was done with his morning appointments and was getting a late start on a couple of house calls he planned to make that afternoon. The emergency in the courtroom caused him to abandon his agenda and head to city hall.

Meanwhile, someone had fetched some water and a towel. For a few minutes, the brothers bathed their mother's face and tried to get her to sip a bit of water. She was just starting to regain her senses when the doctor strode into the room. He took a quick look and told the Brodies to sit their mother up on a bench. After some poking, prodding and pulse counting, he announced his initial diagnosis: hypotension, an episode of extreme low blood pressure.

"What has this woman had to eat or drink today?" he asked no one in particular.

Martin had been with her since daybreak. He tried to recall. "Well," he said, "she didn't eat much breakfast. Drank a little coffee. At lunch … she didn't really eat."

"She had another cup of coffee,"

Cleve offered. "… But she didn't drink much of it."

"I only saw her take a couple of sips," Eliza volunteered.

"Hasn't she had any water?" Doc Tebbetts asked incredulously.

All the Brodies were silent. No one recalled seeing her drinking that morning or during lunch.

"Well, she's dehydrated," the doctor said, exasperated. "We need to get fluids into her fast."

Doc arranged to have Louellen carried over to his office. Cleve went with her. Martin and Eliza decided to stay at the courtroom to be with Hiram.

Judge Robinson, having ascertained what had happened, called counsel for both sides to his bench.

"I'm prepared to postpone this afternoon's testimony until tomorrow, due to the health of the mother of the accused," the judge said quietly. "Counsel, your thoughts?"

"Your honor, if it please the court, I have two more trials to prepare for," the district attorney said. "I would prefer to finish the proceedings today. But, of course, it is your courtroom."

"I'll consider that, Johnny," the judge told the DA. "And your views, sir?" he asked Flannery.

Flannery saw a real concern for Hiram's mother in the Judge Robinson's eyes. He wondered if it was a good time to roll the dice. He decided his case needed a break, a little bit of luck. It was fourth and goal and time for a game-winning play.

"We appreciate your honor's kind offer," the slick West Plains lawyer said. "But we have no assurance that my client will find his mother's health improved tomorrow. In fact, tomorrow may be an even more difficult day, should worse come to worse. I beg your honor to consider allowing us to wrap up matters today. I promise to make the case for the defense short and as amicable as possible."

Judge Robinson considered for a moment. Both sides appeared to want to continue. He, too, had a heavy docket later this week. He would prefer to have part of tomorrow free. The weather promised to be good. Fish might just be biting on the Eleven Point. He made up his mind.

"How soon are you prepared to continue?" he asked Flannery.

"In 10 minutes," the attorney replied. The judge raised his wispy eyebrows and looked at the DA.

"We're ready, your honor," he assured the judge.

"We're back in session in 15 minutes then," he said, turning his back on the attorneys.

XXX

Flannery quickly gathered the Brodie family. He told Hiram he'd changed his mind. He didn't want his client to take the stand now. He asked if they trusted him. Hiram immediately said yes. Martin, considering Hiram's confidence in the lawyer, agreed. Eliza also nodded her approval.

Flannery left them and approached Sheriff Lawson, conversing with him a few minutes. Then the defense lawyer went back to Hiram, Martin and Eliza. He asked a series of seemingly off-the-cuff questions about the family. He asked Martin how he managed to work and take care of Louellen. He asked about the family's property, its income and its debts.

He also asked if any family members were helping any sick or disabled relatives. Eliza mentioned her widowed mother. The old woman was often down in her back. When she ran low on supplies, Eliza would put together a basket of food and other necessities. When at her mother's place, Eliza sometimes helped with chores the woman couldn't handle.

Flannery nodded and smiled. It was a kindly smile, but not a warm one. Soon enough, the bailiff walked up to alert the huddled Brodies that Judge Robinson was ready to reconvene the trial. Flannery and Hiram returned to the defense's table and stood, waiting for the judge to gavel the room back in session.

When asked to call his first witness, Flannery rose dramatically and told the court he would call only one witness. That witness was Sheriff John Lawson. Even Hiram looked shocked.

Flannery began by asking Lawson some general questions about the known moonshiners in the area, without asking for specific names. Sheriff Lawson said moonshining was still common in the county, despite the end of Prohibition a few years earlier.

The lawyer asked what kinds of problems the moonshiners generally caused. Lawson said they provided alcohol to people who sometimes got rowdy or violent.

"And do purchasers of legal, licensed liquor occasionally get rowdy or violent?" Flannery asked.

"Yes," Lawson said.

"Has Hiram Brodie ever been arrested on any charges other than those he faces today?" the lawyer continued.

"No," Lawson said with some hesitation. The prosecutor started writing and his assistant started shuffling papers. Flannery knew what they expected. He cut them off at the pass.

"Has Hiram Brodie ever been accused of breaking any laws?" Flannery asked.

"Yes," Lawson said, offering nothing more.

"Please tell us about those accusations, sheriff."

"Well, someone complained that he'd pointed a gun at them and run them off his property," Lawson said.

"Who made that accusation?" Flannery asked.

"Kyle Jennings," Lawson replied.

"Kyle Jennings, the brother of Jake Jennings, the witness we heard from earlier today?" Flannery inquired.

"Yes," Lawson said nodding.

"How would you characterize the relationship between the Brodie family and the Jennings family?"

"They don't like each other," the sheriff said bluntly.

"Have the Brodies also accused any of the Jennings clan of breaking any laws?"

"Yes, Hiram Brodie accused Kyle Jennings of trespassing," the sheriff said.

"Same day Hiram supposedly threatened Kyle Jennings?"

"The same day," Lawson said.

At the point, the DA objected, claiming this line of questioning had no relevance to the current charges. Judge Robinson frowned and rubbed his tired eyes.

"Mr. Flannery, how do you respond?"

"Your honor, I'm confirming the fact that Mr. Brodie's arrest was plotted by, prompted by and promoted by Jake Jennings and, perhaps, some of his close relatives. It was an attempt to bring down a rival who was doing no more – and, admittedly, no less – than the Jennings family was doing at the very same time."

"Your point, counsel?" the judge asked seeking more clarity.

Flannery raised his voice and his intensity as he said, "It's obvious, your honor, that my client was targeted for actions for which these agents – had they been so enlightened – could have arrested the Jennings family and any number of other illegal distillers. They were blinded and coerced into pursuing Hiram Brodie and Hiram Brodie only. This case could send my client to jail for several years, so it only makes sense to ask, 'Why him? Why not the Jennings brothers? Why not other moonshiners?' "

Judge Robinson sighed. "Against my better judgment, objection overruled. Continue Mr. Flannery."

"Thank you, your honor," the momentarily victorious lawyer said. He then turned back to the witness.

"Sheriff Lawson, have other moonshiners given the law more trouble than Hiram Brodie?"

"Most certainly," Lawson answered. "We have a few boys on the other side of the county that gamble, steal, fight regularly and also make a fair amount of moonshine."

"In your opinion, sheriff, would those criminals – I assume they are criminals, you describe them as criminals –"

"Objection!" the DA shouted. "Those men are not on trial and haven't, to my knowledge, been convicted of any crime. I protest counsel's use of the word 'criminals'."

"Sustained," the judge said evenly.

"Very well," Flannery said. "Sheriff Lawson, would the arrest and/or convictions of these boys on the other side of the county be a higher priority in keeping your county safe? In your opinion?"

"In my opinion, yes, they are a greater threat to public safety."

"I see," Flannery nodded. He paused and turned back toward his chair then stopped and slowly turned around. "Just one more question, if you please. Supposing Hiram Brodie was making moonshine – illegally as the prosecution contends. Supposing that's true … do you think it would serve the overall good of the community if my client were to spend a substantial amount of time in prison?"

"Objection," the prosecutor protested.

"Sustained," the judge said impatiently.

"Withdrawn, your honor. No further questions."

On cross-examination, the DA got Sheriff Lawson to agree that laws are laws and punishment is necessary. He also got the sheriff to agree that the evidence against Hiram appeared solid.

"Irrefutable?" the prosecutor asked.

Lawson didn't bat an eye. He said, "Only if you believe 100 percent of what these agents testified to this morning."

"Sheriff, do you believe what they testified to this morning?"

"Not 100 percent. I wasn't there," Lawson said, looking directly at the three agents. Only the lead agent would meet Lawson's stare. Whether the spectators noticed this or not, the judge did.

"No more questions," the DA said.

With that, Flannery rested the defense's case.

A few minutes later, the DA stood up to deliver his closing argument. It boiled down to one thing, and one thing only. Hiram Brodie was caught red-handed making illegal liquor with plans to distribute it for a profit to members of the community.

It was soon Flannery's turn to speak. He knew he had to make his comments brief, pointed and emotional. He startled everyone in the courtroom by agreeing that Hiram, assuming the federal agents were telling the truth, was guilty of making moonshine.

He then briefly summarized the role of Jake Jennings in betraying a fellow moonshiner. This was done partly for mercenary reasons, to garner a larger market share for his own illegal business. He used the feds to put a competitor out of business.

But it was also done, in large measure, for spite. Jennings wanted to get the better of a despised rival. He wanted to heap shame and scorn on Hiram and his entire family. He wanted to hurt the family financially and emotionally. He had even managed to hurt them physically. One had only to look at Hiram's poor, suffering mother that very day. And – should Hiram go to prison – the rest of his family faced want, hunger and ridicule. Jennings had set out to destroy Hiram Brodie. He should not be allowed to use the irreproachable justice system to persecute his adversary. To do so would sully the reputation of justice.

"Was Hiram wrong?" Flannery asked. "Yes. He knows it. I know it. You know it. Should he be punished? Probably so. But, your honor, you have the discretion to punish my client without taking an unreasonable step that would also inevitably punish his family. Sending Hiram Brodie to prison would serve no purpose to reform him that cannot be accomplished by placing him on probation. This would allow him to show that he's learned from this episode, from his mistake, while taking care of his wife and three children as he also helps support his feeble and frail mother in her old age."

He briefly noted the millions of Americans who were still suffering to overcome the devastating effects of the Depression. More people were in need today than could be helped by government funding, charities or the kindness of sympathetic neighbors.

"Don't cast the Brodie family out to join the struggling masses who slip below the surface and drown in hardship and despair," Flannery entreated. "Offer Hiram Brodie probation and allow him to save his family … if only so the Jake Jenningses of the world may not rejoice in their dreadful plight."

Judge Robinson, as expected, had remained inscrutable throughout both closing arguments. He said he would retire that night to deliberate and rule on the case in the morning. In truth, he wanted a short day, so he ordered the court to reconvene at 9 a.m. sharp. He quickly slammed the gavel down and got up to leave.

As the spectators filed out, Martin and Eliza joined Hiram and Flannery at the defense table.

"How do you think it went?" Hiram asked his lawyer.

"We'll know tomorrow morning," Flannery said, with a wry smile. It was a strange smile, a smile that might hide a wonderful secret or a terrible disappointment. It was impossible to tell.

Chapter 19

THE VERDICT AND
THE VILLAIN

The Brodies planned to gather at the courthouse at 8:30 the next morning. Louellen had stayed the night at Doc Tebbetts' office, with Martin and Cleve taking turns sitting by her bed. Every time she woke up, they encouraged her to drink water and eat something. Crackers went over best, but she still didn't eat much.

Not wanting to be far from his mother, Hiram had spent the night tossing and turning on a cot in the doctor's office. The mayor had taken Eliza home and would fetch her back to town in the morning. She was the only Brodie adult who slept that night in a real bed.

By morning, Louellen was somewhat better, but Doc wouldn't allow her to leave. He and his wife, Imogene, would watch her. They made her eat some breakfast, washing it down with a couple of glasses of water. The rest of the Brodies met at the same diner they had visited for lunch the previous day. No one was particularly hungry, but Hiram convinced them all to eat. He joked that it might be his last meal as a free man for a while. No one laughed.

They drank coffee, talking in quiet tones about anything and everything except the trial. It was soon time to head to the courthouse. The Brodies slowly filed out of the café, crossed the street and walked up to the second-floor courtroom.

Hiram joined Flannery and his assistant, both looking as suave and swell as ever, at the defense table. The other Brodies settled into the row behind them. Sheriff Lawson eventually joined them, exchanging quiet good mornings with Hiram and his family.

The bailiff called, "All rise." Martin felt a tad unsteady, weak in the knees. He hadn't expected the moment to affect him so. Eliza, he noticed, looked pale and lost. Cleve, trying to be stoic, looked almost ill.

Judge Robinson entered and took his position on the bench. He asked the attorneys for each side if they had any further comments or motions. They did not. The judge pulled a single piece of paper from inside his robe and unfolded it on his desk.

"I've made my ruling in this case and, in a moment, will announce my decision," Judge Robinson began quietly. "I want to thank counsel for the prosecution and counsel for the defense for keeping the testimony and arguments concise and on point. If all cases were handled this way, it would save a lot of time for the government and our legal system."

The judge frowned and adopted a more robust and official tone for his next words.

"Having thoroughly weighed all the evidence, and having heard the positions of both parties, I have come to my conclusion. The facts of the case bear only one possible verdict. Hiram Brodie, I find you guilty of violating the law by producing, with intent to sell, alcohol distilled illegally. This verdict carries the following penalties: a fine of up to $1,000 and/or a sentence of six months to five years."

The judge looked up and in a gentler voice asked Hiram, "Mr. Brodie, do you or your counsel have any statement to make before I pass sentence?"

Hiram was prepared for this question.

"Yes, your honor. I only want to say I realize I broke the law and ask for the court's mercy so I can continue to take care of my family."

The judge nodded. He looked at Flannery.

"Does defense counsel have any comment?"

Flannery rose, his head held high, looking stately, almost noble.

"We only reiterate what our client has said," Flannery declared. "We ask the court to show mercy to a man who has learned a hard lesson and wants only to take care of his family. Thank you, your honor."

Judge Robinson nodded and turned to the district attorney.

"Has the prosecution any statement before I pass sentence?"

The DA rose and said, "We ask the court to show no favoritism to this criminal. We asked that the full weight of the law come down upon him to set a necessary example that will deter illegal production of alcohol in this county."

The judge continued to stare at the prosecutor without nodding or smiling. Finally, he looked down again at the piece of paper on his desk and studied it.

"Then I shall proceed," Judge Robinson announced. "Hiram Brodie, you are guilty, as we've established. I cannot consider withholding punishment within the scope spelled out in the statutes for this crime. While your attorney made a strong and compelling plea for leniency in the form of probation, I cannot condone a sentence that charitable. However, testimony has uncovered some mitigating circumstances concerning your targeted persecution by the federal agents involved in your arrest."

The judge paused and stared – or maybe glared – at the three federal agents in the row behind the prosecution. He then looked down at his paper again before looking directly at Hiram.

"I therefore sentence you to one year – but not a day longer – to be served in the Drury County Jail," Judge Robinson said. "You will report to Sheriff John Lawson by sundown today to begin your incarceration. This court is adjourned."

With that, the judge meekly banged his gavel and rose to disappear swiftly through the door leading to his chambers.

The sentence was a half-triumph for Hiram and his attorney. The newly convicted moonshiner would have to serve time, but not in the federal penitentiary. He would be in Kenneth in custody of Sheriff Lawson and Deputy Sanger.

The family gathered around Hiram for a subdued celebration. Oscar Flannery stood, hands on hips, looking at the floor. He looked like a jilted lover. He had hoped to avoid any jail time, but Judge Robinson had bought his arguments only to a point. It was a bittersweet victory, if that, for the dashing West Plains lawyer.

The Brodies didn't notice Flannery's disappointment. They were glad Hiram would be just a few miles away. They could visit him. A year wasn't so long, not when he had avoided two, three, even five years in the state pen.

After a few minutes, Hiram broke away to thank his lawyer. Flannery put on his mask of practiced self-confidence.

"I appreciate all you've done for me," Hiram said. "I want to thank you. You were sure worth your fee."

Flannery looked at the relieved hillbilly, who was just about to lose a year of freedom. He saw honest gratitude. He felt moved. He thought of discounting his legal fee or waiving it altogether. He did what any lawyer worth his salt would do. He just said, "Thanks."

XXX

That afternoon, Hiram said goodbye to his brothers and his mother. Eliza gave her husband a stiff hug and he responded with a soft pat on the back. Neither said a word, just exchanging a long, sad look before parting. Sheriff Lawson then took Hiram to the county jail to get him settled in for what all of the Brodies hoped would be a short year of incarceration.

Louellen was upright, sharp-minded and solemn during the farewell. She had recovered fairly well that morning, but was still a tad unsteady. Doc Tebbetts had said he thought it would pass in time and that she'd regain most if not all of her usual vitality. She hugged her son, and he hugged her tightly. When she finally let go, a tear was trickling down her cheek.

The family watched Hiram turn and enter the sheriff's office. Then the remaining brothers led Louellen and Eliza to the Hiram's truck and Martin's car. Cleve drove Eliza home in the truck, while Martin followed in his car with his mother seated beside him.

When the truck and car reached Hiram's home, the kids were waiting. They had gotten their mom's permission to skip school that day. They had been waiting anxiously to find out what had happened to their father.

When the truck pulled up, Eliza hurried out of the car to her children. She bent down and collected Nancy in one arm and Jenny in the other. She had tears in her eyes, but she was smiling. She also glanced up at Dusty, who was impatient for someone to tell them what had happened. It was Martin who spoke up.

"Kids, we have some good news and some bad news," he said solemnly. "The bad news is that the judge found your daddy guilty of moonshining. Now, he could have sentenced him to up to five years in federal prison. But the judge only gave him a year. The good news is he'll serve his time in Kenneth."

"That means you can go visit him every once in a while," Cleve added. Dusty, who was considering the news pretty much all bad, had perked up at this last statement. So, he would be able to see his dad … and his dad wouldn't be drunk if he was in jail, right?

Eliza continued to fuss over the girls, who were now crying as much as she was. Martin moved over to Dusty and put his hand on the boy's shoulder.

"It'll be all right, Dusty," his uncle said. "Course, you'll hafta be the man around the house for now. Help your mama and look after your sisters."

"I will," Dusty replied. He felt tears welling up in his eyes. He was too old to cry. If he was the man of the house, no one could see him crying. He turned away from his uncles and his mother and walked into the cabin. For the first time, he noticed how big it looked inside. It seemed so empty. How could it seem to expand and be so lonely with only one person missing?

That night, after his grandma, Martin and Cleve had left, after his sisters were asleep, after his mom was in bed, Dusty finally let loose and cried. He cried silent, sad tears. A lump grew in his throat. It seemed to be the size of an apple. He could barely swallow. He didn't think he could ever get sadder than he was that night.

XXX

Dusty found it difficult to pick up the pieces and move on. He had always been good student, but things had changed this year. He didn't warm up to the new teacher. Mrs. Rice started the school year by reviewing some of the same lessons they had already learned last spring. It was boring.

Dusty found his mind was wandering, mostly thinking about his dad in jail. He couldn't stop thinking about Jake Jennings the role he had played in Hiram's arrest. He made fantastic plans to avenge his father. He would daydream about making the Jennings family pay for their treachery. He would have his retribution. His family would praise his heroic deeds, and his father would thank him. He would be the savior his family needed now.

Day by day, these daydreams grew wilder and more detailed. But deep inside, Dusty realized they were unrealistic. They were fantasies. He couldn't think of anything he could really do to get even with the evil Jennings clan. That made him feel weak, useless and frustrated.

Meanwhile, Nancy and Jenny were dealing with some of the same feelings their brother was experiencing. And to top it off, now that their father had been convicted, a few of the snottier kids were belittling them and taunting them. Jenny generally yelled back at these antagonists, calling them names and besmirching their family heritages as best she could.

Nancy, who wasn't prone to back down from a confrontation, also could give as well as she got. But the barbs of her schoolmates stung her more than they did her little sister. Her sensitive side was overloaded by feelings of guilt, shame and indignation.

One morning Amos Lane asked her, "Hey, Nance, how's the jailbird doin' today?" The other boys surrounding Amos snickered.

Nancy tried to think of a smart comeback, but nothing came to mind. She considered making fun of the fact that Amos' father walked with the help of a cane, but she couldn't think of a clever retort. Tears began to well up in her eyes as her face turned red and then redder. She turned and ran out of the schoolhouse and into the woods. She found a fallen log and lay alongside it, bawling like a five-year-old.

Janey Forsythe, back in school and wearing her ugly but indispensable glasses every day, saw what happened to Nancy. She sympathized with the Brodies. She knew what it was like to be teased and badgered and put down because of her father's failings. She understood, to a degree, what Dusty, Nancy and Jenny were going through.

When class started and Nancy was still absent, Janey asked permission to visit the outhouse. Instead, she searched the edge of the woods until she found Nancy crying.

"Don't cry," Janey said. "Don't pay attention to boys like Amos. You'll be fine."

"I-I don't feel fine," Nancy said. "You don't know what it's like."

Janey wasn't sure about that: She'd had plenty of her classmates make fun of her, sometimes because of her dad. But that didn't matter now, all she wanted to do was help her friend.

"A year seems like a long time," she said, "but it'll go by fast. You and me can get together, go for walks or just sit and talk. If you need me, I'll be around to help you."

"Thanks," Nancy said, sniffling back her tears. Then, a second later, the tears returned, as hard or harder than before. Janey was out of comforting words, so she just held Nancy's hand until the wounded girl was cried out. They went back to the schoolhouse together. Mrs. Rice was on the verge of demanding where they had been and why they were gone so long. She recognized that Nancy had been crying. Graciously, she let it go and continued with the lesson.

XXX

Dusty also took occasional offense at comments made by his classmates – especially those he didn't much like. It was probably good that Will Todd had not returned to school that fall. His presence would have added gallons of fuel to the fire that was smoldering just below the surface within Dusty.

As it happened, Dusty did get into a tangle or two with other boys, most notably Amos Lane. The two got into a heated exchange late one morning. An apple had disappeared from the Lane boy's desk, and the only person he could remember being near it that morning was Dusty.

It was actually Donna Bakken, who had a big crush on Amos. She had taken the apple to tease him. Donna, the stout girl who had played first base on the successful Avery baseball team last spring, was not the most attractive girl in school. Amos, like most of the boys, barely noticed her. Taking the apple was her way of getting his attention. At least that was her plan.

But Amos quickly accused Dusty doing the forbidden and taking the fruit. Dusty had no idea why he was the top suspect. Eventually, Amos made a sneering comment about Dusty winding up in jail, perhaps in the cell next to his dad.

That did it. Dusty barreled into Amos and both tumbled to the floor. Mrs. Rice called on some of the other boys to break up the struggle, but most of them wanted to watch and see who would win. In short order, it was Dusty. His sorrow, frustration and anger poured out in a series of blows that soon had Amos covering up and finally giving in. At this point, the contest decided, a few boys intervened and pulled Dusty off his battered adversary.

Mrs. Rice had promptly demanded both boys leave the school and not come back until the next morning. At that point, either they would shake hands and make up or she would suspend them.

Dusty collected a couple of things from his desk. He looked at Nancy and Jenny, sitting on the other side of the room. Their faces were impassive, but Dusty could read through the masks they wore. This was one more parcel of shame added to the heap of disgrace the Brodie family was suffering. In the months to follow, Dusty was to recall the sadness of his sisters on more occasions than he could count.

Amos and Dusty left the school and headed different directions. Amos headed toward his home, which happened to be the way Dusty usually went. Dusty decided instead to walk toward Avery.

The apple? Donna still had it. She was embarrassed by the violence her innocent theft had caused. She took it into the woods during lunch and ate it, tossing the core as deep into the brush as she could.

XXX

Dusty had no real destination and no plans. He found himself wandering into Ivan's general store. He didn't have much money on him, only a nickel and a couple of pennies. He thought about buying a bottle of pop, but he wasn't sure he wanted to blow most of his cash on a temporary and frivolous beverage.

Ivan can out of the back and saw him standing by the cooler.

"Morning, Dusty. What brings you into to town today? I thought school was in session."

"It is," Dusty answered. "I just don't feel like being there." There was enough truth in that sentence that Dusty didn't feel very much guilt about his response.

"Well, you want a bottle pop, then?" the store owner asked.

"I … I don't think so," Dusty said. "Better save my money."

"That's a good plan, son," Ivan nodded. He, like everyone in the area, knew Hiram was serving his sentence in Kenneth. He also knew that the Brodies, especially Hiram's three kids, were in for some hard times. Ivan wanted to make a profit, to make a living like any other merchant. But he wasn't heartless.

"Say, Dusty, if you can give me a hand carrying a couple of boxes of cans in here, well, I suppose I could pay you with a pop," Ivan said in an offhand manner. He eyed Dusty and waited.

"Sure, that's fine," Dusty said.

Dusty carried the boxes, put them where Ivan indicated and went over to the cooler to get his reward. Just then a vehicle pulled up outside. It was Percy Jennings. He'd decided it was too nice a fall day to spend at the high school. He was playing hooky, and he was unapologetic about it.

Percy stepped happily into the store saying, "Howdy, Ivan. Are you taking wooden nickels today?"

"Now, why would I take a wooden nickel if folks are willing to pay with real money?" the storekeeper replied.

"I don't know, maybe this winter you'll need 'em to start a fire in that old stove," Percy said. "Wooden nickels burn a lot better than those metal ones."

"Well, them metal ones will buy a lot of wood, you know," Ivan grinned back at Percy.

"All right, here's a real nickel for you," Percy said, flipping the coin to Ivan and turning toward the cooler. It was only then that Percy saw

Dusty standing there, drinking a cola. It was an awkward moment. Percy's father had been the one who had turned Hiram in. The older boy didn't know what to say to Dusty.

"Well, if it isn't the kid with the rifle arm," Percy said. He hoped praising the lad's skills would start them off on the right foot. "How ya doin', Dusty? Ivan, this boy won me and my friends a pocket full of money at the fair, didn't ya Dusty?"

Dusty was hesitant to talk to Percy. After all, Percy's dad was the enemy. Dusty had been fantasizing about mangling and maiming Jake and Kyle Jennings. It seemed wrong for any Brodie to talk to anyone named Jennings. But Percy had always treated him fine. And now he was smiling at Dusty. Maybe he wasn't as bad as the rest of his family. Or maybe he was.

Dusty decided to answer. "Hi, Percy," he said quietly.

"So, what did you do with all that money?" Percy asked.

"Well, nothing … Dad took the money before I could spend it," Dusty replied.

"All of it?" the older boy asked. Dusty looked down at the floor but said nothing. "Oh … I, uh, I'm sorry to hear that. And … I'm sorry about your dad."

Dusty looked up at Percy, his eyes dark and distrusting.

"He's in jail because your dad snitched on him. My dad said I should never trust a Jennings."

"Well, look, Dusty, I know how you feel," Percy said. "But I didn't do it. My dad did. How would you like it if I blamed you for things your dad did? It wouldn't be fair."

Dusty pondered that.

"No, I guess not," he said. "But how can I trust you? You'll always be a Jennings. And I'll always be a Brodie."

"True," Percy said firmly. "But you'll always be Dusty, and I'll always be Percy. Neither one of us is our pa. I'd like to be friends. But I see you're still mad. I don't know what I can do to make you feel better. So maybe we shouldn't be friends. Would you rather be enemies?"

Dusty then pondered this for a moment. He asked himself what his dad would do. Then he asked what Uncle Martin would do. Finally, he considered what his grandma would do. He thought she would try to live peacefully. She didn't like the feud between the two families. He decided he should be a little bit like his grandma. He would forgive … but he would never forget.

"All right," Dusty said thoughtfully. "I guess we can be friends. But I have to stick by my dad, even if that means that someday we can't be friendly anymore."

"Deal," said Percy, shaking Dusty's hand.

"A good deal," said Ivan, who had been listening unobtrusively from across the store. "I think that deserves a couple of candy bars. On the house."

He tossed each of them a chocolate bar.

"What, no free pop?" Percy asked with wide, innocent eyes.

"OK, one more pop apiece," the softhearted entrepreneur said. Percy turned to wink at Dusty. "Then get out of here before you boys drive me into the poorhouse."

XXX

Percy and Dusty walked out into the early fall sunshine. Percy stretched and looked wistfully at the sky. It seemed like such a perfect day. He wondered why there was hatred and greed and sorrow and poverty in this beautiful world. Would it ever change?

"So, where you headed, Dusty?" Percy asked.

"Guess I'm going home," Dusty said, taking another swig of his second soda pop. "I sorta got kicked out of school this morning. I got into a fight. Amos accused me of stealin' his apple."

"You plan on walkin' back?" the elder boy asked. Dusty nodded. "Wanna ride in my car?"

"Sure," Dusty said enthusiastically.

Percy's Model A Tudor was old, a 1928 model that had seen better days. Still, Percy and his friends had tinkered with it many long hours, and now it purred like a kitten. Well, maybe it grumbled like a bear. But it could move. Percy was known for running his car at high speeds up and down the county roads. Riding with him sounded like fun.

Dusty climbed in on the passenger side as Percy fired up his vehicle, put it in gear and popped the clutch. They were off down the dusty, pitted road toward the Brodie home.

It was a joy for Dusty to ride down that road with the car travelling along at such a clip. The wind in his hair and the noise from the four cylinders made conversation difficult, but by the time they neared Dusty's home, they were both smiling and laughing. It was a grand bonding experience for the two boys from rival clans. It seemed like they were cementing an authentic friendship.

As they approached the lane that led up to the Brodie house, Dusty yelled for Percy to slow down. The teenager driver did so.

"You don't need to take me up to the house," Dusty said. "There's a big rut where the road washed away during that storm last week. Uncle Cleve even bottomed out there with the truck."

"OK, friend," Percy said. "Then I'll let you off here. Hope you don't get in trouble over that fight this morning."

"I don't think mom'll say much if I tell her I was accused of stealin' something I didn't take," Dusty said thoughtfully. "I believe I was in the right. And my sisters will back me up."

"Take care then, Dusty," Percy said. "See ya later."

"See ya, Percy," Dusty replied. Percy put the Ford back in gear and accelerated down the road, kicking up a little gravel and a lot of dust. The Brodie boy watched until his friend was out of sight and the dust drifted back down to settle on the road. Then he headed up the lane toward home.

XXX

Dusty was feeling pretty good when he reached the cabin. He skipped up the steps, opened the screen door and barged into the house.

"Mom, I'm home," he announced. He heard scurrying sounds coming from his parents' bedroom.

"Mom, you in there?" he asked, walking toward the open door.

As Dusty peered into the room, he saw his mother in bed, partly covered by the sheet but obviously undressed. He saw something else as well. Something he would never forget.

It was another man, hastily trying to pull his trousers up with one hand. The other hand held the man's socks and boots. It didn't take a genius to figure out what was going on. His dad was in jail and his mother was making love to another man. And Dusty quickly recognized the man. It was Kyle Jennings, the brother of Jake Jennings. Percy's uncle.

Dusty stood paralyzed, shocked by what he was seeing. The man stopped wrestling with his pants and stared back at Dusty. His mother's initial look of shock turned quickly into a frown. Then she scowled at him.

"You get the hell out of here," she demanded. "You're not supposed to be home yet. Go on, get!"

It took a couple of seconds for the words to sink in. Dusty kept staring at the guilty couple. When he finally broke out of his dumbfounded trance, he turned and sped out of the house.

Chapter 20

THE DEPARTURE

Since Hiram's trial, Louellen had been taking it easy. She had experienced no more bouts of low blood pressure, but she was still feeling frail.

At times, she had trouble concentrating. She didn't realize the effects of her earlier heat stroke were lingering. The stroke had subtly affected her cognitive abilities while doing slight damage to her kidneys. She was having trouble urinating.

These kidney issues would fade, and she would recover to some degree in the next few months. But the inability to remember things was bothering her.

Louellen would go outside and forget why she was there. Sometimes, in the afternoon, she'd forget what she had done that morning. Had she eaten breakfast? Was she drinking plenty of water as Doc Tebbetts had insisted? Sometimes she wasn't quite sure. On a couple of occasions, she couldn't remember what year it was … or if her boys were all still living in her home.

In the days after Hiram's trial and jail sentence, she had mourned his absence. She went to visit him in the Kenneth jail any time she could persuade Martin or Cleve to drive her. Both men reminded her it could have been worse. Hiram could be serving multiple years in the penitentiary. Still, the mother grieved for her son.

She had thought that after his arrest, conviction and imprisonment, her summerlong forebodings would go away. But her sleep was still unsettled. At night, many of her dreams were as dark and tense as ever. Her anxiety rose as she tried to comprehend the murky sense of dread that revisited her every few days.

These intermittent waves of uneasiness caused her to wonder if, after all that had happened that summer, some other potential evil lurked around the corner.

The dread returned with a vengeance on the morning that Dusty had gotten into the fight with Amos and been dismissed from school. Some vague foreboding crept over Louellen as she was piddling around in the kitchen. She felt her heart begin to race. Her breath became quicker and uncomfortably shallow. Louellen sat down in a kitchen chair. She leaned her head onto the table and focused on breathing as slowly, regularly and deeply as she could.

By and by, the feeling waned. She felt a touch of calmness return. She realized she was breathing normally again. Although the episode had been fleeting, the old woman was convinced it meant something. Was her health failing? Was she sensing more trouble ahead for the Brodie family? She couldn't read the signs. There were no clear omens. She was puzzled. What, if anything, were the spirits telling her?

She decided a little nap would do no harm. She had just settled onto her bed and closed her eyes when she heard footsteps outside. Someone was coming her way, and they were in a hurry.

XXX

When Dusty reeled out of his house, retreating from the shocking sight of his mom and Kyle Jennings together, he had started running. He had no destination in mind. He just ran. After a few minutes, he realized he was running toward his grandma's place. He couldn't think of anywhere else to go, so he continued running toward her.

As Dusty raced into her house, Louellen struggled to her feet and looked with curiosity at her grandson. He stopped in front of her, red-faced and panting. He had a look of hurt and horror on his face. It was as if he had seen a ghost in the middle of the day.

"What's wrong, child?" Louellen asked.

Dusty wordlessly ran to her and hugged her close. Louellen forgot about her fatigue. She was now focused on providing solace for a boy who obviously needed whatever strength she had.

"Grandma, hold me," Dusty said. He couldn't help. He started to cry. Suddenly he was no longer a young teenager; he was once again a scared little boy. "Just hold me, please!" he cried.

"Of course, Dusty, of course," his grandmother said, hugging him and rocking slowly back and forth to sooth her beloved boy. "You're safe with me. Tell me what troubles you."

After a few minutes, during which Dusty cried more than he had in years, he began to calm down. He did feel safer in the cosy embrace of his gentle grandma. With difficulty, Dusty pulled himself together and – pushing his emotions deep inside – began a matter-of-fact description of all he had done, heard and seen since being banished from school that morning.

When he got to the part about what he had seen in his mom's bedroom, Louellen put her hand to her mouth to cover her expression. She didn't want Dusty to see how angry she felt toward her daughter-in-law. Louellen had long suspected Eliza of hiding some secret. But this was beyond what she had imagined. And it happened with Eliza's husband in jail just a few miles away.

Meanwhile, Dusty continued – trying to maintain a dispassionate manner – to describe everything he had seen. He repeated word for word what his mom had said when ordering him to leave. At this, his grandmother dropped all pretense of impartiality and muttered, "Damn that stubborn woman!"

XXX

When Nancy and Jenny got home from school, they expected their mother to ask where Dusty was. They didn't want to be the ones to tell her that Dusty had been kicked out of school that morning. They expected their brother to get into big trouble for getting into a fight.

Eliza, however, didn't mention her son. She only told her girls to sit down at the kitchen table. She wanted to talk to them. The sisters looked at each other. Neither understood what was going on. They climbed into their chairs and waited to hear what their mother had to say.

XXX

When Martin returned home from the post office that evening, he found his mother and his nephew seated at the kitchen table. Both looked sad, maybe worried – he couldn't quite make it out. But something was wrong.

"Someone die?" he asked, hoping he was wrong.

"Maybe someone should," his mother said, staring harshly at her son. Now Martin was really troubled. He had rarely seen his mother look so severe, so angry. It was a look he associated with her disciplining him or his brothers when they were mischievous boys. He half expected her to go out and cut a switch to tan his backside.

"I wanna know what's goin' on," Martin said, impatient to find out the cause of this unconcealed hostility.

Louellen looked at Dusty, who was looking down into his lap, a sorrowful and glum expression on his face. For a moment, Martin thought his nephew had done something to vex the old woman.

"Your sister-in-law has brought shame on this family," Louellen said, frowning and furrowing her already-wrinkled brow. "Dusty found her in bed … with another man."

The news stunned Martin. He couldn't believe this could happen, especially so soon after Hiram's incarceration.

"Do you know who she was with?" Martin asked, his temper rising just short of a boil.

His mother grimly nodded yes.

"Well, who?"

Dusty, still looking down, spoke quietly.

"It was Kyle Jennings."

Martin's temper hit the boiling point and soared beyond.

"You sure?" he asked.

Dusty looked up at his uncle nodding solemnly. He was certain.

"I oughta shoot him and beat the hell out of her," Martin said. Then he immediately wished he had held his tongue for Dusty's sake.

Martin said no more, but paced the small kitchen floor, fuming and studying what he could do.

At length, he settled down a bit, controlling his fury enough to discuss with his mother what response or action to take. They debated back and forth as Dusty sat and listened. At one point, having heard enough, tiring of inactivity, the boy got up to go outside. But his grandmother grasped his wrist and firmly but gently compelled him to stay.

"This is a terrible thing for a young boy to know," she told him. "I understand you just want to get away and be by yourself now. I would want to do the same thing. But we are talking about YOUR mother. We will not make any decisions or do anything about this without considering your wishes. You need to stay, to listen … and to tell us what you think is the right thing to do."

Martin may have agreed only partially with his mother on this point, but he saw the wisdom in including the boy in the discussion. After all, with his dad in jail and his mom acting shamefully, Dusty had every right to be included. Like it or not, his nephew would have to start growing up in a hurry. He eyed Dusty then nodded at the chair. Dusty hesitated a second or two and sat.

The unpleasant discussion lasted well into the evening. The upshot was that nothing could be done until morning. Once the sun was up, all three would march to Eliza's den of iniquity. Louellen and Dusty would pack up his sisters' things and bring Nancy and Jenny back to Louellen's place. Martin would then send Eliza packing. And good riddance to her.

As for Kyle Jennings, Martin would take Cleve to visit with Hiram in the Kenneth jail. There they would decide what they would do to their philandering foe.

XXX

Things were crumbling right and left for Eliza. From the time she started her illicit affair with Kyle Jennings, she was on a road to self-destruction. Kyle's confident appearance and deceitful manner made him a master manipulator of women. With studied guile and unfailing persistence, he was a difficult predator to fend off. And Eliza made only faint, feeble efforts to stop him.

At first, it was exciting to sneak away from home for an hour or two of forbidden pleasure. She soon came to depend on Kyle for validation that she was still an appealing, attractive woman. Eliza was soon addicted, a victim of his back-country – but effective – charm. She craved his explicit fervor and met his lascivious urgency with her own womanly need.

In the quieter interludes, when they lay together, their passions temporarily spent, Kyle engaged his satiated mistress with idle questions. He asked about her family: her mother, her kids and eventually her husband. In the sweet repose of their trysting environs, Eliza felt free of inhibitions and worries.

She had spoken openly of her dreams and desires. She talked honestly of her conflicting views of motherhood and her desire for a carefree, hedonistic, sensuous existence. She also spoke of the cooling affections she felt for her hard-drinking husband.

Little by little, Kyle pried bits of information from Eliza about Hiram's still, including its location and when Hiram was likely to be starting up production. Throughout the summer, Kyle had filed away a nice mental dossier on Hiram's activities.

From there, it was a matter of luring the federal agents to look in Hiram's direction – while ignoring what might be going on near the Jennings properties. It was funny how readily those agents took the bait. Led by Kyle's brother, Jake, the agents had scoped out the location of Hiram's still. Once Kyle had drawn from Eliza the exact timing of Hiram's return to his hidden distillery, it was an easy matter to notify the agents and help set up their foolproof ambush of the rival moonshiner.

After Hiram's arrest, Eliza began to worry about what she had done. For a few tortured weeks, she faced an internal battle: To whom did she owe her allegiance? One day, she would feel she was justified in derailing Hiram's liquor production. Another day, she would convince herself none of it was any of her doing: The agents would have caught Hiram eventually anyway. Still, some days, she cried over her betrayal of her husband. She couldn't help feeling ashamed of consorting with the enemy.

After the arrest, Kyle redoubled his Casanova antics. He convinced Eliza there was no way to retrace her steps. She couldn't turn back. When the district attorney had approached her about testifying against Hiram, she could see no alternative but to agree. And she continued to meet Kyle. She couldn't resist. It was like the man had control of her, body and soul. And she honestly didn't want their affair to end.

Then came the day that Dusty arrived home unexpected and found the wicked couple together. After Eliza drove her son from the house, she made a hasty decision. She realized she couldn't stay in Hiram's home any longer. She feared she couldn't continue to live in Drury County. She would have move away.

She tried to convince Kyle Jennings to take her off somewhere. To Springfield, Rolla, St. Louis: It didn't matter. Eliza had to go. Her mind was made up. She tried cajoling Kyle to leave at once. But the philandering hillbilly had no intentions of going anywhere. Avery was his home. His ancestors settled here. His family was established here. Here he would stay: There were plenty of other bored and attractive women in the hills. Eliza could go jump in a lake.

Kyle had told her so – after he had dressed and pulled on his boots. Then he marched out of Hiram Brodie's house, having done with Hiram's wife all he had needed to do.

Eliza was stricken by his rejection, but as the minutes ticked by, her panic turned to anger. By the time Nancy and Jenny got home from school, she had a new plan in place. She wouldn't be thwarted by any despicable Drury County rake – no matter how much she had thought she had loved him just hours before.

Eliza had one desperate play left. When her daughters got home from school, she was prepared to put her plan in motion. And she would waste no time.

XXX

The next morning, Martin and Louellen were up early. Martin retrieved his 12-gauge shotgun, checked it over and loaded both barrels. He wasn't taking any chances. He would be prepared if Kyle Jennings were stupid enough to be hanging around Hiram's cabin.

Louellen made a quick breakfast. She wasn't hungry, but she forced herself to eat to make sure she had the strength to get through this day. Strangely she had slept well without any disturbing dreams.

His grandma woke Dusty up just after dawn. He, on the other hand, had not slept well. He had stayed awake, alternately fighting back tears and anger. Finally, exhausted by the day's events, he had fallen asleep sometime after 3 a.m.

He was surprised at how lively he felt now that he was fully awake again. He was still juggling an array of emotions as he hurriedly wolfed down his breakfast.

When Martin and Louellen agreed it was time to go, Dusty was ready. He dreaded seeing his mother again, but he badly wanted to rescue his sisters from the woman he now viewed as evil.

Because of Louellen's recent health issues, Martin insisted they drive to Hiram's place. It was the long way around, but it took less than 10 minutes. The plan was for Louellen to pack up the girls, put their things in the car and drive them back to her home. Martin would follow on foot once he had booted Eliza out of the cabin.

Dusty's grandmother wasn't a great driver, but it was only a few miles. She assured Martin she could make the trip with no problems. Besides, Dusty would be with her if anything went wrong. In the worst case, the grandkids could walk her home slowly, stopping to rest as often as needed. The avenging trio, representing three generations of Brodies, piled into the car. Martin headed up to the gravel road leading toward Hiram's place.

The nearer they drew, the tenser they became. When they finally turned up the rough, narrow road, Dusty remembered the rut that Cleve had hit earlier. He warned Uncle Martin to take it easy over that area. Martin had been so deep in thought he'd almost forgotten about the small trench. He slowed and inched his way along, his car jerking and bouncing up the pathway. He cleared the obstacle without bottoming out then accelerated gradually, his attention once more on what he planned to do when he got to the house.

Soon enough Martin and his passengers arrived. The house was quiet. No smoke rose from the chimney. Nothing stirred in the yard. It was almost eerie.

"Stay here," Martin said. It was a command, not a request.

Martin pulled the shotgun from behind the car seat and cradled it in the crook of his arm. He walked resolutely to the door and knocked.

"Eliza, come on out here," he said firmly. "We need to talk."

Martin waited for 10 to 15 seconds before calling out again. Still there was no response from the house. He looked back at his mother and nephew and motioned them to stay put. He swung the screen door outward and pushed the front door open. He peered inside, squinting as his eyes adjusted from the outdoor light to the dim interior of the cabin. Finally, he slowly ventured in.

Louellen and Dusty were holding their breath, hoping there would be no violence or conflict. Everything stayed quiet for 30 of the longest seconds either of them had ever experienced.

Eventually, Martin came out, shotgun dangling from his hand. He looked calm but unhappy. By the time he got back to the car, the two passengers had imagined all sorts of possible outcomes to his inspection of the cabin. Finally, he approached the driver-side window.

"They're gone," he said. "Eliza, the girls, no one's in there."

"Where would they go?" his mother wondered, echoing Dusty's thoughts.

"Wherever it is, they intend to stay gone awhile," Martin said. "They packed up their clothes and a few other things. I think Eliza's moved out."

"And taken the girls?" Louellen asked.

"Looks that way," Martin said. "C'mon in and take a look."

Louellen climbed out of the car and hurried as best as she could to the front door. Martin was already entering again. Dusty wanted to rush ahead with him, but he forced himself to lag behind and walk with his grandma.

When they went inside, they saw everything Martin had described was accurate. The already sparse cabin looked bare, abandoned. Gone were most of the girls' clothes and belongings. The same for their mom's things. Dusty saw that Nancy's favorite books were missing from the shelf.

It hit Dusty hard. This had been the only home he had ever known. Now his dad was in jail and wouldn't be back for a year. And his mom had disappeared, too. And worst of all, he had no idea where his sisters were.

At that point, he realized something about his sisters: Good, bad, fun or annoying, he loved them. He missed his mom and dad, for sure. But he was heartsick at the departure of Nancy and Jenny.

His grandmother walked over to stand behind him. She softly put her hands on his shoulders.

"Dusty, I'm so sorry," she said. A moment later, Dusty heard her softly sobbing, her hands still clamped upon his shoulders.

"Why did she go without me?" Dusty asked, not really speaking to anyone in particular. "Doesn't she love me? Doesn't she care?"

As Martin looked at his nephew, most of his anger turned into sorrow. Sorrow for a young boy who didn't deserve to be deserted by the woman who gave birth to him. From that moment on, Eliza would never really be a mother to Dusty again. Martin realized this even if Dusty did not.

"WE love you, Dusty," his grandmother said softly in his ear. "Don't ever doubt it, no matter what happens. The Brodie family is one, and we all love you."

Despite his grandma's good intentions, Dusty felt no love at that moment. Only rejection. He felt abandoned, alone and isolated in a strange and miserable world. Would he ever see his sisters again? Would they get along without him? Could he survive without them?

Dusty wondered about this new world he had been thrust into. Could a world that held this much sorrow hold any happiness? No, this world was overflowing with misery. There was no room for joy. At that moment, it seemed there would never be another sunny day for the rest of his life.

Chapter 21

THE TRAGIC TRIAD

Martin helped his mother gather up some of Dusty's things. There was no question about it: He would stay with them. If Martin doubted it for a minute, Louellen's fierce eyes and determined expression killed that notion for good.

While Dusty stood stunned, struggling to understand what had happened, his uncle and grandmother carried a few handfuls of the poor boy's belongings to the car.

"Dusty, anything else you want to take?" Martin asked.

Dusty looked around the emptied room. He didn't seem to recognize it. He didn't say a word. Then his eyes lit on the one thing he decided he wanted: his dad's rifle. His dad wouldn't need it until next fall. Dusty could do a lot of hunting before then.

"I want dad's .22," he said firmly.

Martin looked at Louellen. The grandmother shrugged.

"Fine," Martin told him. "Take it."

Dusty retrieved the rifle from the rack on the wall and headed out to the car. At the front door, he turned and took one short look at the house that had been his home. He saw nothing he cared to hold on to. He went out to his uncle's Ford, put the gun in the back and climbed in the front seat.

A minute or two later, his uncle and grandmother came out of the cabin, carrying a few odds and ends. They got into the car on either side of Dusty. When Martin turned the car around and headed away from the house, the boy didn't look back. He'd had enough of that place for now.

XXX

Once they were back at Louellen's and had unloaded the car, Martin told his mother he was going to drive up to Kenneth and tell Hiram all that had happened. He would pick up brother Cleve and fill him in on the way. Louellen nodded. Her mind now was focused on looking after Dusty.

After dropping them off at the homestead, Martin drove into Avery and stopped by the post office. He informed his co-worker, Ruby Guthrie, that he had to take the morning off.

"And don't be surprised if I'm not here tomorrow," he added.

"What do I do if anyone wants to know where you are?" she said, clearly piqued by the short notice and Martin's abrupt manner.

"Tell 'em it's personal business … and none of their business," Martin said. He was out the door before Ruby could reply.

A short time later, he arrived at Cleve's house. He found his brother in the garden, checking late-planted lettuce, spinach and cabbage as well as his last-planted stand of sweet corn. Martin, in his succinct manner, told Cleve about Eliza's infidelity and abrupt departure with both nieces.

Cleve's temper rose as Martin quickly told the tale. The younger brother was in favor of heading directly to the Jennings home and filling Kyle with a deadly amount of lead. Martin talked him out of the knee-jerk violence. He reminded Cleve that it was Hiram's call. They would go to Kenneth and discuss it with their brother. Whatever he wanted, they would do. Cleve agreed.

When they arrived in Kenneth it was nearly 10 a.m. They walked in the sheriff's office and found the deputy, Cliff Sanger, sitting at the sheriff's desk, reading a magazine. When asked, Cliff told the brothers that the sheriff was out checking on a report of stolen livestock. The Brodies then asked the deputy if they could speak with Hiram. Sanger didn't see any harm. He took them back to the cells and left them with their brother.

Martin had been dreading how to break the news to Hiram. Of the three brothers, he had the worst temper. Martin was afraid Hiram would hit the ceiling. After greeting one another, Hiram waited. He could see his brothers had something to say but were stalling.

"Well, what are you two doin' here?" Hiram said. "Out with it."

Martin sighed. In quiet, calm language, he told his brother that Dusty had caught his mother in bed with Kyle Jennings.

Hiram, as expected, fumed and frothed. He let out a string of oaths that would make a mule blush. He vowed immediate and severe retribution. He cursed his jail sentence and his inability to proceed directly to the Jennings farm and take his revenge.

The deputy burst in to find out what the commotion was about. When Cleve gave him a short version of the story, Cliff's jaw dropped.

Meanwhile, Hiram continued to rant. The three men standing outside the cell let the mercurial man erupt, overflow and slowly settle into a gentle white-hot anger. Then Martin told him the rest of the story. He explained how he, his mother and Dusty had found the cabin abandoned, with Eliza and the girls gone, apparently for good.

Again, Hiram raged. He threatened extreme bodily harm if he ever got hold of his wife. He bellowed that no one had the right to take his daughters away from him. Finally, almost as an afterthought, he asked about Dusty.

"He's stayin' with me and mother," Martin said. "We'll take care of him."

"What you want us to do about Kyle?" Cleve asked. "We could fill him full of holes today. You just say the word."

Cliff's eyes grew wide with concern. What could he do to stop these two brothers from carrying out some form of instant frontier justice if they took a mind to go after Kyle Jennings?

Hiram frowned and thought. He gave a quick glance at Cliff, considering what he could or could not say in front of the deputy. Then he glared at Cleve with stormy eyes.

"You don't do nothing to Kyle," Hiram muttered through gritted teeth. "He's mine. It may take a year, but I'll take care of him. And I'll fix him so's he don't fool around with any woman again."

The deputy felt a weight lift from his shoulder, and he almost felt like he could breathe normally again. The crisis was averted … for the time being.

"We'll respect that, Hiram," Martin said, looking at Cleve to join him in the promise. "But when you're out of here, we're with you."

"Hell, yes," Cleve nodded. "What should we do for now?"

"Keep Dusty away from Kyle," Hiram ordered. "Keep him away from all them Jennings skunks. And tell ma I took the news well. Tell her I'm being good in here. I'll make sure I get out right on time. Don't let on what's in store for those Jennings sons of bitches."

XXX

Louellen was trying to get Dusty to eat some lunch, but her grandson wasn't the least bit hungry. She even offered to make a batch of chocolate gravy with fresh biscuits. He declined. It was the first time she had ever seen the boy turn down chocolate gravy. It pained her heart.

It had been a hard summer for Dusty. Too much was happening too fast. First that heathen Rafe had tried to maim or kill him. Then his dad had taken away his money. Before he could realize what was happening, his dad had been arrested, tried and jailed. If that wasn't enough, he had walked in on his mother committing adultery. Now she had run off without a word of goodbye, taking his sisters who knew where. It was all too much for an adult to handle, let alone an innocent child.

One thing puzzled Louellen Brodie. She had been having premonitions all summer. She had seen warning signs of impending calamity. And, true enough, bad things had been happening – to Dusty, to Martin, to Hiram and to her granddaughters.

But those events had come, taken place and passed. Were they the last of the troubles her family would face? Would the forebodings end or would they return? She closed her eyes and considered. Maybe the peril was over. Perhaps the Brodies had survived the ominous snares that had littered their path. Silently, she prayed that their troubles had ended. But, she asked the spirits respectfully, if there were more troubles ahead, would they please provide a warning?

She opened her eyes, realizing she had been standing there for some minutes unaware of Dusty. Where had he gone? Should she try to find him? Or should she let him go? Perhaps he needed time alone to think. Time to take in and process all that was happening.

Maybe it was best to let him reflect upon his woes, take stock and resolve his feelings. He was a good and strong boy with a sharp mind. Dusty would figure it out. She had to tell herself that. She had to believe in him. More than that, she had to believe he would learn to believe in himself.

XXX

Dusty had indeed walked away from his grandma's house that afternoon. He had headed down to Dermots Branch. He sat on the bank, watching the water pirouette past, rolling gently and breaking into little eddies that appeared, vanished and reappeared in new forms.

Life, he realized, was like that river. As you floated along, it pulled and twisted you, changing course without reason or rationale, just meandering aimlessly without warning. And no matter how you figured it might turn, the river moved according to its own whims. It took you wherever it wanted. And once it took you, you were obliged to go along. There was no turning back, no retracing your path. No opportunity to try again. You went where the water wanted you to go. You had no choice.

Dusty imagined that all summer he had been shunted about, maneuvered and steered though events and experiences that he had not wanted to endure. He couldn't understand what had made this summer so strangely different from all his other summers.

He always yearned for the end of the school year so he could feel free of responsibilities and released to enjoy that special world that all boys crave. The pleasant aspects of this past summer had flown past him like sudden breeze. The harsher elements had hung on like an all-day storm, forcing him to bottle up his youthful zeal and deal with the solemn and serious issues that had arisen one after another.

The more Dusty pondered these things, the more he felt cheated. It was as if life had dealt him a cruel hand. He had been shackled by sadness just as the season for fun was ripening around him. He was drowning in self-pity. He began to grow angry at the lack of control he had to change his destiny. It was all unfair. It was all unjust. Why was this happening to him?

Dusty stood up, continuing to look at the river rolling past. And suddenly he realized he wasn't really moving with the water at all. No, he was stuck here on the bank. All this water and all the debris it carried would move downstream, around the bend and join the Eleven Point River. From there it would make its way out to sea. It would leave behind all the heartache and frustration it witnessed today. But Dusty, he couldn't just drift downstream. He had to stay here where the misery and anguish would continue to eat at him day after day after day.

He bent down and picked up a rock. He aimed for a log that was lodged about midstream. Dusty concentrated and hurled the rock. It thwacked off the log. He picked up another and threw, harder this time. The sound was even louder and sharper. Suddenly he imagined the log was the body of Kyle Jennings. Right now, Dusty hated that man with his entire being.

He picked up more rocks and threw harder and harder and harder. As his velocity increased, his aim suffered. Soon he was missing the log more than he was hitting it. But his temper was up, and he kept heaving the rocks ferociously.

Finally, it dawned on him that he was wasting rocks. He wasn't hitting his target. He was doing absolutely no damage to the log that he now viewed as an animate enemy. He remembered a lesson his dad had taught him long ago, when they were knocking cans off a rail fence. A rock thrown at almost any speed could stun or kill a rabbit or a squirrel, but no game ever dropped dead or was even stunned if the throw missed.

Dusty readjusted his thoughts. His next rock nailed the log dead center. In fact, it bounced back straight at him, plunging into the river halfway between him and the waterlogged timber. From that point on, he hardly missed. He stood there hurling rocks at the wooden effigy of Kyle Jennings until his arm started to hurt.

By then he knew that, if he ever got the opportunity, he could nail Kyle Jennings in the head with a much-deserved missile. It would be like David versus Goliath, just like in the Bible. And just like in the Bible, the bad man would suffer.

XXX

On his way back home, after dropping off Cleve, Martin went to the schoolhouse. The students had been dismissed for the day, but Mrs. Rice was grading some of the day's schoolwork.

"Sarah Jane, I need to talk to you about my nephew and my nieces," Martin said.

"Yes," Mrs. Rice said carefully. "I noticed none of them were in school today."

"Well, there's a reason for that," the uncle explained. "Dusty is going to be staying with me and my ma. The girls likely aren't coming back to school anytime soon."

"My heavens, why not?" Mrs. Rice said, sounding offended. "Surely you think girls deserve an education just the same as boys."

"It ain't that, Sarah Jane," Martin said as calmly as he could. "Just listen a minute. Dusty is staying with me. The girls are with their mother. That's all you need to know. None of us pulled them out of school to stay home and cook and clean. Dusty will be back in a day or two. You can count on that much."

"Martin Brodie, I think you owe me – and the school – an explanation," Mrs. Rice said, glaring at her visitor.

"I don't owe you a damn thing, Sarah Jane," he said coolly. "I just told you everything I came to say. Good day now."

He stomped out of the classroom, got into his car and drove home with a thousand thoughts swirling around his head. He had no experience being a parent. How could he take on that responsibility? He already had to take care of his mother. Maybe Cleve should take the boy.

Then he realized that was no good. First of all, Cleve knew even less about being a responsible parent than he did. And, in any case, his mother would never let Dusty live with Cleve. Dusty was theirs to watch over, whether they liked it or not. But he sure wished he didn't have to deal with stupid teachers who didn't know how to mind their own business.

XXX

The next few days passed relatively uneventfully for the Brodies. It was as calm as it had been all summer. Dusty returned to school. Martin returned to work at the post office. And Louellen returned to doing most, but not quite all, of the chores she usually handled.

But the tranquility wasn't going to last. It turned out Louellen's dreams were not over. After a few nights of respite, that terrible foreboding feeling returned with a vengeance. Louellen had dreamed that one of her sons – she couldn't see which one – was hanging over the edge of a cliff.

It was a dark, moonless night, windy, with mists creeping past in the background. She found herself on her knees at the overhang, grasping the son's wrist, trying to hold onto him. She was trying to keep him from falling into an impenetrable darkness that hid some unseen hole or crater. In her dream, she knew that letting go meant certain death. She held on with all the strength she could muster.

Meanwhile, she kept pleading with the unknown son to use his other hand to pull himself up. For some reason, he refused to try. She kept begging him to climb toward her, but he only grasped her wrist with the single hand. The other never moved from his side.

Louellen felt her strength ebbing. She knew she couldn't hang on much longer. She tried desperately to pull the victim up, but even with both her arms, she could not raise him even an inch. At last, her strength flagged and she could no longer hold the struggling son. Still, he did not try to reach up with his free hand. Her fingers burned and went numb. Suddenly her precious child slipped from her grasp.

And then it was Louellen falling, looking up at the clifftop. Sensing she was near the bottom, she waited for the inevitable impact as she crashed onto the ground.

And then she woke, wondering why her body didn't hurt and surprised to find herself undamaged by the dream. This had been the most intense vision she had yet experienced. She slept very little the rest of the night. In the morning, she rose before dawn to check on Martin. She told her son she wanted him to drive her into Kenneth that morning. On the way, they would stop and check on Cleve.

XXX

Martin dutifully took his mother to check on Cleve. He was fine, in a good mood even. They asked if he wanted to go with them to see Hiram. Cleve thought a minute but declined. He had a few things to take care of that day. So, Martin and Louellen went to see Hiram in Kenneth. Satisfied, for the moment, that her sons were safe and sound, Louellen relaxed on the way home. Maybe the dream was … just a dream.

Cleve was also dreaming. His dream was a happy daydream. In the time since Hiram's conviction, Cleve had resumed his courtship of the widow, Jeannie Allworth. He had strong feelings for her, but he always treated her with a proper respect. He didn't want to frighten her off by assuming too much and coming on too strong.

For her part, Jeannie had been alternatively demure and flirtatious toward Cleve. Sometimes she welcomed his attentions, even inviting him to her place for an intimate but innocent dinner. On other occasions, she had baked him a pie or homemade bread. On his birthday, she had even baked and decorated a cake for him. Such kind attentions buoyed the bachelor's hopes. Cleve began to think more and more that her affections were real and serious. He had resolved to rachet up his amorous endeavors.

He planned to visit Mrs. Jeannie Allworth that very night. Cleve had spruced himself up, put on his second-best clothes (to avoid looking unduly flashy) and – a last-minute inspiration – had gathered a handful of late-season black-eyed Susans.

These in hand, he walked out and seated himself in Hiram's truck – which he had been using regularly since Eliza had disappeared. He drove to Mrs. Allworth's house singing the happiest and most romantic songs he knew. He was merrily hopeful, restrained by a thin strand of apprehension. Tonight, if all went well, he might propose that he and the lovely Jeannie take their modest relationship to the next level.

When Cleve drove up the dirt road that led to Jeannie's beautiful little cottage, he was surprised to see a vehicle already parked out front. Jeannie didn't drive, so he knew at once that she had company. As he neared the house, he recognized the vehicle. It was the battered and rusting Model T that Kyle Jennings drove.

All of Cleve's hopes scattered into the air as a hot geyser of jealousy shot up his spine. In his mouth was a bitter taste of betrayal, of love snatched suddenly from his grasp. At the same time, his disappointment in the lovely widow pained his yearning heart. But that was only the background. At that moment, he hated Kyle Jennings with a passion beyond love and anguish.

For the next few minutes, Cleve acted in a surreal fog, not fully conscious of what he was saying or doing. He was aware that he was a man out of control: a man who wanted to be out of control.

The angry suitor charged up to Jeannie's door and, without knocking, barged in to confront Jeannie and Kyle seated on a soft armchair and sofa, respectively. The couple was astonished by his sudden and unwelcome entrance. Cleve immediately started railing at Kyle, using words and phrases that could be found in no civilized people's dictionary. He was pointing an accusing finger at the hated Jennings demon, punctuating every new oath.

Meanwhile, Jeannie jumped up and waved an arm at Cleve, ordering him to leave her property instantly. Kyle, who had been taken aback by the sudden attack, gradually regained a shred of composure. As Cleve continued to harangue him, Kyle rose slowly. Gradually, so gradually that Cleve took no notice, he began approaching the angry intruder. He deftly cut the distance between the two men until he was sure he had the initiative to launch a physical strike.

Cleve was still mining his vast deposit of invectives, swearing a blue streak at his nemesis.

Then Jeannie cried, "For god's sake, stop it, Cleve!"

As the profanity-spewing swain turned to address her, Kyle made his move. He leapt at Cleve, leading with his right fist. He struck a solid blow against the outraged man's left cheek. Cleve staggered backward. Kyle got in a couple more blows before Cleve recovered enough to start reciprocating.

Somehow, the two men ended up outdoors, which was just as well for Cleve. If Jeannie had been a violent person, she might well have joined Kyle in pummeling the trespasser. Cleve, though battered and bleeding from the nose, finally managed to get in a string of effective punches. One uppercut was sufficiently violent to send Kyle reeling. Shaking his head, he turned to see Cleve coming at him.

Kyle sprang toward his vehicle, jerked open the door and pulled out a double-barreled 12-gauge shotgun. Before Cleve could react, Kyle aimed the weapon and pulled one trigger.

The blast caught Cleve in the right arm, with a few pellets peppering his shoulder and his right breast. Cleve wavered, dazed and incredulous, and tried to resume his forward movement. Kyle was shocked that the blow had not stopped his adversary. He hurried aimed again and pulled the second trigger.

The two men had been so intent on destroying one another that neither had noticed Jeannie hurrying forward to break up the murderous battle. The second shot missed Cleve but struck the widow Allworth in the throat. She fell backward, mortally wounded but not yet gone.

The two combatants turned in horror to see her lying on the grass, blood gurgling from her neck. The noises she made, trying to speak or scream or pray, were grisly, almost unhuman. In a short minute or two, the noises faded and stopped. Mrs. Jeannie Allworth, the object of the competing men's affections, was dead.

Cleve turned to look at Kyle. The latter met his eye but said nothing. A few helpless seconds later, Kyle piled into his car with his empty shotgun and drove off. Cleve, faint from shock and loss of blood, dropped to his knees. Then everything went blissfully black.

Chapter 22

THE ENDURING MYSTERY

Sheriff Lawson was sitting at his desk, muddling through some tedious paperwork. The sun was heading toward the horizon and it was past time to go home. He hated administrative duties, but they were part of the job, so there he was. Just as he decided the deskwork could wait until morning, the phone rang.

Deputy Sanger, who was leafing through a magazine, got up to answer it. It was Claude Wilkens, a farmer who owned the land adjacent to the Allworth property. He was calling from Ivan Reynolds' store in Avery.

"Evening, Claude," Sanger greeted the farmer. "What's going on down there?"

"Sorry to bother you this time of day," the farmer said. "Ah … it may be nothing, but I was just walkin' into town this evening, and I heard two shots from the direction of Jeannie's house. At least they sounded gunshots. A shotgun, I'd say."

"Did you go up for a look?" the deputy asked.

"Naw, I was headed on into town," Claude said. "I had me in mind to have a beer or two then go home and turn on the radio for a while."

"You see anybody up that way today?" the deputy asked.

"Well, a car or two went by early this evening," Claude said. "Not sure who. But AFTER the shots, an old Model T came roaring by me, headed away from Jeannie's. I can't swear to it, but it looked like that old Ford that Kyle Jennings drives."

Sanger jerked his head around to look at Lawson. "Claude heard gunshots from near Jeannie Allworth's place. He thinks he saw Kyle Jennings' truck. You want me to run up there and take a look?"

"No, you stay here and make sure our guests are settled for the night," the sheriff said. "I'll drive over and take a look."

The sheriff got up and took the phone from Sanger. "Claude, I'm on my way down there."

"I'll be here at Ivan's," Wilkens said. "You mind if I tag along?"

"Suit yourself," the sheriff said. "I'll pick you up."

XXX

Kyle had driven recklessly as he left the Allworth home, speeding through Avery on his way home. He had a split lip, pain in his left ribs and a sharper pain on top of his head. He reached up and felt a knot rising. For a little man, Cleve packed a surprising punch.

Kyle's heart was thumping, his mind was racing and he didn't know what to do. He tried to focus on getting back home. He'd tell Pop and Jake what happened. They'd know how to handle this situation. Then the panicked man wondered about Cleve: Could he have survived? Kyle didn't think so. When he had left, Cleve had been bleeding and seemed to be struggling to breathe.

At one point on his flight home, Kyle thought about slowing down and chucking the shotgun into the ditch. Or maybe stopping to bury it. He tried to weight the pros and cons, but his mind couldn't focus. He decided to wait until he got home and let his pa and brother help him figure it all out.

During the drive, Kyle's mind flitted from thought to thought. Then another thought appeared, this one for the first time: Had anyone seen him drive away from the scene?

XXX

When Cleve regained consciousness, the light was fading from the sky. He felt a terrible ache in his right arm between the elbow and the shoulder. Then he remembered Jeannie Allworth and her agonizing death.

224

Cleve lifted his head and turned to see the inert form of the lovely woman lying just where it had fallen … how long ago was it now? Cleve had no sense of time. He tried to rise, but the slightest move made his head spin. He collapsed back onto the ground and had one final thought before passing out again: Kyle Jennings.

XXX

The sheriff picked up Claude and drove out east of town. They went up and down a couple of hills, passing Claude's place and coming to the small hill where Jeannie Allworth's home sat. There were no lights at the house. As they drove up the dirt road, both men saw a vehicle in the yard.

"That's a truck," Claude said.

"Yeah it is, and it kinda looks like Hiram Brodie's truck," Lawson added.

"By golly, it might be," Claude said. They turned into the small, narrow drive. A few seconds later, the headlights played over a prone form in the yard not far from the truck. "That's a body."

"I think you're right, Claude," the sheriff said. "Pull that rifle out of the back seat. Just in case we need it."

The sheriff drove up near the body. He jumped out, drew his revolver and carefully but quickly made his way over to the motionless figure. Claude cautiously followed.

"It's Cleve Brodie," Lawson said, checking the man's pulse. "He's alive, but he's in bad shape."

"John!" Claude croaked. "There's another one."

Claude started toward the second victim, Lawson following on his heels. Claude recognized her first. "It's Jeannie. I think she's dead."

The sheriff bent to examine the woman. He saw lots of blood. Her neck was mangled. He found no pulse. "She's gone," Lawson said. "She took a blast right in the neck."

"My god," Claude said. "Who would do such a thing?"

John Lawson didn't know yet. He had a more important priority. He sprang up, saying. "We gotta get Cleve to Doc Tebbetts. Help me get him into the car."

XXX

As the sheriff sped back to Kenneth, Claude held onto the injured man, who half sat and half lay in the seat between them. Claude soon was saturated with Cleve's blood. It seemed the trip took three times longer than normal.

Finally, they pulled up in front of Doc's office and roused the old physician. The three men carried Cleve into Doc's office. Lawson then asked Claude to hurry over to the jail.

"Tell Cliff to drive back to the Allworth house to secure the crime scene," Lawson said. "You can ride with him, and he'll drop you off at home. And Claude, don't mention Cleve's injuries just yet, especially in front of Hiram."

The sheriff didn't have time to talk to Hiram right now. The prisoner would demand to know all the details, and Lawson just couldn't deal with that.

Meanwhile, Doc Tebbetts had been examining Cleve. He shook his head.

"He's lost a lot of blood," Doc said. "My goodness, that arm is in bad shape. I think I can stop the bleeding, but I can't do anything about that arm. We need to get him over to the hospital."

"You'll have to call my brother and have him help," the sheriff said. "Can you go with him?"

"Of course I'll go with him," Doc said, sounding offended. "He's my patient."

"You and Fred will have to get him over there by yourselves," Lawson said. "I have a murder scene to investigate."

"Murder? Aren't you jumping the gun? He's not dead yet," the doctor said.

"No, but Jeannie Allworth is," the sheriff said grimly. "Someone shot both of 'em. I sent Cliff up to her house to watch over the place.

I gotta get back there. Good luck with your patient, Doc."

Lawson left before the stunned doctor could reply.

The sheriff leaned on the gas and quickly returned to the site of the shooting. In the short time he'd been there, Cliff Sanger had done all he could do.

The sheriff found his deputy seated on the running board of his Ford, looking pale and sick. Darkness had closed in. Lawson soon realized they could accomplish no more until daylight. He filled Sanger in on what he knew so far. Then he told the deputy to go back into Avery and get someone to help him move Jeannie's body.

"Where should I take her?" Cliff asked, still looking ashen and a feeling bit ill.

"Take her to Doc's office in Kenneth," Lawson said. "Put her in one of the back rooms. Then run on up to the hospital and tell Doc to do a quick exam on the body. And don't tell anyone but Doc that she's been shot."

As Cliff climbed unsteadily into his car, Lawson took one more look around the grim scene. Much as he detested his responsibilities so far that night, he knew the worst was yet to come. He had to drive to Martin's place and relay the bad news to the family. Then he had to tell Hiram.

XXX

Martin couldn't imagine who'd be coming up to the door after dark. He peered out the window and saw the silhouette of John Lawson, his hat giving away his identity. Martin opened the door and greeted the sheriff.

"Hello, John," the wary man said with a hint of curiosity.. "What brings you up here tonight?"

"Bad news, Martin," the sheriff said. "Cleve's been hurt. He's in bad shape."

"How'd it happen?" Martin asked. Louellen and Dusty came to the door in time to hear the rest.

"He was shot in the arm; shotgun blast; 12-gauge," Lawson said.

"Who done it?" Martin said in low almost menacing tone.

"Don't know yet," Lawson said. "Cleve's up in Kenneth at the hospital. Doc says he needs a good surgeon. They ... uh ... they might not be able to save the arm."

"I'm heading up there," Martin said resolutely.

"I'm going too," Louellen said. No one tried to talk her out of it.

"Me too," Dusty said. His grandmother nodded to the boy. That settled it.

"All right, I'll take you all up there," Lawson said. "We'll stop at the jail and get Hiram so he can go to the hospital with y'all. Now get your boots on and let's go."

The sheriff could easily fit all of them in his large Ford Flathead V8 sedan, but Martin wanted to take his own car. Lawson, knowing he would have to drive back to the crime scene at some point, agreed. But he told Martin to follow him. They'd make better time and be safer if he led with the siren blaring. Martin realized that made sense.

Louellen rode with her son, but John had Dusty jump in beside him. Despite the tense nature of the trip, the boy enjoyed riding in the big car with the siren howling. It was undeniably exciting.

"Dusty, when we get to the jail, I want you to stay in the car. I'll go in and get your dad," the sheriff told him. "We'll be out in a flash. You understand?"

"I understand," Dusty answered.

The trip was much quicker than Dusty expected. They roared through Avery and on to Kenneth. Soon they pulled up at the sheriff's office. Lawson disappeared and quickly came back with a barefoot Hiram following close behind. His boots were in one hand as he struggled to get his overalls up and fastened. They headed for the hospital, just a few blocks away.

"What exactly happened, John?" the anxious prisoner asked.

"Well, that's not clear yet," the sheriff replied. "He was up at Jeannie Allworth's house. Claude was walking to town and heard a shotgun. Two shots. He called me, and we went up there. We found Cleve hurt. He was bleeding but still breathing. Got hit in the right arm, only one blast."

"And the other shot?" Hiram asked, feeling the sheriff was holding something back.

"Well, I didn't want to mention it yet," John said, glancing at Hiram and rolling his eyes toward the backseat where Dusty sat.

"He's old enough," Hiram said, also casting a quick glance back at his son. Dusty was hanging on every word even if he didn't understand completely.

"Well, we found Jeannie, too," John sighed. "She got the other blast. She didn't make it."

Dusty was stunned. His uncle had been shot, hurt bad, and Jeannie Allworth had been killed. But Dusty wondered why the sheriff didn't say who did it.

Hiram was still lacing up his second boot when Lawson stopped the car in front of the hospital and killed the motor and the siren.

Martin had somehow managed to just about keep up with the more powerful police vehicle. He and Louellen were right behind the other three as they hurried toward the hospital doors, wondering what news would greet them inside.

XXX

Kyle Jennings was involved in serious discussions with his dad and his brother about what to do. They quickly discussed and rejected the idea of Kyle turning himself in and claiming self-defense. If they were lucky, no one would ever figure out Kyle was at the scene.

Talk then turned to another topic: Should Kyle lay low for a few days? Maybe he should stay out of sight until Jake and Pop found out if the law was looking for him. Pop suggested his son hang out at the little shack they had built near their very well-hidden still.

"That'd be the first place they'd look," said Jake, shaking his head.

"It would be," his dad agreed. "If they knew where it was."

Both boys looked at Pop like he was a genius. Of course, no one knew where it was. At least no one in law enforcement. Why, they'd even paraded the federal agents past the site two or three times just for kicks. It was so well concealed that the agents hadn't had a clue they were within 100 yards of an operational still.

"No one's ever been up there but you and me and Percy," Pop said with a sly laugh.

"Well, maybe a couple of customers," Jake said smiling. "Remember them three brothers. They paid 50 percent over the usual price – and we didn't even give 'em the good stuff."

Jake elbowed Kyle, who joined his brother, laughing and remembering the event.

"You two took customers up to the still?" Pop said tersely. "What in hell were you thinkin'?"

"They wasn't from around here," Kyle said defensively. "They was from over in Cunningham County. We'll never see them boys again."

"Well … maybe not," Pop said as he thought a bit. "But it ain't a good idea to have no one other than family up there."

"So, then, it's settled?" Jake asked, trying to move on from the subject of visitors. "Kyle will stay at the still for a few days until we see if anyone is lookin' for him?"

"Awright," Pop said, slapping Kyle on the knee. "Let's get you packed for a little camping trip. And don't drink all the merchandise."

XXX

When the sheriff and the rest of the Brodies entered the hospital, they found Fred Lawson – the sheriff's brother – pacing the floor. He didn't know anything yet. Doc Tebbetts had gone into the emergency room, and that's the last Fred had heard.

Just then, Doc came out a door down the hall. He saw the Brodies and headed their way.

"He's in surgery," Doc reported. "He's alive, and with luck, he'll stay that way." The listeners let out a collective sigh.

"But it's not all good news," Doc said. "The blast really messed up his arm. I couldn't do much for it. And the surgeon, he's good now, but even he isn't sure he can save it."

"When will we know anything?" Hiram asked.

"No telling," Doc answered. "For now, we sit and wait."

It was well over an hour later when the surgeon came out. The news was not good. The hospital team could not save Cleve's right arm. They had amputated just below the shoulder.

Louellen took it particularly hard. It was just like her dream. A son of hers had reached out to her with only one arm because the other was useless. The spirits had shown her the future, a future she couldn't prevent. She vowed she would forever after heed her dreams and visions.

The doctor made it clear that no one could see Cleve yet. He would be unconscious for a while. That was a good thing. It would help him heal. The family might as well go home, get some rest, come back tomorrow and get an update on his condition.

Louellen wouldn't hear of it. She demanded to stay. Hiram also wanted to stay.

"No, Hiram, I can't let you," the sheriff said. "Why, if anyone finds out I brought you here, I'd be in a boatload of trouble. I gotta take you back to the jail tonight."

Hiram wanted to argue, but he understood the lawman had already broken the rules by letting him out – even for a couple of hours. The prisoner reluctantly agreed to go back to the jail. But he made Lawson promise to start looking for the shooter at daybreak. The sheriff affirmed that was his intention.

Martin also wanted to stay, but he didn't like the idea of Dusty staying at the hospital all night.

"Can anyone take Dusty home?" he asked.

The sheriff certainly didn't have time. His brother, Fred, volunteered, but Louellen vetoed that idea.

"He needs you with him, Martin," she said. "You take him home and stay with him until morning. I'll be fine here."

Fred again volunteered, this time to stay with Louellen until the family got back in the morning. They considered the idea, and finally agreed, thanking Fred profusely. He tossed it off as just something one neighbor does for another.

With that settled – and so much more unsettled – the group broke apart. The sheriff and Hiram headed back to the jail. Martin and Dusty headed home. And Fred and Louellen sat down to a long, restless wait.

It was torturous night for all of them. But it would be even more torturous for another resident of Drury County.

XXX

Martin and Dusty drove in silence. Martin would rather have been at the hospital keeping vigil with his mother. But Louellen's wishes always held sway with her middle son. As they neared the house, Dusty broke the silence.

"We can't just go to bed like nothing happened," he said.

"What do you mean?" his uncle asked.

"We, well, we oughta do something," the boy said. "We oughta find out who shot Uncle Cleve."

"Well, yeah," Martin said as he studied the situation. "I been thinkin' about that."

"Then what do we do?" Dusty pleaded.

"I've a good idea who's behind this," Martin said, staring ahead through the windshield. "But can we prove it?"

"Well, then we need to figure out how to prove it," Dusty said. "I know I won't be able to sleep tonight, not knowing who it was that shot my uncle."

"Yeah … I reckon I won't sleep either," Martin said, as he pulled the car into his yard and turned off the engine. "Stay here. I gotta get a couple of things from the house. I won't be long."

XXX

Kyle Jennings waited until well after midnight. The moon had set and it was fully dark when he started out for the secluded still. In the pitch-black night, he made his way carefully but quickly up a hill and down through a hollow before turning left to go up another hill.

232

Halfway up, he turned to his left again, walked about 30 yards farther and stopped.

The refugee looked carefully around him. He had to make sure no one had followed him. It was a still night with a nip in the air, but calm, with just a faint breeze.

Peering into the blackness, his eye caught some movement from a clump of trees below, very near the path he had taken up the hill. He stared at the spot for a good two minutes. He observed no further movement. Maybe it was only a gust of wind. Maybe a small animal. At any rate, it appeared to be a false alarm.

He took one final survey of the area below him. Seeing nothing, Kyle headed through a little thicket of brush and into the small, level clearing that harbored a very large and productive still. At the far end of the tiny glade was a ramshackle hut. This would be Kyle's home for a couple of days or more. Might as well settle in and get comfortable, he thought. At least there would be a few jugs of the good stuff to help him pass the time.

A few seconds after Kyle had disappeared into the bushes, two figures rose from behind that small clump of trees lower on the slope. The taller one began picking his way noiselessly up the hill. The shorter one followed a few paces behind. Both were armed with rifles.

XXX

True to his promise to Hiram and to himself, Sheriff Lawson was up before the sun. He had caught maybe three or four hours of sleep. He carried a jar of hot coffee to his car, started the engine up and went to pick up his deputy, who also had managed a few hours of much-needed sleep.

The two spoke little on the way to Jeannie's property. They examined the scene again, more methodically this time. They tried to replay the events as best as they could. A struggle in the house had spilled outside. Someone had fired two blasts, both back toward the house. Cleve had gone down nearer the shooter than Jeannie. His wounds had concentrated around his right arm. Hers had seemed to be centered around her neck.

Then they combed the yard, covering a circle some 40 or 50 feet from where the victims had fallen. They discovered nothing of any real consequence.

"Well, what now?" the deputy said.

"I don't see anything we can do here," Lawson admitted. "I think we might as well take a run over to the Jennings place. Let's see if Kyle admits to being in the neighborhood last night. If so, we'll ask him why he was in such a hurry to get out of town."

About 20 minutes later, the officers pulled up in front of the Jennings farm. Jake was the first to appear. He came out of the barn, holding a pitchfork, tines pointed upward.

"What brings the sheriff's department out so early in the morning?" Jake asked with a too-friendly smile.

"Just enjoying the fine weather," Sanger said. "How are things going, Jake?"

"Just great," he said, his smile growing even bigger.

"Jake, we'd like to have a quick word with Kyle," Lawson said, not smiling back at the genial host. "We heard he was in Avery last evening. Wonder if he might have heard a gunshot or two."

Jake's smile melted slowly away.

"Don't know nothin' 'bout that," the reticent man said. "Kyle ain't here this morning."

"Where is he?" Lawson asked.

Jake's face sunk into a frown as he replied. "Don't know. Let me get Pop. You can ask him."

Before Jake had taken three steps toward the house, Pop Jennings came out. He was smoking a pipe and holding a coffee mug in his hand. Lawson wondered whether the coffee was laced with something stronger. Or whether the cup held any coffee at all.

The sheriff repeated his queries to the old man, who was just as convivial as his son and just as ignorant about Kyle's whereabouts.

Sanger looked at Lawson, who shook his head. They'd get nothing out of these two. But a couple of things were suspicious: Why were these two so chummy? And why wasn't Kyle available? The officers left, having acquired little information, but Kyle was certainly still atop their list of suspects.

XXX

Martin and Dusty, also sleep-deprived, got to the Kenneth hospital about 8 a.m. They found Louellen sitting with a cup of coffee talking to Doc Tebbetts, while Fred Lawson snored softly in a chair nearby.

The news was good. Cleve had regained consciousness in the early-morning hours and had spoken briefly. His memory was foggy, but the surgeon told Louellen that was normal at this point. Doc confirmed this to the doubtful woman. The surgeon had said they probably could go in to visit him later that morning. But he warned them not to upset Cleve. That meant not mentioning his missing arm.

At the suggestion of Doc Tebbetts, Martin and Dusty took Louellen for breakfast. He promised to stay and await any news from the surgeon or the nurses. Then he would have to go back to his office to keep appointments with his patients.

After the Brodies headed for the diner, Doc called his office. He had his assistant arrange for the body of Jeannie Allworth to be moved to the office of the coroner. Doc had studied her wounds late the night before and instantly concluded it was death from a shotgun blast. Soon enough the medical examiner would agree and rule the death a homicide.

While Doc was waiting for the Brodies to return from breakfast, Sheriff Lawson dropped in to check on Cleve's condition. As Doc was catching him up on the news, a nurse came scurrying down the hall.

"Dr. Tebbetts, Cleve Brodie is awake," she said. "He's agitated and insists on talking to one of his brothers or you."

"Can I go in?" Lawson asked, looking from Doc to the nurse and back again.

"I can't see that it'll hurt," Doc said. "Just don't ask him too many questions. He needs to stay as calm and relaxed as possible."

Doc looked at the nurse, who seemed unsure. Doc smiled at her, and she smiled back weakly and nodded, leading the two men into the room where Cleve was recovering.

Cleve recognized Doc then also the sheriff.

"I got shot," he said, looking up at them with wide and wild eyes. "He shot me. Then he shot Jeannie. I think she's dead. He killed her."

"Calm down now, Cleve," Doc said soothingly. "We're listening. Just take it slow and easy."

Cleve's head fell back on his pillow. He took a few labored breaths, licked his lips and mustered a bit of composure. He said, "Kyle Jennings pulled a shotgun out of his car. He shot me in the arm. Then he shot Jeannie in the neck. Kyle shot her. Oh, the blood, the blood. Poor Jeannie. Right in the neck."

The surgeon, who had been called by another nurse, arrived and immediately ordered her to give Cleve a sedative.

"That's enough talking for now, Mr. Brodie," the young doctor said gently. "Just lay back and relax. We can talk about the details later. For now, you need to rest. You need sleep."

The soothing murmurs of the surgeon, along with the sedative, helped Cleve drift quickly into sweet slumber. The young physician then turned to the older doctor and the sheriff.

"Now you two get the hell out of here and don't rile my patient again," he said quietly but sternly. The two men felt like chastened schoolboys. "He's not out of the woods yet. He needs a lot of rest. Do you understand?"

Doc and Lawson said yes, mumbled apologies and left the room. Cleve would remember none of this conversation. When he awoke several hours later, he would repeat it all again.

But the short conversation gave Lawson an important break. He now had an eyewitness accusing Kyle Jennings of the shootings. The sheriff hurried from the hospital to his office to fill in his deputy. They would make another trip back to the Jennings farm. This time they expected a lot less artificial hospitality.

Less than 15 minutes later, Lawson and Cliff drove up to the house of Jonas and Orville Wambsganss, two brothers who were known to be trustworthy enough to act as temporary deputies. They brought another key asset to the small posse. They were reputed to be the two best shots with a rifle in the entire area.

Jonas and Orville agreed to provide support for the sheriff and the deputy. They, like the Brodies, had no particular love of the Jennings clan. The thought of putting a Jennings in his place appealed to them. And they were just about tough enough that they certainly didn't fear Kyle or Jake.

The Wambsganss brothers retrieved their rifles: Jonas favored a Remington and Orville preferred a Winchester. As soon as they joined the lawmen in the sheriff's sedan, Lawson headed for the Jennings place prepared, if necessary, to face armed resistance.

XXX

After the sheriff had left the Jennings farm earlier that morning, Jake had waited a while before hiking up into the hills to the still. He went to warn his brother that the sheriff was on his trail. Jake and Pop agreed that Kyle should stay out of sight for maybe a week. He would have to wait in the shack until a family member could confirm the coast was clear.

Like his brother the night before, Jake stayed alert in case anyone was tailing him. He detected no one else in this part of the woods. After halting outside the hidden plateau, searching for any signs of followers, Jake was satisfied he was alone. Jake entered the brush at the same place Kyle had the night before. He called softly for his brother. The last thing he wanted was to be mistaken for a lawman and get winged accidentally.

When his brother didn't answer, Jake's senses went on a higher degree of alert. He looked around and noticed the still had been tampered with. In fact, someone had mangled parts of it. He didn't understand. His brother wouldn't sit by quietly while their valuable still was sabotaged. Was it already damaged when Kyle had arrived last night?

Jake began to wish he'd brought his rifle with him. He edged over to the shack, noticing the door was barely ajar. Kyle wouldn't have left it that way, would he? Maybe he had gotten into the stash of moonshine and tied one on last night. He might be sleeping it off. But why hadn't he done anything about the destruction of the still? Jake couldn't puzzle it out.

He crept up to the door, stood to one side and called his brother in a loud whisper. No response. He tried again, a little louder. Still nothing. Then Jake reached out and pulled open the shanty door.

It was immediately evident that a struggle had taken place. The cot was turned on its side, the old tan blanket on the dirt floor. The only chair in the room was busted. Several shattered jugs and jars littered the floor. Kyle was absent.

Jake then noticed dark stains under and near the broken chair. He bent down to examine them. It was blood. Fresh blood. Somebody had been fighting, and someone had been injured. He was afraid to think of where his brother was and what had happened to him.

Jake rose slowly and began moving back toward the camouflaged entrance to the hideaway. By the time he got through the brush and onto the hillside, he was scampering down the hill back to the house. How could he explain what he'd just seen? What would Pop say? How were they going to find Kyle?

XXX

The sheriff and his gang pulled up into the Jennings yard late in the morning. This time, Pop Jennings came out holding a gun. Lawson quietly told his men to spread out so the old man wouldn't be able to fire at more than one of them.

"What do you want now?" the old man asked.

"Need to talk to Kyle," Lawson said firmly. "Tell me where he is or I'll search every building within two miles."

"You ain't comin' in any of MY buildings," Pop Jennings said, raising his gun.

"Put that gun down now or we'll fire," the sheriff said. "I mean it, Pop."

The old man saw the odds were against him, especially with the Wambsganss boys drawing a bead on him. He figured one of them might be off target, but he knew they both wouldn't miss. He was on the horns of a dangerous dilemma.

At that moment, Jake came running into the yard. He was flushed, fatigued and his eyes were full of fear.

"Pop, I can't find Kyle," he said, not caring at this point if the lawmen heard him.

"Waddaya mean can't find him," Pop said sourly. The old man now realized there was no profit in engaging in a gun battle. It was four armed officers against him and his unarmed son.

"I went to the still," Jake continued. "Someone had smashed it up a bit. But the cabin – wrecked, blood on the ground, Kyle's gone."

Now Pop was worried. Had someone captured or killed Kyle? Did the sheriff have anything to do with this? If he found out who was involved, he vowed, they wouldn't live long.

"Put your gun down, Pop, so we can figure this out," Lawson said. The old man complied. The deputies lowered their rifles. The two sides came together to discuss the sudden and disturbing disappearance of Kyle Jennings.

XXX

The sheriff, his three deputies, the Jennings family and a slew of volunteers began a search early that afternoon for the missing moonshiner. They traipsed up and down all the hills in the vicinity of the still. The manhunt went on for several days without success.

After the third day, Pop Jennings relented to Lawson's demand to see the still and look for clues. It was all the way Jake had described it. There was nothing to indicate where Kyle was or whether he was still alive.

The Jennings family suspected one of the Brodies. The sheriff didn't respond to that accusation. There wasn't a shred of evidence yet. As the days went by, the search efforts waned and eventually died out. Lawson had no option but to believe Kyle was nowhere near the Jennings place or the damaged still.

One afternoon, a couple of days after the search had ended, Deputy Sanger was discussing the situation with the sheriff. Sanger asked the sheriff if he thought it could all be a ruse by the Jennings clan to make it look like Kyle had been attacked. Maybe they were just covering up his escape. Maybe he was no longer in the county – or even the state.

"I thought about that, Cliff," Lawson responded. "I thought it over a long time. Why would they destroy the still but not take us up there right away to show us it had been ruined? If that was a trick, they'd have played it on us the first day. And why would they tear up the still just for an alibi? They'd want to keep it operating.

"No," the sheriff continued, "I think someone else went up there. Someone with a grudge. They tore up the still and fought with Kyle up there. It's just a question of who had a motive."

"Well, the Brodies have the strongest motive," Cliff said. "But Hiram was in jail. And Cleve was in the hospital. That only leaves Martin, right?"

"I thought about that, too," Lawson said. "It's possible." He paused in thought. "Maybe he did. But I sure hope he didn't."

XXX

There were others in the county who suspected Martin. Most people soon learned that he had taken Dusty home from the hospital the night Kyle had disappeared. He would have had the opportunity. Martin would likely have suspected one of the Jennings brothers of shooting Cleve, even if he didn't have proof. It didn't matter that Cleve hadn't named Kyle as his shooter yet. That news didn't come out until after Jake had found that Kyle was missing.

Lawson and Sanger did as thorough a job of investigating Martin as they could. But nothing beyond circumstance turned up. The sheriff and the deputy questioned all the Brodies and all their friends, to no avail.

For his part, Martin said next to nothing. When asked about Kyle's disappearance, the quiet man only grew quieter. He would neither confirm or deny an involvement.

Meanwhile, Dusty wouldn't say much about what happened that night either. When asked, he just said he and his uncle couldn't sleep, so they went and sat on the bank of the river, fishing, listening to the water and looking at the stars.

Martin would never be charged in Kyle's disappearance. There was just no proof. No one could do more than speculate about what had actually happened. The cloud of suspicion hovering over Martin never quite blew over, but in time it faded.

Then, a few years later, a tale began to circulate that proposed another explanation. A habitual drunk from Cunningham County, south of Drury County, was well into his cups one night when he told a sad story about his disabled brother and the dangers of bad liquor.

Apparently, three brothers had made their way over to Drury County in search of some moonshine. Back up in the hills, they had each bought a large jug of white lightning from a couple of dubious moonshiners. The drunken storyteller didn't reveal any names: Perhaps he didn't remember or perhaps he never knew their names.

On the way back home, the three brothers took occasional nips out of their own individual jugs. The next day, one of the brothers had trouble seeing. But he kept nipping at that gallon jug of moonshine. Within three days, he couldn't see at all. His two brothers took him to a doctor, who diagnosed methanol poisoning. The brothers concluded it was due to drinking bad moonshine. The afflicted man never regained his sight.

The remaining brothers vowed revenge, according to the inebriated narrator. A week or so later, he and the other brother returned to that still in Drury County. He confided that they had caught one of the moonshiners up at the isolated still. They had overcome the man and made him watch as they wrecked the still.

That deed done, they completed their revenge by viciously beating the seller of the tainted liquor to death. They had taken his body away, disposed of it in an appropriately secluded location and come back home by early the next morning.

The brothers apparently had vowed to take the tale with them to the grave. But, under the spell of potent spirits, this brother had spilled the beans.

By the time this rumor came to the attention of Sheriff Lawson, the name of the narrator had been lost. All law officers had to go on was second-hand – or fifth-hand – hearsay. No one was ever able to track down the self-professed killer. It didn't matter: Without a body, no conviction was ever likely anyway.

Whatever had become of Kyle Jennings, one fact was indisputable: When Hiram Brodie said there were lots of places in the hills to hide a body so it could never be found, he was right.

Chapter 23

THE DUST SETTLING

Folks in the hills are predisposed to distrust strangers. They are born, raised and usually die in near isolation from newfangled or different ideas. Developing close relationships with outsiders doesn't come easy for many residents of the Ozarks.

This applied to the Brodies as well as nearly all of their neighbors. The majority of the earliest settlers saw little value in becoming too familiar with strangers. Anyone who wasn't close kin was likely to be considered a foreigner. Even families who had been part of the community for three generations were considered relative newcomers.

Dusty was surrounded by a small group of near relatives who spent most of their time with each other and maybe a few close neighbors. Dusty and his sisters had been raised in an atmosphere where quiet suspicion was considered a prudent practice.

The past months had reaffirmed this outlook. His recent experiences had helped cement Dusty's distrust of others. This tendency would govern his thoughts and shape his personality for the rest of his life. From the autumn of 1938 onward, Dusty would find it difficult to open up to people and build intimate relationships.

Just a year before, Dusty had been a young boy, barely 12 years old. He was a happy-go-lucky kid whose primary thoughts revolved around having fun. Yes, there were chores. Yes, there was poverty and want. Yes, he had to observe certain behavioral boundaries to avoid his parents' discipline. But those things were negligible in his world. Left to his own devices, he would run through the woods, hunt, fish, swim and play. In calmer moments, he could enjoy sitting in the grass watching Dermot's Branch rolling by or the clouds gliding overhead.

Recent events had changed Dusty in ways he would never fully understand. He had once been talkative and engaged – a bit like his dad or his Uncle Cleve. Now he was on the way to becoming more like his Uncle Martin: reserved, taciturn, withdrawn.

It was much too simple to say he'd grown up in these 12 months. Dusty had been swept from childhood into his teen years on the waves of intense drama, near catastrophe and deep, unfathomable heartache. His dad had been taken away. His mother had left him. His sisters had disappeared in a twinkling.

Dusty struggled to fit into a household that had for many long years consisted of only his grandmother and Uncle Martin. He found himself navigating new feelings, asking new questions and – perhaps for the first time – questioning the answers. He felt bound to his home and his family, yet he began to feel a strange yearning to get away. That feeling was growing stronger.

All that would play out later: For now, Dusty realized his place was with his grandmother and his uncle. The trio were experimenting, adjusting and learning how to develop a daily routine into which Dusty would fit. Martin still went work at the post office. Louellen still ran the house and kept food on the table. Dusty tried to accustom himself to a new slate of chores.

Of course, there was school. Schoolwork – always a priority for the Brodie clan – was Dusty's principal duty. His grandmother would stand for nothing less. Martin, for his part, also sternly encouraged his nephew to devote himself to education. That was fine: Dusty had that part down. It was the way his two guardians strove to instill a strong work ethic that caused the boy to resist.

After Uncle Cleve had recovered enough to come home from the hospital, Louellen had made her recovering son's comfort her immediate mission. She smothered Cleve with constant care and an abundance of concern. She would do anything to ensure his wellbeing.

That suited Cleve just fine. He liked the attention. He also liked the aid and support she arranged for him.

That's where Dusty came in. If the boy had finished his chores around the homeplace and was caught up on his homework, Louellen expected him to labor for his one-armed uncle.

During the school year, Dusty found himself working many weekends – and sometimes until dark on school nights – doing his uncle's bidding. He was expected to chop wood, tend livestock, clean the barn and perform any other task Cleve came up with.

Dusty liked his uncle … well, maybe "liked" was too strong. What he hated was the extra work. A 13-year-old boy needs some leisure time. Dusty felt he wasn't getting his share. At this point in his maturation, he needed time to think, time to reflect and – perhaps most important – time to dream of a different future.

At night, if Martin turned on the radio, Dusty would sit and listen, often doing homework by the light of the fireplace. The country music singers sounded like they inhabited a magical world, a place where music was just the soundtrack to a carefree, adventurous life.

Dusty dreamed of becoming a country music star, stepping up to the microphone at radio stations, bars and theaters across the nation. And, maybe someday, the holy grail: Playing onstage at the Grand Ole Opry.

During the next spring and summer, the young teenager spent many days working either at the homeplace or at Cleve's place. Most of the time, he was tired and sweaty … and bored.

For some reason, what vexed Dusty most was working in his uncle's massive garden. Half the things growing there were vegetables that Dusty couldn't stand to eat. Take peas, for instance. Picking peas was a kind of torture. Dusty hated peas. He couldn't force himself to swallow them. Why would anyone waste time growing these useless, nasty things? If not for his relatives, he would take a hoe and chop every pea plant into tiny pieces.

Martin saw what was going on and tried to get his mother to stop sending the boy over the help Cleve. "He don't need to be over there every day," Martin argued. "Cleve lost an arm, but he ain't bedridden. He can do for himself."

"Now, you know Cleve can't do near what he used to," Louellen would reply. "He needs help. Dusty's young and strong. It'll do him good to work hard."

"Fine," Martin said, knowing he was bound to lose the argument no matter what he said. "But someday Dusty will be grown and gone. Who's gonna help Cleve then?"

"You and me," his mother would say.

"You and me and Hiram," Martin would correct her.

XXX

Despite the many long days of farmwork, the summer passed quickly. He thought often about his sisters. He wondered where they were and what they were doing. He wondered if they remembered him. He hadn't heard a word from or about them. Was his mother keeping Nancy and Jenny from writing him? Or did they just not care anymore?

He tried not to think much about his mother. She had cheated on his dad and had run off, leaving Dusty behind without a goodbye. He may have needed her love, but at this point, he was convinced he didn't want it.

Dusty did get to visit his dad at the jail every week or so. It was good to talk to him. Dusty was anxious for his release. He wanted to go back to living in the cabin. Even if it was just him and his dad.

Uncle Martin and his grandmother weren't so sure. They both thought it likely that Hiram would rebuild his still and start making moonshine again. Even if he didn't, Hiram almost certainly would continue to drink heavily. Jail wasn't going to change that habit.

Louellen had been puzzling over this issue practically since Eliza had disappeared with the girls. She concluded Hiram couldn't raise a child on his own. She and Martin began to talk about what they were to do once Hiram had served his sentence.

The summer drew to a quiet end. This was a blessing for the Brodies, especially Louellen. With a lull in the drama or stress – at least compared to last year – the grandmother had regained some of her vitality. Per orders from Doc Tebbetts, she was eating plenty, drinking plenty of water and stopping to rest when she got winded. Although she would never be as spry as in the past, she was able to continue running her own house. And, to her relief, her sleep had been mostly quiet. The spirits were not delivering any warnings of dire distress.

XXX

School started in early September. For the first time ever, Dusty was glad summer vacation was over. It had been no vacation for him. Sitting in the school room might be boring at times, but it was easier than choring all day under a hot sun.

His friends returned to school gregarious and boisterous as usual. But they found Dusty to be more silent and subdued. Maybe he had changed a bit. He was still friendly most of the time. He laughed at their jokes and shenanigans, but he seldom joined in like he had in the past.

Dusty seemed to have particular trouble relating to the girls at school, especially those near his own age. He sensed something was changing. And it wasn't just with him. Girls and boys were moving in different directions, separating into two groups with different interests. It was weird. He didn't know how to talk to girls who suddenly cared how their hair looked or gathered in groups to watch, whisper and giggle at the boys.

Dusty just didn't feel comfortable around these girls. They seemed to be thinking about things he couldn't fathom or understand. So, around members of the opposite sex, he remained mostly polite, mostly superficial and always on guard.

For a few weeks, Dusty patiently tolerated the teaching style of Mrs. Rice. Then he began daydreaming in class. Most of his thoughts centered on how things would be when his dad got out of jail. Would they go hunting or fishing together? Would they wake up and eat breakfast together? Would they sit on the porch at night and talk? If so, what would they talk about?

These thoughts were running back and forth in Dusty's head when he should have been paying attention to Mrs. Rice. It hardly mattered. He did his homework at night. He understood the material.

He had the right answer nearly every time she called on him. So, he figured, what was the big deal if his mind wondered now and then?

XXX

One day in late September, Percy Jennings and Henry Franks stopped by the Avery baseball diamond. Dusty and a bunch of his friends were in the middle of a pickup game. They only had enough players for six kids on each team, but they were making the most of it. At least everyone was getting plenty of chances to bat. And, with every fielder playing on the batter's pull side, they were getting plenty of chances in the field.

"Hey, ain't that the Brodie kid? The one that beat Kenneth almost single-handed last year?" Henry asked.

Percy peered out on the mound and recognized Dusty.

"Yeah. That's him," Percy said flatly.

"What's wrong? I thought you liked the kid?" Henry said.

"I thought I did," Percy said. "But his uncle killed my uncle."

"They never proved that, Percy," Henry reminded him.

"No, but I don't need no proof," Percy said frowning at Dusty, who delivered another bullet toward the plate. "I'll never be friends with a Brodie again."

Later that afternoon, Dusty and a few other ballplayers went over to Ivan's store for a bottle of pop. Percy and Henry were there. Dusty walked in and saw Percy standing by the counter. Their eyes met. Neither said anything. They both knew there was no chance they could put aside the enmity of their families. Neither would ever speak another civil word to the other.

XXX

A few weeks later, Hiram was released from jail, having served a year – but not a day more, thanks to the high-priced West Plains attorney. Hiram's family – minus his fugitive wife and missing daughters – greeted him with hugs and handshakes.

Dusty was glad to have one parent back. He ran to his dad to embrace him. The boy got a brief hug, a hand on his shoulder and a quick ruffling of his hair from his newly freed father. Louellen drew a longer and more emotional hug from her son. Martin and Cleve made do with hearty handshakes, Cleve of course with his left hand.

His mother insisted Hiram come directly to her place so she could cook a celebratory meal. Her prodigal son was returning, and she figuratively slew the fatted calf. She served plates of food: pork, rabbit, squirrel, biscuits and gravy, greens and not one but two pies, apple and peach. She even stirred up a batch of chocolate gravy for Dusty.

After they all had their fill – and a little bit more – they sat talking. Hiram had decided he would return to his cabin. Dusty wanted to go with his dad. Louellen and Martin suggested he let his dad get settled before moving back. Hiram disagreed. He wanted his boy home with him. Eliza may have taken his daughters away, but no one was taking his son. The grandmother and uncle couldn't sway either the father or his son. Dusty packed a few things and went back with his dad to their old home.

For the first few days, Dusty and his father got along great. They did eat breakfast together a couple of times. They did go hunting together one afternoon. They did go fishing the first Saturday morning that Hiram was home.

But it didn't take long for Hiram to return to his former vices. Liquor quickly regained its hold on him. After a couple of weeks of harmony, Dusty came home from school one afternoon to find his dad had gotten hold of a jug of moonshine. Whether it was the remnants of his own production or a purchase from a neighbor, Dusty never knew. What he knew instantly was that his dad roaring drunk. Unfortunately, the emphasis was on the roaring part.

Hiram immediately laid into Dusty, accusing him of shirking on household chores. He scolded the boy for not keeping the kitchen clean, the dishes washed, the floor swept. These were things Eliza and his sisters had done. Dusty had no concept of how to do them.

As Hiram continued to tug on the jug of alcohol, he became more demanding and more menacing. He made Dusty get to work straightening the place, cleaning the kitchen and even cooking supper. When Dusty burnt the eggs, his dad's wrath exploded.

Hiram verbally abused his son and took a swipe at the boy with his big right hand. The blow caught Dusty on his lower jaw: Luckily it was a glancing blow, with Dusty avoiding the full weight of the impact. Dusty looked up to see his dad's eyes burning with rage. He didn't wait for a second blow to fall. He used all the agility he had to duck and scamper to the back door. Out he went, darting past the springhouse and into the woods.

XXX

Louellen had been worried about Dusty. She knew Hiram too well to believe he would abandon alcohol for long. Since her son's release from jail, she and Martin had made a couple of trips to the cabin to check on Hiram and particularly on Dusty. Both times things were quiet. The father and son seemed happy together. Louellen was cautiously hopeful, but she was far from convinced.

The old woman had been free of dreams, visions and omens during the recent months. But now, her sleep on occasion was being disturbed by fleeting images, slightly fretful impressions that left her uneasy. Were her dreams once again trying to tell her something? She wasn't sure. The uneasiness was subtle, a trifling dissonance. But she had promised to heed such feelings, and so she kept her senses open for any coherent message.

On the day Dusty had come home to find his dad in a drunken rage, Louellen had felt a cold shiver run up her spine. Louellen had been trying not to think of Dusty all the time, but she missed having him around. She continued to worry about the boy. When Martin came home from work, she asked him to walk her over to Hiram's. Martin, who had felt no premonitions of impending menace, nonetheless agreed.

They reached Hiram's well after Dusty had run away to escape his father's fury. At once, the visitors realized Hiram had been drinking heavily. They tried talking to him, but he was muddled, confused and groggy. They couldn't get him to say where Dusty was. All they could get out of him was a string of offensive epithets about the boy and a final slurred comment: "Good riddance!"

With nothing more to gain by talking to the well-stewed drunk, they returned home. Along the way, they discussed plans to get Dusty away from Hiram before he could hurt the boy.

XXX

After running out of the cabin earlier that afternoon, Dusty didn't slow down for several minutes. When he did, he leaned against a large tree, catching his breath and listening to hear if his dad was pursuing him. When he heard nothing, he started moving again, taking a long route through thick underbrush until he came to a little cave where he and his friends used to play once in a while.

He huddled up just inside the opening and quietly cried. He spent the night there with nothing but the clothes on his back to keep him warm. In the morning, he didn't go back home. He went straight to school.

In next afternoon, Dusty cautiously returned home to find his dad asleep on his sisters' old bed. A nearly empty bottle of moonshine, a different jug than he'd been emptying yesterday, sat on the floor next to the bed. Dusty stealthily made his way to the kitchen, found some leftover biscuits and some jam. He silently wolfed down a quick meal then stole out the back door to the spring for a drink to wash it down.

Dusty returned to the back door and was just creeping into the kitchen when he heard his dad moving around. Would Hiram wake up in a foul mood? Dusty decided he didn't want to know. He backed away from the door and ran. His only thought was finding a safe haven. He headed to his grandmother's house.

Louellen welcomed her grandson, relieved to see him unharmed and resolved that he would stay with her and Martin. When Martin came home that afternoon, his mother expressed her intention to provide Dusty a permanent home until he was ready to go out on his own. Martin had expected this. He knew Hiram was unprepared

– perhaps unable – to take care of the boy and raise him. He quickly determined that he and his mother would take over as his guardians.

A few days later, when a more-or-less sober Hiram came looking for Dusty, Martin and Louellen met him outside their home. They made it clear to Hiram that they could not tolerate the way he had been treating his son. The boy was living with them. If Hiram wanted to come visit, he'd better come sober.

Hiram cursed and threatened his relatives. He claimed it was his right to have the boy and treat him however he liked. It was none of their business. Technically, or at least legally, he probably was correct. But that didn't deter Louellen and Martin.

Over the next two weeks, Hiram came to his mother's house several times to claim possession of his son. On each occasion, Louellen gave him a severe dressing down. She recalled his shiftless ways, his unpredictable temper and his history of careless indifference to Dusty. She told him he was not cut out for parenting.

Meanwhile, Martin, in his quiet and stoic way, firmly informed his older brother that he agreed with his mother. And he would do all in his power to make sure the old woman got her way in this matter. The only way Hiram would regain custody of Dusty was to go through Martin.

Hiram may have thought he could take his younger brother. Martin may have had doubts about his ability to win if a fight ensued. But both men knew it would be a vicious and severe battle. In the end, Hiram thought the situation through. Eventually, grudgingly, he decided sheltering, supervising and sustaining a troublesome teenager was a responsibility he didn't want to take on.

Dusty would finish his high school days living with his grandmother and his uncle. He would see his dad regularly, but Hiram would never again have the final word on how to raise his son.

XXX

Louellen was satisfied. Having Dusty in the house, of course, would mean continued extra work for the old woman. But she accepted her new burden. Louellen had raised three boys and now, through circumstances no one had expected, she was raising another one. She took on this duty with a solemn commitment to do her utmost to bring Dusty up the best way she knew.

The good news for her was that she could continue to instill a sense of pride in Dusty for his Indian heritage. She taught him to cherish her Cherokee values and helped nurture within him the spirit of a grand and noble warrior.

At night, she would tell and retell stories of her ancestors. She would recite their deeds of heroism and perseverance, traits she expected Dusty to absorb via her words.

Martin would often sit in the room with them, listening to the same stories he had heard as a young boy. The power of his mother's words was such that the grown man once again felt moved by an appreciation of and pride for his family legacy.

Louellen took excellent care of Dusty. She continued to make sure he ate well. She continued to spoil him with chocolate gravy if the bill of fare contained items that he found distasteful. She kept his clothes clean, even if they were old and plain.

The one negative, from Dusty's perspective, was that his grandma still insisted he go help Uncle Cleve with chores. Cleve demanded more work and harder work from Dusty every time the season changed. Dusty continued to hate those thankless tasks he performed for Cleve, who never offered any thanks or gratitude. It was the one change in his life that he detested. But, because it was his duty and because he so wanted to please his grandmother, he did his best.

Having Dusty around for keeps meant changes for Martin too. He had spent a year as his nephew's interim keeper, but now this was his permanent role. He tried to balance discipline and instruction with a bit of latitude and encouragement. In many ways, he succeeded. But he was still Martin: tightlipped, unexpressive and more than a bit emotionally withdrawn. He appreciated and esteemed Dusty, but he never learned to show anything resembling affection.

Dusty, for his part, appreciated what his grandmother and uncle were doing for him. He learned a lot from both of them. He knew they cared for him. But that didn't fill the hole in his heart. His mother had left him behind. She had taken his sisters away. His dad couldn't put down the bottle and make a decent home for him. So much had been lost in such a short time. Despite the efforts of Louellen and Martin, he never felt quite at home in their house.

The years rolled by as Dusty entered high school. He continued to play baseball, now for the Kenneth High School team. He continued to excel in the classroom. And he continued to work hard helping both of his uncles with their chores.

But he longed to get away and start a new life of his own. He wanted to see more of the world. He had read about exotic, faraway places in his school books and in books he borrowed from the small Kenneth library. He began to imagine ways to take off, see new sights and experience his own personal freedom. He wanted to follow that little river to the wide-open sea.

XXX

The summer between his junior and senior years, Dusty got an un-expected letter. It was actually two letters in one envelope. They were from his sisters, Nancy and Jenny. From the writing, he could tell they had both matured. They sounded almost grown up.

The letters informed him that they had talked their mother into letting them come back to Avery to visit their grandma, their dad and – most importantly – Dusty himself. Dusty couldn't believe it. His mind raced with a million questions he wanted to ask them. But before he could try to sit down and draft a response, he ran to tell his grandmother the good news.

The sisters came into Kenneth on the bus in early June. The whole family was there to meet them. Many hugs and kisses followed. Everyone was surprised to see how they'd grown. Nancy was blos-soming into an attractive, smart-looking girl. Jenny was developing into something like a coquettish teenager, perhaps a bit spoiled, but bright-eyed and cheery.

After a quick meal at a small diner, the family took the girls home. They stopped by Hiram's cabin for a quick look, a brief journey down memory lane and some quiet reflection on days gone by. Then it was onto to their grandma's house for lemonade, tea and, of course, some desserts Louellen had spent the entire morning baking.

After a while, Dusty and his sisters drifted off toward the river, sharing news, telling stories and reminiscing about their childhood together. Dusty learned that his mother had taken the girls to Kansas City, settled on the north side of the city and gotten a temporary job. Within six months, she remarried, and the girls had a new stepfather. Neither of his sisters liked the man. At any rate, the union didn't last a year.

More recently, Eliza had taken up with a tall widower from Iowa who had moved to Kansas City to work in the stockyards. The man, son of a farmer and grandson of a farmer, had a son and daughter of his own. They had just moved to Kansas City to stay with their dad. The Brodie girls didn't know it yet, but Gerald and Maureen would soon be their stepbrother and stepsister.

Dusty recounted Cleve's shooting, the disappearance of Kyle Jennings and Hiram's drinking issues since his release from jail. In ways, he was glad his sisters had not been around when their father was at his most abusive. Still, he had missed them, and they had missed him.

The week they spent in Avery passed much too quickly. Just as they were falling back into their old habits of teasing and insulting one another, it was time for the girls to go back home.

As they parted at the small bus depot, the girls broke down and cried. Dusty tried to hold back his own tears, but he sniffled, choked up and had difficulty saying goodbye. It hurt to watch them board the bus and depart. But he promised to come and see them in the big city before school started in the fall. And they vowed to come back for another visit as soon as they could.

Once they were gone, Dusty was left with one question he had wanted to ask but never found the right time to bring up. Why had his mother left him behind? Why did she only take his sisters with her? It was a question Dusty would ask his mother several years later.

Eliza never gave him a viable answer. She would die without explaining her reasons for abandoning her son.

XXX

The summer before Dusty's senior year of high school was a blur with one day accelerating into the next. He did manage a short trip to Kansas City. He met his mom's fiancé: Owen had just asked Eliza to marry him and, to no one's surprise, she had agreed. Dusty found he liked Owen, who seemed always upbeat and chipper in an "aw shucks" sort of way. Owen treated Dusty immediately like one of the family. He would turn out to be a fine stepfather to the boy from the Ozarks.

He also met his soon-to-be stepbrother, Gerald. Gerald was the same age as Nancy, so Dusty had no trouble finding things to talk about. Baseball, naturally, was a common interest. They were both St. Louis Cardinals fans. Dusty and Gerald hit it off pretty well, though neither knew quite how to handle the prospect of gaining a new brother so suddenly.

Dusty really liked his new stepsister, Maureen. She was smart, funny, thoughtful and a real joy to be around. Just as important to Dusty, she got along famously with Nancy and Jenny. A year younger than Nancy and two years older than Jenny, she seemed to fit perfectly between the sisters. They formed a sort of female Three Musketeers comradeship: One for all and all for one.

Like his sisters' stay in Avery earlier that summer, Dusty's visit to Kansas City was too brief. When he got on the southbound bus to head home, Dusty still had dozens of things to say to his sisters and dozens of things to ask them.

Over the years, they would get together frequently, but the closeness and intimacy they had shared growing up together would never completely return. They were always on good terms, but Dusty often felt they were on different wavelengths. The abrupt gap in their relationship had resulted in distinct sets of experiences that had shaped them in subtly different ways. For the rest of his life, Dusty would feel vaguely like an outsider, especially if his sisters reminisced about adventures that had taken place while they had been separated.

Dusty pushed through his senior year despite an unrelenting case of senioritis. It was impossible to concentrate on schoolwork when the door to the wide and wonderful world was opening just ahead. Dusty kept his grades up, but his daydreaming reached epic proportions. He could slip into a fantasy world at the drop of a pencil.

Meanwhile, Dusty had figured out what he wanted to do. World War II continued to rage with no sign of ending soon. He would join the Navy the day he got his high school diploma – a stipulation his grandma and his uncle insisted on. He would see the world from the deck of a warship. He would help quell the beasts of Germany or Japan (he wasn't sure where he and his ship would be assigned). He would help make the world safe for democracy and free of tyranny.

Before he knew it, he was walking across the little stage at the end of the Kenneth High School basketball gym, accepting his sheepskin and feeling like he was now a full-fledged adult. After the ceremonies, many of his classmates were hugging and shaking hands. Some of the girls were even crying.

Dusty understood why, but all he could think about was getting to the nearest recruiting office and signing up. There was no mourning for an era ended. There was no long, lingering last look around the school. Dusty's high school days ended suddenly and decisively.

XXX

When Louellen, Hiram and Martin dropped Dusty off at the bus depot in Kenneth for his voyage to boot camp, they tried to maintain their composure and wish him luck. He stood stoically as they each bid him farewell. They made him promise to write. His dad made him promise to be a good soldier. His uncle made him promise to come back home safe.

His grandmother made him promise to remember his Cherokee heritage, to be a brave and true warrior, to defeat the enemy for his people. With that, she hugged and kissed her grandson and released him into the world.

Dusty would take few material belongings with him on the bus. But he did carry a boatload of memories, thoughts and emotions. The lessons he'd learned from the good and the bad things that occurred during his childhood would help him maneuver an unknown and unpredictable future.

It was time to move forward. The poor boy was on his own. The lone wolf was starting his solitary journey. He was finally moving where the waters would take him. And, from now on, what happened to Dusty Brodie was up to fate and to Dusty Brodie.

The End

www.ingramcontent.com/pod-product-compliance
Lightning Source LLC
Chambersburg PA
CBHW072107300726
48975CB00003B/736